A.W. Faber-Castell
The Magic Pencil 2

AF117308

The Magic Pencil 2
Copyright © 2022 by Castell Trading Pty Ltd

All rights reserved. No part of this publication may be reproduced, distributed, or transmitted in any form or by any means, including photocopying, recording, or other electronic or mechanical methods, without the prior written permission of the author, except in the case of brief quotations embodied in critical reviews and certain other non-commercial uses permitted by copyright law.

Tellwell Talent
www.tellwell.ca

ISBN
978-0-2288-5917-8 (Hardcover)
978-0-2288-5916-1 (Paperback)
978-0-2288-5918-5 (eBook)

I would like to gratefully acknowledge family, friends and colleagues who have contributed in many ways to bring my writing to fruition.

Author: Count Andreas Wilhelm von Faber-Castell

For author A.W. Faber-Castell (Count Andreas von Faber-Castell), every pencil holds the promise of magic. From the time he was a young boy he has always regarded pencils as small magic wands that inspire creativity and make the imagination visible.

Known as Count Andy to his colleagues, he is the last surviving member of the 8th generation pencil dynasty to have been actively involved in the running of the famous company, which began in Germany in 1761.

Andy was the company's undisputed champion for developing children's products – the main contributor to Faber-Castell's success over recent decades. One of his claims to fame was the launch of his beloved Connector Pen. He was its sole champion initially, but with passion and persistence he ultimately brought the disbelievers in the company on board. The pen became famous worldwide, and it has been the number one colouring product in Australia for the past twenty-five years.

Kunnikunde

Anna Johann

Mr Broombridge

Cornelia

Andy Belle/Andy

Lady Heger-Steel and Jim Steel

Roger Less

Andy and his friends

Fritz the Painter

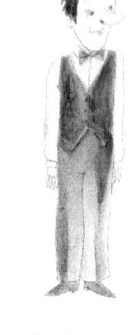

Hermann the Plumber

Rollover von Cracklingen

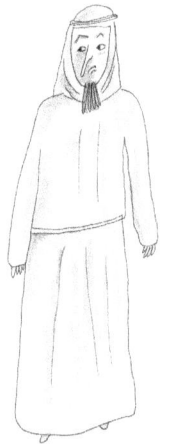

Werner Little Werner

Ohama Bin Schaden

Dr. Ulrich Folterknecht

Gusto Calamari

Moses Clay

Table of Contents

CHAPTER ONE 1
CHAPTER TWO 4
CHAPTER THREE 8
CHAPTER FOUR 12
CHAPTER FIVE 17
CHAPTER SIX 21
CHAPTER SEVEN 25
CHAPTER EIGHT 30
CHAPTER NINE 33
CHAPTER TEN 37
CHAPTER ELEVEN 41
CHAPTER TWELVE 46
CHAPTER THIRTEEN 51
CHAPTER FOURTEEN 55
CHAPTER FIFTEEN 59
CHAPTER SIXTEEN 63
CHAPTER SEVENTEEN 67
CHAPTER EIGHTEEN 72
CHAPTER NINETEEN 76
CHAPTER TWENTY 80

CHAPTER TWENTY-ONE 84
CHAPTER TWENTY-TWO 88
CHAPTER TWENTY-THREE 94
CHAPTER TWENTY-FOUR 98
CHAPTER TWENTY-FIVE 102
CHAPTER TWENTY-SIX 107
CHAPTER TWENTY-SEVEN 111
CHAPTER TWENTY-EIGHT 114
CHAPTER TWENTY-NINE 117
CHAPTER THIRTY 122
CHAPTER THIRTY-ONE 125
CHAPTER THIRTY-TWO 128
CHAPTER THIRTY-THREE 133
CHAPTER THIRTY-FOUR 137
CHAPTER THIRTY-FIVE 139

1

Time is the thief of memory, and it stole freely from the good people of Stone.

The stupendous, explosive drama of the night they combined forces to drive the evil countess from their village should have been burned vividly in their memories forever. Yet just a little over a year after that spectacular and extraordinary event, they referred to it simply as 'the incident.'

And they couldn't agree on what 'the incident' was. For some, it could only have been an illusion or hallucination. Others recalled it as just a careless misfiring of a ceremonial cannon. There were even those who described it as an alien encounter of some kind, when a small boy shot down a UFO with his powerful laser gun (a version that every other small boy in the village hoped was true). From there the rumour grew that it had actually been an alien's gun that the boy had somehow stolen from the aliens …

However, despite the varied memories, one belief the villagers shared was that on the sensational night in question they came together as a powerful, united force to rid their town of the greedy, nasty Countess Kunnikunde Ritter von Krumm, after which, life in Stone returned to normal.

Or, should we say, just about normal. The one big change in the year since that dramatic night was the establishment of Johann Ritter von Krumm's new pencil factory, right next to the old one which had been taken over and ruined by Countess Kunnikunde and her henchmen. Most of her former workers wanted to join Johann's new company, knowing full well that he had been the driving force behind much of the success of the old company, especially with his new and exciting product ideas designed for children. Not surprisingly, with Johann at the helm of his own business, developing innovative products and applying astute marketing strategies, the new factory took off like a pencil-sized rocket. Its stratospheric rise surpassed even its owner's high expectations.

Despite her absence from the old factory, Kunnikunde was still very much in control of it. She had placed another Ritter von Krumm there as a puppet manager to run it on her orders. Her nephew, Farty Ritter von Krumm, was a male version of his horrendous aunt. With Kunnikunde's continuing influence, the Ritter von Krumm pencil company gradually fell apart, its once great soul slowly eaten away by an obstructive bureaucracy and an incompetent advisory board headed by Mr Broombridge.

Johann's son, Andy, on the other hand, was unencumbered by any such millstones and his soul was in fine shape! He was a happy ten-year-old and doing well, thanks in part of course to his magic pencil, which had up-loaded vast amounts of knowledge into his brain and given him enhanced physical skills. But these weren't unconditional gifts from the pencil; it insisted that Andy not use them to draw attention to himself. Andy accepted the pencil's rules and tried very hard to follow them, which he somehow managed to do ... with the occasional lapse, of course.

This morning at school was a good example of such a slip-up, when Andy dared smile during assembly. Now, if he had been at any other school, smiling wouldn't have been a problem. In fact, it may have been seen as a sign of a happy, pleasant child. But not here at the fearsome Miss Heger's school.

'Andy!' she screeched. 'What are you grinning at like an idiot? What are you thinking about, you naughty boy? You're not here for fun—school is serious!'

With that, Miss Heger stormed over to Andy and in the blink of an eye let loose two stinging blows with her large right hand. Slap! Slap! In the same motion, she turned around and stalked off, assuming that she had hit her target.

The hand may be quicker than the eye, but Andy was even faster and ducked just in time to avoid the headmistress's blows. Instead, the two boys standing closest to Andy, Otto and Franz, copped the full force of Miss Heger's thumping hand. They stood holding their burning cheeks and glared at Andy.

'That wasn't fair,' the magic pencil whispered.

'Just a reflex action,' Andy said. 'Sorry'. He shrugged apologetically at Otto and Franz who, clutching their stinging cheeks, made fists of their free hands and shook them at Andy before turning and walking away.

But Andy's relationship with the pencil easily survived such occasional lapses in judgement. The two had developed a trusting friendship and had fun conversing with each other. The whole family enjoyed the pencil's black humour and were happy to have it around.

Right now, Andy was particularly happy, and it had nothing to do with the pencil. Today was the last day of school for the term and the long summer holiday was ahead of him. *No Miss Heger for eight blissful weeks*, he reminded himself for the umpteenth time since the final bell rang. And he wasn't the only one rejoicing; all the children of Stone were in a joyous mood.

Andy even entertained the idea that he might never see Miss Heger again because he'd heard she was getting married to a man named Jim Steel, the former head of Kunnikunde's guards. It occurred to Andy that she might give up teaching once she was married. He could only hope.

2

The instant he arrived home, Andy rushed upstairs to his bedroom and flung his school backpack into the darkest corner of his wardrobe. 'Good riddance!' he yelled and started dancing wildly around the room.

The sudden appearance of his mother, Anna, in the doorway pulled him up short. 'Shush, Andy!' she said in a loud whisper. 'You must be quiet. Your father is in a meeting downstairs with Mr Broombridge, Rollover von Cracklingen and Farty Ritter von Krumm.'

'Can I listen in?' Andy asked cheekily.

'Absolutely not!' Anna shot back. 'Please just stay here in your room for a little while. And keep the noise down. I'll let you know when they've gone.'

Andy waited till his mother left and then slumped on his bed with a disappointed snort. 'It's not fair!' he whined to the pencil. 'Why can't I—'

'Be quiet, Andy!' the pencil commanded, cutting him off. 'I'm trying to listen.'

'You can hear them?' Andy said excitedly.

'Yes, of course.'

'Can you make me hear them too?'

'Yes,' the pencil responded with a tone that suggested he would be rolling his eyes if he had any.

'You never told me you could do that!' Andy cried.

'You never asked me.'

Suddenly, Andy could hear the voices of the people downstairs as clearly as if he were sitting right next to them. The first voice he heard was Farty von Krumm's yelling at Andy's father, Johann.

'The crest! My precious crest!' Farty cried. 'You are using *my* brand icon in your advertising material! How dare you!'

'Was my grandfather not a von Krumm?' Johann calmly replied.

This was a red rag to a bull. Farty completely exploded. 'That's only because he married a lowly von Ritter baroness!' he screeched. 'By doing so he lost all rights to use our von Krumm family crest. Do you understand?'

Before Johann could respond, Rollover von Cracklingen interrupted.

'My dear Johann,' he said soothingly, 'we are here to make peace.'

'Tell that to Farty,' Johann retorted, glaring at his enraged relative.

'Farty's just very passionate about protecting the family crest,' Rollover said. 'And that's the key word, Johann—family. It's very important that our family remains united. So, you must accept that the only legitimate Ritter von Krumms are Kunnikunde and her daughters, Pink and Rose. The rest of us don't count. The best thing for everybody, Johann, is for you to retire immediately. Just go quietly and enjoy the rest of your days in peace.'

'But there are *conditions!*' Farty interjected aggressively.

'Conditions?' Johann asked. 'Whose conditions? What conditions?'

'*Our* conditions!' Farty screeched, losing his temper again.

'Kunnikunde and the family,' Rollover declared, 'demand that you never make another pencil in your life and that you immediately stop advertising your products and talking to the media about them.'

'Rollover! Rollover!' Johann replied, shaking his head in disbelief. 'Impossible! Ridiculous! I've worked extremely hard to establish the business. It is now very successful and starting to make good profits.'

Rollover von Cracklingen abandoned all pretence of fostering family unity and harmony. 'Just shut it down, you fool!' he shouted. 'That is the command of your sister-in-law, Countess Kunnikunde Ritter von Krumm!'

Mr Broombridge, who Johann had almost forgotten was in the room, abruptly piped up. 'Or,' he said, 'we could rent it from you. I have checked it out and discovered that you have some very nice new machines and equipment. Of course, the rent has to be very small.'

Johann's good nature had been stretched to the limit. He rose from his chair, trying hard not to raise his voice but failing.

'Gentlemen!' he barked. 'This conversation is over! I ask politely that you leave this instant.'

As the three unwelcome visitors rose from their seats and made for the door, Rollover von Cracklingen paused to glare at Johann. 'You have four weeks to shut down your factory,' he threatened, 'or face the consequences!'

'Please, Johann, you can't win against us,' Mr Broombridge mumbled with a measure of appeasement. 'You should know that.'

'You will regret your hostile attitude,' Farty von Krumm hissed. 'You are a parasite sucking on the Ritter von Krumm name. Kunnikunde and the family will shun you. Your name will be wiped from the family history!'

'Consider yourself erased!' Rollover von Cracklingen shouted as he stormed out, taking the other two with him.

'That's OK! So be it!' Johann called after them before shutting the door, somehow resisting the urge to slam it off its hinges.

As soon as he heard the door close, Andy shot out of his room and down the stairs.

'Dad! Dad!' he called. 'What did they mean by "face the consequences"? What will happen?'

'Nothing but empty threats,' Johann said. He stared hard at his son. 'How did you ... were you eavesdropping?' He raised his finger and was about to scold his son when the pencil intervened.

'Any threat by Countess Kunnikunde must be taken seriously,' the pencil said. 'Sir, I suggest you increase the security around the borders of your factory—I smell sabotage.'

Johann was about to respond when the pencil continued. 'Worse still, I sense an attack by a horde of devils.'

'A horde of devils!' Andy gasped. 'How can we defeat that?'

'It will be made up of several groups, each one led by a powerful alpha demon. I have to identify those leaders and then try to turn them against one another. If I succeed, and they start fighting amongst themselves, it will greatly weaken them. The horde will lose speed and momentum and forget its prime purpose.'

Andy and his father could do nothing but stare at the magic pencil; this was all beyond their understanding.

'In order to prepare myself,' the pencil went on, 'I have to return to the spiritual world to seek more powers. In the meantime, Andy, don't get into trouble; just stay in the house. By the way, sir,' the pencil said to Johann, 'it was me who enabled Andy to listen in on your meeting. I thought it was important for him to hear it.'

At that, the pencil flashed a bright blue, and the spirit was gone. For now, it was just an ordinary pencil again, lying inert on the desk. Andy and Johann gazed at it for several seconds, then at each other.

'A horde of devils?' Johann muttered. 'Hard to believe.'

'But you *must* believe it, Dad!' Andy cried, waving his arms around and becoming very agitated.

'I do, Andy ... I do. Now, calm down. Go and watch a movie in my study and I'll call you when dinner is ready.'

This ruse worked because Andy's parents strictly controlled the amount of television he watched, especially movies. He rushed happily into the study with his dog, Sassy, following keenly behind.

3

After the movie and a big dinner, Andy slept soundly. It was shortly after dawn when the magic pencil's voice woke him.

'Wake up, Andy! Wake up!' it called out from the bedside table.

Andy sat up greatly relieved his mysterious friend was back. He was now so used to having the magic spirit around that he couldn't imagine a day without it.

'How was your trip?' Andy asked, as if the pencil had been on an overseas holiday.

'The airports were a nightmare, of course, but'—the pencil cut himself short and laughed when he saw Andy's shocked expression—'Just kidding,' he said. 'Even though a spirit can travel millions of times faster than the speed of light, it still took me several human hours to reach my destination.

'Once there I had a briefing and was given some training by senior spirits in how to handle Lucifer's growing army of little devils, as we call them, who he has provided with special powers in order to spread hate, jealousy, greed and anarchy. One of the most recent devils he has recruited is, unfortunately, your Aunt Kunnikunde.'

'But I thought she already was a devil,' Andy said, frowning.

'Not quite,' the pencil replied. 'Previously she needed assistance from other devils to work her evil. Now she should have enough powers herself to pursue her single-minded obsession ... money.'

'What added powers does she have?'

'Don't know yet, but we'll find out soon enough. One thing for sure, though, she'll be back any time now and we have to be prepared.'

'Yes! Yes!' Andy cried. 'I'll run into town and warn everybody that Kunnikunde will soon be back, and we should start setting traps to catch her and put her in Commander Wurstling's gaol.'

'You'll do no such thing!' the pencil ordered. 'Such a plan won't work, although its simplicity does have some merit. And right now, I don't think Kunnikunde is our main problem. I sense that Lucifer's other newly recruited devils, equally evil in their own way, are already approaching.

'The spirits gave me some names. The first one is Gusto Calamari, head of the infamous Calamari crime gang. The second one seems to be Ohama Bin Schaden, head of a vicious terrorist group. Both these violent thugs want only one thing—the mighty laser gun that is rumoured to have shot down an alien UFO. They've heard that it is in the possession of a boy in Stone. There is a third violent thug who also wants to find this unfortunate boy.'

As the 'unfortunate boy,' Andy's eyes were on stalks and his breathing was increasing rapidly.

'His name is Dr Ulrich Folterknecht,' the pencil continued, 'and he was the one that hypnotized your parents to sign over their possessions to Kunnikunde last year. He is also the head of the dreaded TSP—the Teutonian Secret Police. His mission is to prove that aliens do not exist. He will arrest anyone involved in the laser gun and UFO rumour. He has vowed to torture them and put them in gaol for a very long time. His prime target is not just this troublesome boy but also his parents.'

Andy gasped in such a huge breath and held it so long that he started to feel dizzy.

'Oh no!' he finally blurted out, feeling wobbly on his feet. 'Oh no!' he repeated, starting to panic. 'We have to warn Mum and Dad!'

'Calm down!' the magic pencil demanded forcefully. 'All in good time ... just let me finish. It's important for you to know your enemies. The last one on my list is Moses Clay, a senior operative of the New Colonies Secret Service. Although he's not a bad man, he could be influenced by the evil countess and hence become a threat.'

Andy seemed defeated already. 'Do we have anyone on our side at all?' he groaned dismally.

'Yes, we do,' the pencil said. 'Fritz the painter and Hermann the plumber are also targets. And Jim Steel, the soon-to-be husband of Miss Heger, is also of value to us. So is Miss Heger but only unwittingly. Another helpful ally could be Roger Less, a secret agent of Her Majesty the Queen of Britonnia. His primary intention is to expose and apprehend both Gusto Calamari and Ohama Bin Schaden. But he will also sabotage the operations of the Teutonian Secret Police and the New Colonies Secret Service if he gets the opportunity. I know we had another ally, but I ran out of time and couldn't scan the name into my memory.'

Andy had calmed down somewhat. 'What about the chief of police, Commander Wurstling?' he said. 'He would be on our side.'

'Yes ... you're right, Andy. I was just about to mention him. The commander will be an ideal weapon with which to distract and confuse our enemies. And let's not forget the good people of Stone who stood so solidly behind your parents. We are definitely not alone.'

'That's fantastic!' Andy cried. 'Yes, we can win ... we can win easily and kick all those devils out of Stone for good! I will now warn Mum and Dad. Then I'll put on my karate suit—that will scare all those bad people! And when I see Aunt Kunnikunde, I will set Sassy onto her!'

'No! No!' the pencil objected sternly. 'You won't do any such thing. I have a plan ... but it will only work if everyone involved on our side follows it step by step and trains and operates as a team.

Only then will we have a chance—a very small one I might add—of defeating the forces of evil that Lucifer is pitting against us.

'We still don't know what new powers he has passed on to your aunt, or what his own involvement will be. There could be other evil spirits helping Kunnikunde. No one knows yet.'

Andy looked a little less gung-ho than he had been just minutes before. But he was still keen to do something, so what the pencil said next pleased him immensely.

'Andy, I want you to sneak into town and find Fritz and Hermann. Ask them to come here late this afternoon. And if you can locate Jim Steel, get him here as well … but without his future bride, please. Be as inconspicuous as possible; the fewer people who see you the better.'

'Yes, sir!' Andy cried, saluting. 'Your plan sounds like a great adventure!'

'We don't want an adventure. An adventure is what happens when you don't have a plan.'

Andy didn't quite get it, but he nodded gravely, looking suitably chastised. Minutes later he was dressed and rushing downstairs. He was out the front door in a flash, unobserved, with Sassy hot on his heels.

4

To stay out of sight for as long as possible, Andy took the forest route into town. He hoped he might run into his friends Jurgen, Hansi and Hartmuth but knew it was a bit too early in the morning for them to be out of bed on the first day of the summer holidays.

When Andy reached the end of the forest, he paused and gazed out across the green carpet of cornfields on the outskirts of Stone. 'What's that?' he said aloud, pointing skywards for Sassy's benefit. She was more interested in a hare she'd spotted disappearing between the cornstalks just a few metres away.

'It's a drone!' Andy answered himself, unaware that Sassy had bolted after the hare. He watched the tiny helicopter moving from side to side as it hovered over the town. It was moving erratically, stopping and starting continuously, as if it were hunting for something. Andy was so transfixed that he almost failed to notice that the drone had suddenly turned and was heading straight towards him.

He instantly flung himself into the cornfield and ducked down, only then realising that Sassy wasn't with him. Before he could call out to her, he heard the whirring of the drone's propellers directly above him. He knew it would have a camera, so he resisted looking up and hunched down as far as he could among the cornstalks. Seconds later, the loud bang of a shotgun rang out over the cornfield and blasted the drone out of the sky. The drone tumbled through the tall leafy corn plants and landed right next to him.

He heard someone crashing through the cornfield towards him, cursing loudly. Whoever it was stopped short of him and yelled, 'Got you, you sneaky spy! No one is allowed in or over my field—especially spying competitors!'

When Andy heard the sound of a tractor starting up shortly afterwards, he assumed the sharpshooter was the local farmer protecting his crop.

'A tractor!' Andy gasped, suddenly aware of the danger he was in if it came towards him. Fortunately, it didn't, and he heaved a sigh of relief as he heard it chugging off in the opposite direction. Andy stayed hidden in the corn until the sound of the departing tractor faded away completely, by which time Sassy had found him.

'Get the birdy, Sassy,' he ordered, pointing at the disabled drone. Sassy obliged, probably thinking it was the strangest bird she had ever retrieved. Once she had it firmly in her jaws, Andy burst out of the cornfield with Sassy in pursuit. Together they ran through some high grass and into the cover of the forest. When he finally stopped for a breath, Andy felt a piercing pain in his right thumb. He was shocked to see a bee in the process of inserting its stinger right under his thumbnail. 'Yow!' he cried, shaking his hand violently, flinging off the bee. When he inspected his thumb again, he saw the tiny venom sac the bee had left behind. With another yelp of pain, he flicked the sac off. He remembered his father telling him not to pull bee stingers out because it would squeeze the remaining poison into the wound and make things worse.

As it was, the pain brought tears to his eyes. He stuck his thumb in his mouth and sucked on it hard for several seconds, then rushed off towards home. Sassy followed close behind, carrying the damaged drone in her mouth.

Once home, Andy ran straight upstairs to his room. He jumped onto his bed and lay down moaning and sucking his thumb as hard as he could to try and ease the pain.

'That was quick,' he heard the pencil say. 'Why are you sucking your thumb?'

'A bee stung me for no reason at all!'

'You must have disturbed it or scared it. Otherwise, it wouldn't have stung you.'

'I had no intention of scaring or hurting the stupid bee,' Andy cried. 'I wish all nature's creatures liked me as much as I like them.'

'I could arrange that,' the pencil remarked casually.

Andy sat up. 'I didn't know you could do a thing like that!'

'You never asked.'

'Do it! Do it!' Andy cried. He was so excited he almost forgot the pain. 'Could you stop a tiger from chasing me?'

'Yes.'

'Or a shark from eating me?'

'Yes.'

'And you could make all humans like me?'

'No! Humans are the only ones exempted from this spell. Now, pick me up and hold my point against your skin.'

A bright blue flash followed, engulfing Andy and, unexpectedly, Sassy who had chosen that instant to jump up on the bed and present Andy with the damaged drone. Her front paws touched Andy's legs, connecting her to the magic power flowing through his body.

'Oh my goodness!' the pencil exclaimed with a hint of panic. 'That's not good!'

'What? What?' Andy cried with alarm. It was the first time he had heard the pencil sound unsure of himself.

'Your dog!' the pencil yelled. 'Your crazy dog became part of my spell to make all animals like you. It is totally unacceptable to perform these spells on animals, especially a dog like Sassy.'

'Why?' asked Andy.

'Hello? Hello?' the pencil cried. 'Is there a brain in your little skull?'

'Of course,' Andy retorted hotly.

'Does Sassy like chasing rabbits?' the pencil asked rhetorically.

'Yes.'

'Does she run after birds and lizards and anything else that moves in a field?'

'Of course, she does,' Andy said proudly, patting Sassy's head. 'She's very fast and almost catches them.'

'Well then, noodle head,' the pencil said facetiously, 'from now on she'll catch everything she chases!'

'What?' Andy asked, mystified. 'How come?'

'There really are noodles in your head instead of brains. *Because* ... my spell will make all the animals like her, and they won't run away! This is a disaster. It breaks all the laws of nature.'

'Can't you cancel the spell?' Andy asked.

'No, I can't. What I would normally do is rush back to the spirit world to find a spell that would reverse this one, but there is no time now. You must keep Sassy on a lead whenever you take her outside. Until I can reverse the spell, she can't be allowed to roam freely ... understood?'

'Yes, understood,' Andy muttered, looking momentarily intimidated. But then he puffed out his chest and said defiantly, 'By the way, Sassy has never killed anything!'

'That's because she's never caught anything,' the pencil retorted sharply. 'Now it will be a slaughter if she's running loose in the forest and fields.'

Andy was a picture of misery, sitting on the side of his bed with his head slumped and sucking hard on his sore thumb, which now seemed to be hurting more than ever.

'Let me see that thumb,' the pencil demanded.

Andy held up his shiny wet thumb which had swollen considerably.

'Touch my point to it,' the pencil said.

Andy picked the pencil up with his left hand and very gently touched the pencil point to the tip of his thumb, causing a tiny blue flash. Instantly, the pain went away.

'Oh!' Andy gasped. 'That's incredible—the pain's gone!' He pressed hard on his thumb with his forefinger just to make sure he wasn't imagining it. He might have asked the pencil why it hadn't done that much earlier, but he was too relieved to think of it.

'It was my pleasure,' the pencil said.

'What?' Andy said, looking up from his thumb.

'Oh, sorry,' the pencil chirped, 'I thought you said thank you.'

'No, I didn't say—oh, yes ... sorry. Thank you.'

'So, a little teensy bee stopped you from completing your important mission?' the pencil asked.

'No, it wasn't the bee sting,' Andy said defensively. 'Something happened before that, which frightened me. And I thought you should know about it as soon as possible.'

5

Once Andy explained his harrowing encounter in the cornfield with the drone and the trigger-happy farmer, the pencil's tone softened somewhat.

'Yes, that would be frightening, Andy,' he acknowledged. 'You did the right thing abandoning your mission and getting home safely.'

Together they inspected the damaged drone, which Sassy had dropped on the bed.

'It is a yellownise,' the pencil explained, 'of the highest quality. Normally it is only sold to the military. Look at the sophisticated camera. Let me touch it—I may be able to download some of the pictures it took.'

When Andy touched the pencil point to the camera, he could immediately see clear images in his mind. They were mostly pictures of houses but some were of people. There were also moving video images, and at the very end, the angry farmer could clearly be seen raising his shotgun and aiming it at the drone.

'Good work, Andy,' the pencil said. 'I don't think that drone was spying on the farmer's cornfield.'

'So, what was it—' Andy's question was interrupted by a loud knock on the door.

Andy's mother came in. 'Andy, please come downstairs to the study and bring the magic pencil. Your father and I want to have further discussions.'

'Further discussions?' Andy said quietly to the pencil as he began to follow his mother downstairs.

'Yes,' the pencil said. 'While you were trying to reach Stone, I used the time to brief your parents. Your father came up here looking for you, so I took the opportunity to speak to him.'

Andy entered the study to find his father, Johann, looking anything but happy. His mother simply looked worried.

'This is really not the time for me to be sidetracked with threats of dangerous thugs and evil spirits,' Johann declared. 'I will ask my friend Commander Wurstling to provide us with round-the-clock police protection so we can get on with life as usual.' He frowned at Andy and shook his head. 'I just can't believe your magic pencil's hysterical idea that half the world will be after us.'

'But, Dad!' Andy was trying to think of something useful to say when the pencil spoke up.

'Sir,' he said, addressing Johann respectfully, 'is what you want to believe always correct? I doubt that. Does what you don't want to believe never happen? I doubt that too. All I'm asking politely is to take me seriously and see if what I said to you and Countess Anna happens or not. My predictions have been proved correct in the past, as you well know.'

Before Johann could respond, they all heard a forceful banging on the front door and someone shouting, 'Attention! Attention!'

'Andy, run upstairs, please,' Johann said, 'and stay out of sight.'

With the banging on the door getting even louder and more aggressive, Andy was only too happy to oblige.

'Sir,' the pencil said, 'do you remember the instructions I gave you this morning about what to do if something like this should happen?'

'Yes, I do,' Johann replied as he turned towards the front door. Before he could take more than a couple of steps towards it, the door was smashed open by a battering ram.

The first person to walk in was an angry-looking rotund little man with glossy black hair that seemed to be glued to his head. Three much larger men with him had close-cropped hair and looked almost twice as big as him. They wore long black leather coats and rather stupid expressions on their faces. What alarmed Johann more than their intimidating size were the violin cases they carried. He doubted any of them even knew what a violin was.

'I'm-a Gusto Calamari,' the little fat man declared gruffly, 'and I wanna talk-a to your boy!'

'How dare you enter my house like this!' Johann roared with unrestrained outrage.

'Umberto! Rudolfo! Alberto!' Gusto called out. 'Unpack-a your instruments!'

The only music these instruments could play would be funeral dirges. The three machine guns the men took from their violin cases were now all pointing at Johann.

'For Gusto Calamari,' the little man said, 'the time is money! I wanna see your boy—now! I know he is here! Don't-a make-a me angry!'

'He is in the cellar ... hiding the g—um, making some sort of toy,' Johann said. 'Please don't hurt him.'

'If I get-a what I want-a, he won't-a be harmed,' Gusto said with an eager grin on his face. 'Show me this-a cellar.'

Johann led the gangster to the kitchen where the door to the old air-raid shelter was. As the coolest room in the house, Johann now used it as his wine cellar where he often held wine tastings with his friends. It was furnished with comfortable lounge chairs and coffee tables. There was also a cheese fridge and a variety of dried meats hanging from the wall. Off to one side was a small tool room.

The door to the cellar was very heavy and it creaked on its hinges when Johann pushed it open. He leant in and called out, 'Son, you have some visitors!'

'Please ask them to wait for a couple of minutes!' Andy's voice called out. 'I'll be right up ... I'm just hiding the laser gun away!'

'Alberto, Rudolfo,' Gusto commanded, 'you come-a with me.' He jerked a thumb at Johann. 'Umberto, you stay and watch-a this guy. And if-a the boy tries to escape-a, you grab him.'

With that, Gusto and his two henchmen started down into the cellar. Umberto stood blocking the cellar doorway, his gun trained on Johann. A second later, with silent commands from the magic pencil, Sassy bolted at high speed across the kitchen and threw herself at Umberto with all the force she could muster. Taken off guard, the big thug stumbled backwards towards the open cellar door. He frantically threw his arm out and just managed to stop himself from falling. But his reprieve was short-lived. Thinking quickly, Johann gave Umberto a hard kick, sending him tumbling down the steps. He quickly slammed the door shut and bolted it securely.

He patted Sassy vigorously. 'Good dog, Sassy! You are a very good dog.' Sassy happily wagged her tail and then went and sat beside the kitchen cabinet where she knew her treats were kept.

'OK, Sassy,' Johann said with a chuckle, 'you certainly deserve a big treat.'

6

Sassy was delighted with the big ham bone she received and immediately rushed upstairs to show it off to Andy. But he was preoccupied, talking on the intercom with Gusto in the cellar. Because the house was rather large, Johann had had an intercom system installed that serviced most rooms, including his wine cellar. The magic pencil had taken good advantage of it in his plan to trap anyone who might come to the house and threaten the family.

Through the intercom, Andy could hear Gusto shouting angrily.

'Boy, wherever you are, come out and show-a yourself! Rudolfo ... find-a the light switches! Alberto search-a every inch of this darn dungeon!' Unintentionally, Gusto had used a very apt description for the cellar, considering his current predicament.

Safely upstairs in his bedroom, Andy was speaking into the intercom exactly what the pencil was instructing him to say. 'Mr Calamari ... I don't have the laser gun anymore,' Andy said. 'A Mr Ohama Bin Schaden stole it last night.'

Gusto didn't believe him but pretended he did to keep him talking, while he stealthily approached the wine tasting area where he figured Andy's voice was coming from. 'You mean the terrorist leader?' he asked, his pistol poised, ready to shoot if he had to.

At that tense moment, Rudolfo found the switches and the cellar lit up. It was then that Gusto realised he had been talking to an intercom and not Andy in person.

Andy heard the gangster boss emit a loud, unintelligible sound that suggested he wasn't at all happy about being tricked. He vented his spleen briefly then calmed down. 'My sweet boy, you must think-a Gusto Calamari is stupid, eh?'

He turned and whispered to Alberto and Rudolfo, 'Get upstairs, you idiots! The boy speaks through an intercom so he must still-a be in the house. Take everything apart and find-a that darn boy! Go! Go!'

Gusto then sat down in one of the armchairs and, with an evil grin, started to talk to Andy to keep him distracted while his men went off to search the house for him. 'OK, clever boy, if Ohama has-a your gun then he would probably already be back in-a the desert.'

'I don't believe so,' Andy responded, repeating the pencil's words he could hear in his head.

'And why not?' Gusto demanded.

'Because I have the chip that makes the laser gun fire. Without it, Ohama Bin Schaden has nothing but a large, impressive-looking toy weapon.'

'And where do you keep-a this-a chip?'

'It's in a very safe place,' Andy replied.

'Good! Very good!' Gusto cried. 'You give-a me the chip, nice boy, and I will get-a your gun back from Ohama. Deal?'

'OK, deal,' Andy agreed.

Gusto was just about to respond when Rudolfo surprised him.

'Boss,' he said, 'we have a problem.'

Gusto exploded. 'What!' he yelled. 'You can't-a find him? He's definitely in-a this house somewhere!'

'No, boss,' Rudolfo said unhappily, 'the problem is that we cannot open the cellar door.'

'Idiot!' Gusto shouted. 'Get Umberto to open the darn-a door now—or I'll feed-a him to my crocodiles!'

Umberto took this as a direct command to blast the door open with his machine gun. He'd forgotten that his boss thought he was still upstairs *outside* the door. He opened fire and Alberto joined him.

RATATATATATA! ... RATATATATATA! ... Mayhem ensued. Ricocheting bullets and fragments of door and stone wall began flying around the room, smashing many bottles of Johann's fine wines. The noise in the confined space was deafening.

'STOP! STOP! STOP!' Gusto screamed to no avail. 'You wanna kill us all! Imbeciles!'

It was only when Rudolfo intervened that the gunfire ceased. In the sudden, merciful silence the only sounds that could be heard were the dripping of wine and the occasional tinkling of glass fragments caught up in the liquid as they fell onto the stone floor. The pungent smell of burnt gunpowder, mixed with wine aromas, hung in the air. This lull lasted for less than ten seconds before the cellar was filled once again with a deafening noise but not from gunfire.

This time it was Gusto Calamari going totally ballistic. His swearing was almost as rapid and loud as the machine guns. He cursed everything under the sun—the laser gun, the Son of God, the cellar, Ohama Bin Schaden, Andy—but most of all his "stupid! stupid!" henchmen. Gusto's fury reached a crescendo when he realised that Umberto was in the cellar with him.

'Umberto!' he screeched, stabbing his finger at the ceiling. 'I told-a you to stay up-a there!'

'They shot me with a white cannonball,' a quivering Umberto tried to explain, his eyes locked on the pistol Gusto was waving around.

Gusto made a noise like a wounded bull then fired three shots from his pistol—shattering several more wine bottles. Umberto, Alberto and Rudolfo hit the floor in unison.

'Next time I will-a shoot you three, not bottles!' Gusto shouted.

He fired another shot up at the cellar door. 'We have been tricked! I will-a feed this-a family to my crocodiles! And after that, I will-a hang them and then burn them!' He emitted another sound like some animal in pain. 'They will-a pay for making a monkey out of Gusto Calamari!'

His apoplectic rant finished, the gangster boss slumped, exhausted, onto one of the lounge chairs as his three henchmen cautiously got to their feet.

'I thought we had a deal,' Andy's voice chirped over the intercom.

Gusto sat up. 'Deal? What-a deal? What are you talking about?' he yelled, pointing his gun at the loudspeaker.

'I offered you the chip,' Andy said, 'that will make the laser gun work, and you then steal the gun from Ohama Bin Schaden, who I have reason to believe is still in Stone.'

'Why would-a you do that?' Gusto barked.

'Because I'm just a boy,' Andy said. 'How could I face up to Ohama Bin Schaden ... or you for that matter?'

You've done pretty well so far, Gusto thought.

'I just want to get on with my life,' Andy's voice went on. 'I won't be needing any laser guns for that.'

'That-a makes good sense, boy,' Gusto said, his mood brightening. 'So, open the cellar door and let-a me see this chip.'

'I can't do that,' Andy replied. 'But I can tell you another way to get out—but only if you promise never to tell my father. He's gone to get Commander Wurstling and an army of police and will be very angry with me if he knows I helped you escape.'

'OK, I promise,' Gusto said, shrugging his shoulders at his three henchmen, who were all keeping a watchful eye on their volatile boss.

'In the next five minutes or so I will drop the chip down the little mail chute, which is near the big sofa. I will talk to you again when I drop it.'

'OK, I'm waiting,' Gusto said.

It occurred to Rudolfo that his boss didn't have a choice about waiting, but he kept that thought very much to himself.

7

Upstairs, Andy switched off the intercom. 'What now?' he asked the pencil.'

'Get me some knives and forks,' it replied. 'And if you could find a small crystal or gemstone that would be very helpful. And a thick breadboard too. But hurry, we have little time.'

Andy rushed off. He returned quickly with a breadboard, several items of cutlery and a small crystal ornament that had been sitting on a shelf above the fireplace in the lounge room.

'Excellent!' the pencil said. 'Place them all together on the desk ... on the breadboard. We don't want to burn a hole into the desk. Now, close your eyes; the glare from my welding process might damage them.'

Andy did but even so, the blue light engulfing the items on the table was so intense that he had to look away. It lasted about thirty seconds.

'OK, finished,' the pencil said. 'Everyone seems to believe the non-existent laser gun is an alien one, so the chip that operates it should look alien too.'

When Andy opened his eyes, he couldn't believe what he saw.

'Wow!' he cried. The object was a disc about the size of a drink coaster, like a miniature Olympic discus. It was as shiny and smooth as polished marble, and to Andy, it looked as if it were made of liquid crystal and mercury that had somehow solidified. A light at its centre glowed subtly and the disc constantly changed colour across the spectrum.

'This will convince any human that it's not from this planet,' the pencil said. 'Now, drop it down the chute and run back quickly so we can finalise the set-up of Mr Gusto Calamari.'

Andy ran off with the chip to the mail chute, rushing past his bewildered parents—twice. He was back in his room in a flash. He switched on the intercom and spoke the pencil's words into the microphone. 'Mr Calamari, have you got the chip?'

After a brief silence, Gusto's voice erupted in the speaker: 'Mama Mia! Mama Mia! I have never seen a thing like this! Holy Mother Mary—maybe the boy is telling the truth!' Gusto raised his voice and leaned in close to the intercom, which he didn't need to do. 'Boy!' he yelled, distorting the sound in the speaker upstairs. 'Boy! ... Are you there?'

'Yes,' Andy responded. 'Can you please not yell so loudly, Mr Calamari. I can hear you quite clearly at normal volume. Here's how you can escape from the cellar without getting me into trouble. Under the stairs, there is an emergency exit, which my father filled in years ago with sand and gravel because it was no longer needed. There are shovels in the tool room—you can dig your way out.'

Gusto wasted no time. 'Rudolfo! Alberto! Stupid Umberto! Get those shovels and start digging. Alberto ... before you start-a that, open a bottle of wine and cut-a some of the hanging meat for me.'

Gusto made himself comfortable in a lounge chair and turned his attention back to the intercom. 'Can-a you still hear me, boy?'

'Yes.'

'When can we meet so I can thank-a you?' The gangster boss was doing his best to sound friendly.

'In two days, there will be a wedding in town,' Andy said. 'The whole town will be there. It is the wedding of our school's headmistress. The celebrations will take place around midday in a big beer tent next to the church. There I will make myself known to you. The church is close to the hotel you are staying at.'

How does he know where I'm staying? Gusto asked himself.

'Mr Calamari,' Andy said, 'I can't talk to you anymore; if my father catches me, I'll be a goner!'

'OK, boy,' Gusto said sweetly. 'I'll see-a you soon.' As he sat back in the lounge chair with his red wine and dried meat, an evil grin spread over his pudgy face.

Andy asked the pencil his usual question: 'What next?'

'I have to finalise my plan,' it said. 'But first, we have to talk to your parents. We need to get them out of danger, or at least into less danger.'

Andy carried the pencil into the living room to find his parents in deep discussion.

'Good timing, Andy,' Johann said to him. 'We have just been talking about you. Your mother and I have decided to send you to her sister's place for a while, at least until things return to normal. I will drive you there this afternoon, so please get ready.'

Andy was horrified. 'But, Dad!'

'Not buts! This is our final decision. Your mum and I are really worried about your safety. Now, go upstairs and start packing!'

Both parents heard the pencil's dissenting voice in their heads. 'That could have worked two days ago,' it told them, 'but not anymore.'

'Why not?' Johann snapped.

'All of Stone, which includes your house, is under constant surveillance by satellite and drones. You can't take Andy anywhere without them knowing, so he's safer here than anywhere else.'

'Without *whom* knowing?' Andy's mother Anna piped up.

'Countess Kunnikunde for one,' the pencil replied.

'Kunnikunde?' Anna and Johann exclaimed in unison.

'At this very moment, her tame weasel, Mr Werner Little Werner, sits at the edge of the forest across from this house, filming every move this family makes.'

'What?' Johann cried. 'Werner is here? I will confront him at once!'

'This simply is not the time for impulsive actions, sir,' the pencil cautioned. 'Rather, I suggest you all start listening to my plan. Each one of you is in grave danger.'

Anna hugged Andy to her and exchanged a nod of agreement with Johann.

'We are listening,' Johann said.

8

The pencil spoke for at least an hour, explaining in detail what he believed should be done. Andy and his parents listened intently. There was a lot of nodding, some gasps, occasional laughter and at one point an outburst from Andy who jumped up and shouted, 'No way! I will not do that!' He was firmly told to be quiet and keep listening.

The pencil finished his briefing with the caveat that the best-laid plans of mice and men—and spirits—can go awry. 'So be prepared to improvise,' he said. 'Especially, keep listening to me and never ever act out of anger or fear; that will cloud your judgement and only make matters worse.'

'There is a great deal of work in this plan,' Johann said. 'How can you pull it off?'

'Leave that to me, sir. You and your wife must just focus on your roles and nothing else. That will be of immense help to me. Now, if you would both go into the big city and buy everything on the shopping list that I dictated. It's important that you are back here with everything within two hours. In the meantime, Andy and I will conduct some counter-surveillance on Mr Werner Little Werner. And don't worry. I will protect Andy from any serious danger.'

Anna and Johann left immediately for the big city while Andy, with the pencil in his pocket and Sassy right behind him, snuck out the back door, keeping behind a large hedge and the many bushy plants in the garden which bordered the forest. He had his father's binoculars and planned to use them to locate Werner. Then he would use the cover of the forest to sneak up as close as possible to him.

It wasn't long before Andy spotted Werner in a tiny clearing almost totally obscured by thick foliage. With a close-up view through the binoculars, he saw what an impressive surveillance set-up Werner had. At least five cameras were facing the house with four drones lined up beside them ready for take-off. And Werner himself was peering into a large telescope mounted on a tripod. Andy was also alarmed to see two large dogs sitting alert beside Werner. He recognised them as two Dobermans Kunnikunde had bought over a year ago for her personal protection.

Andy knew he would have to be extra quiet and sneaky trying to get close to Werner with those two brutes on guard duty. Perhaps they made him more nervous than cautious because no sooner had he started crawling towards Werner's spying set-up than his knee pressed on a dry twig which snapped with a sharp crack.

The two Dobermans jumped to their feet, ears pricked and staring in Andy's direction.

'Show yourself!' Werner screamed, 'or my dogs will tear you apart!'

'Better show yourself, Andy,' the pencil said.

Andy stepped out of the bushes and began walking towards Werner, who couldn't believe his eyes—or his luck. He looked like he had just discovered a treasure chest. The look of ecstatic astonishment on his face was priceless. Andy couldn't imagine anyone being so happy to see him, not even Sassy. It was as if Werner had seen some sort of rapturous vision, because he threw both arms in the air, threw his head back and began shrieking at the top of his voice. A first, Andy couldn't make out what Werner was screaming, but then he heard the words: 'I have caught the boy! Countess Kunnikunde, I have caught the boy! Countess! Countess! I have caught the boy!'

Andy was momentarily confused, expecting to see his evil aunt somewhere close by. He couldn't see her anywhere and had just begun to think Werner had taken leave of his senses when he heard a loud, hair-raising hissing that even frightened the Dobermans.

Then the evil noise seemed to metamorphose into a swirling spiral of flames, like a small tornado made of fire. Out of this fiery whirlwind emerged a blonde-haired woman dressed in a black business suit. Andy was shocked and a little terrified. He patted Sassy, who was right at his feet, to reassure her … and himself. The woman had her back to Andy, and he assumed it wasn't his aunt. He was sure this blonde apparition wasn't the normally dark-haired Kunnikunde. How wrong he was. The instant he heard the woman's shrill voice he knew it was his horrible aunt.

'You've called me twice now, Werner!' she shrieked. 'The first time because of a stupid broken drone; this had better be good! I can't waste these powers. You know I can only use this power ten times a year!'

Werner was trying to tell Kunnikunde what he was so excited about, madly waving his hands around like some kind of crazy semaphore, frantically stabbing his finger towards Andy behind her.

'Uh oh!' the pencil piped, 'I need to take control of your and Sassy's bodies now!'

A bright blue flash momentarily engulfed boy and dog together. A second later the evil countess turned and saw Andy.

'Aha! My darling nephew!' she cried. 'Werner, excellent work! Well done!'

Little Werner glowed with pleasure and pride. Like him, Kunnikunde was overjoyed to see Andy but without the histrionics. Instead, she put on the sweetest smile she could muster.

'My darling little nephew,' she cried, 'how lovely to see you again! I trust your parents are well?'

9

Kunnikunde's excitement at seeing Andy seemed to manifest itself in little blue flames, which covered her suit. Looking closely at his aunt's face, Andy was shocked to see flames also emanating from her eyes.

Seeing his expression, Kunnikunde enquired sweetly: 'Are you surprised to see me, Andy dear?'

'No, not at all,' Andy said calmly, quickly composing himself.

'Shouldn't you be ... after all the terrible things you've done to me?'

'No, I don't think so,' Andy replied pleasantly with a relaxed smile.

Andy's calm demeanour unsettled Kunnikunde, and she glowered fiercely at him, all attempts at sweetness fading fast. Then she saw Sassy step out from behind Andy and a sinister smile replaced the fierce glower. 'Ah! This is indeed a beautiful day,' she exclaimed. 'Just when I was wrestling with the difficult decision of the best way to punish you, your horrid little mongrel has provided the answer.'

'I know you have an extendable magic arm Aunt Kunnikunde, but I'm not afraid of it and neither is Sassy.'

Kunnikunde guffawed a very unpleasant laugh: 'Ha ha ha! That's true ... I used to be able to extend my arm hundreds of metres, but now look, it only stretches to about three metres. But that is more than enough for me to go wallet shopping in a supermarket whenever I need some ready cash! Ha ha ha! I now have incredible new powers, which you will experience shortly.

'Werner!' she barked, turning around so suddenly that it made the little man jump. 'We will deal with that horrid white mongrel the old-fashioned way, she said, glaring at Sassy.' Kunnikunde looked at her two Dobermans with a malicious smile. 'Have my dogs kill it now!'

Werner whistled at the two guard dogs and pointed at Sassy. 'Kill!'

The Dobermans shot towards Sassy, who didn't seem fazed at all. Because of the magic pencil's accidental spell, all animals liked Sassy. Instead of attacking her, the guard dogs greeted her like an old friend while Werner continued screaming, 'Kill! Kill!' at the top of his lungs. The three dogs glanced at him briefly then ran off into the forest together.

'*Muss ik alles makken!*' screeched a furious Kunnikunde. 'What have you done to my dogs? Werner, go after them and bring them back here. You must punish them for their disobedience'— she turned on Andy—'while I punish this nasty boy!' Her face was a distorted image of hate, greed and jealousy. Her eyes were glazed with such bitterness and vengeance they shone with a desire to kill.

'Do you know, you nasty stupid boy, why I'm going to punish you?'

As genuinely frightening as his enraged aunt was, Andy managed to keep his composure. 'No, why *do* you want to punish me?'

'Because you lost me money!' Kunnikunde shrieked. 'Buckets of it! Money! My beautiful money! That's why! To steal from a broke and grieving old widow... How *could* you? Is that fair? Is that fair?'

'No, it would not be fair, Aunt Kunnikunde,' Andy responded evenly. 'But as it happens, no one stole from you. On the contrary, you stole from others ... and you still do! You're a disgrace to our family name!'

'AAARRRRGGGHHH!' Kunnikunde screamed. 'Family! Family! I *hate* the family! Hate! Hate! Hate!'

Kunnikunde finally snapped. Her eyes rolled back in her head, and she screeched some words Andy didn't understand. Waving her arms wildly above her head, she suddenly threw them forward, sending two bolts of fire from her hands shooting towards Andy.

Boom! Boom! The two fire bolts exploded at Andy's feet creating a huge pall of smoke that completely engulfed him, obliterating him from view.

Kunnikunde now looked like a true devil from the depths of hell. With fire in her eyes and a diabolical grin of pure evil, she began to dance in circles, shouting, 'I've gotten him at last! My first kill! It feels so good!'

'You'll start a forest fire, you silly moo!' Andy called out, instantly ruining Kunnikunde's celebrations. When she saw Andy standing there unharmed several metres from where her fire balls had hit, she froze mid-dance. Her sudden transformation from dancing delirium to dumbfounded disbelief was extraordinary to behold. But as Kunnikunde had often reminded everybody, she was tough. Recovering quickly, she took her rage to another level. This time she shot fire bolts not only from her hands but also from the tips of her shoes. She moved back and forth in a semi-circle in front of Andy, firing bolts continuously for a full minute. The effort exhausted her, but she was convinced that this time she had done the job and finished Andy off.

She bent over huffing and puffing trying to catch her breath. Even if she had straightened up and looked, she wouldn't have seen Andy descending from a tall tree close by; he zoomed to the bottom faster than the eye could see. He seemed to move down in a series of three-metre jumps. Once on the ground, he hid behind the tree. And just in time.

He heard a loud rustling in the forest close by which startled Kunnikunde and put her instantly on her guard. He saw her poised, facing the sound, ready to unleash another barrage of fire bolts.

She was on the verge of letting them go when a red-faced Werner staggered out of the forest, puffing and panting.

'Countess,' he whimpered, 'please forgive me, but I couldn't catch your dogs; they were too fast for me.'

'That's OK, Werner,' Kunnikunde said with uncharacteristic tolerance. 'Overall, you have done well today, even though you didn't get everything right, as usual. Have you prepared for the blowing up of Johann's disgusting factory yet?'

'Oh yes, Countess!' Werner excitedly affirmed. 'I am taking delivery of two bombs the day after tomorrow—one large one and one small one. They are explosives that can't be traced, and they have electronic trigger mechanisms, so I can detonate them by remote control. Each bomb will be in a duffel bag, so they will be easy to conceal. I thought it would be appropriate to schedule the bombs to go off during your advisory board's meeting right next door to Johann's factory. That way everyone will get to enjoy the fireworks! Ha ha ha!'

'Good idea, Werner,' Kunnikunde said distractedly. Something had caught her eye on the spot where she had blasted Andy with her fire bolts. She left Werner standing and went to investigate. When she found a small fragment of what appeared to be clothing, her face lit up. 'Yes! Yes!' she murmured to herself. 'I got him! I finally got the lousy little rat!'

She walked back to Werner with a happy smile on her face.

'Call me when the bombs are ready to explode,' she cackled. 'I love fireworks.' Her cackling was suddenly drowned out by the sound of howling wind, as the air swirled around Kunnikunde like a miniature tornado.

Before Werner could even open his mouth in astonishment, the countess was gone.

10

Andy too was astounded by his evil aunt's spectacular disappearing trick and realised that she was going to be a formidable opponent. He was wondering what to do next when happily he saw Sassy return with the two Dobermans. Werner immediately started shouting at the two guard dogs that they were in big trouble and would suffer terrible punishment at the hands of Kunnikunde.

'Andy,' the pencil abruptly piped up, 'tell Sassy to get the birdies—but don't say it out loud. Just think it with intense focus.'

In his hiding spot behind the tree, Andy pressed his fingers to his temples and tried to send his thoughts to Sassy telepathically. To his amazement, it worked. The little white canine cannonball shot towards the drones which, for her, were the ultimate birds to catch and kill. She grabbed the first one and shook it into little pieces. As she grabbed the second drone, the two Dobermans decided to join in on the fun and destroyed the remaining two drones.

'You rotten, disobedient, lunatic dogs!' Werner shrieked. 'I'll have all three of you put down! Oh my God! Kunnikunde is going to be so angry—those drones were very expensive. Oh my God!'

He began darting around like a lost ferret trying to find the Dobermans' leads. When he finally located them, he approached the dogs, who were happily sitting amidst their destruction.

'Come, little sweethearts,' Werner coaxed, 'it's time for your nice lethal injection at the vet. He's waiting for you right now—mustn't keep him waiting.'

As Werner got closer, all three dogs started growling. They growled louder and louder the closer he got. When he finally reached for one of the Dobermans to try to collar it, the dogs began snarling, baring their teeth ferociously. Werner stopped in astonishment; he couldn't understand what had come over the dogs. Without any control over them, he had no option but to back off, slowly. *Don't run*, he told himself. The dogs watched him go but didn't pursue him. Werner packed the spy gear the animals hadn't destroyed into two large duffel bags, slung them over his shoulders and hurried off into the forest as fast as he could go with the extra weight weighing him down.

'OK, all clear,' the pencil said.

Andy leapt out from behind the tree highly excited. 'Wow! Wow! That was incredible! Those fire bolts were terrifying! Thank God they missed! How could you move me so fast?'

'Teleportation,' the pencil said. 'I thought the safest place for you was up a tree.'

'Wow! Unbelievable!' Andy cried, still high on adrenalin.

'Kunnikunde has developed into a fire witch,' the pencil said. 'Right now, she thinks she has killed you.'

My aunt tried to kill me! The horror of it suddenly dawned on Andy, cutting off his adrenalin rush.

'Let's make sure she doesn't think otherwise,' the pencil went on. 'Let's get home—we have a lot of work to do.'

'Can you teach me how to do that teleportation thing by myself?' Andy asked.

'Now that I've done it with your body,' the pencil replied, 'you can do it any time yourself, unfortunately.'

'Why "unfortunately"?'

'Because I'm not supposed to pass on extraordinary powers to human beings—it's a breach of spirit rules. But I had no choice. I had to act instantly to save your life and that was the only thing I could think of on the spur of the moment. Usually, I have time to plan my responses.'

'Well, I'm glad you broke the rules,' Andy said, 'otherwise I'd be dead! Sometimes rules are stupid.'

'Your logic seems to have some merit,' the pencil said. 'Now, let's go home—the quick way. Picture the front door of your house in your mind then imagine you are there. You will be automatically transported there in a series of incredibly fast stages—almost too quick for the eye to see. We call it telehopping. Now, do it.'

Andy did as the pencil had instructed; seconds later, he was standing at the front door of his house. His adrenalin rush returned. 'Awesome!' he cried, punching the air with both fists. 'Fantastic! Wow!'

He tried the door handle. 'It's locked,' he said. 'We'll go round the back.'

'Why would you do that?' the pencil asked impatiently.

'I don't have a key,' Andy replied.

'You don't need a key, silly boy! Just imagine you're inside and you will be. Come on—we haven't got all day!'

Whoosh! An instant later Andy was standing in the entry hall.

'Oh my God!' he screeched. 'I'm incredible! I'm invincible! That's the best gift ever! I'm invincible!'

'Can we stop overreacting?' the pencil scolded. 'You are far from invincible. We need to get back to work. First, we have to build some sort of large gun that looks alien.'

'Are the gangsters still trapped in the cellar?' Andy asked. 'Yes,' the pencil replied. 'They still have a few more hours of digging to do before they can get out.'

'Well, I'm not going down there,' Andy said, frowning, 'and that's where the tool shed is.'

'I don't need the tool shed,' the pencil said. 'Just take me into your father's machinery shed.'

'OK,' Andy replied. 'By the way, what happens when the gangsters escape from the cellar?'

'I tried to hypnotise Gusto so that he would go straight back to their hotel in Stone and stay there. We'll have to wait to see if I was successful or not.'

11

In Johann's machinery shed the pencil showed more interest in old wheels and hubcaps than anything else. He had Andy collect as many of them as he could in a pile in the centre of the shed.

'Now, get me two thermometers, Andy—we need some mercury in the mixture—and also some of your marbles to create buttons.'

Andy placed the pencil on a bench and raced back into the house. A short time later he returned with the required items.

'Excellent, Andy!' the pencil said. 'Well done. Add the marbles to the pile then break the thermometers and sprinkle the mercury in them over it all.'

Andy did as instructed.

'Now,' the pencil said, 'stand back a couple of metres and then point me at the pile ... and cover your eyes with your other hand.'

Seconds later a massive blinding flash lit up the shed. When Andy opened his eyes and removed his hand, he gasped in amazement at what he saw. Lying on the floor was a large and strange-looking gun—to Andy, it seemed to be some weird futuristic weapon—exactly what he imagined an alien gun would look like. Silver and shiny, it glinted in the sunlight streaming in through the high windows of the shed.

Andy soon noticed that the gun wasn't the only thing gleaming brightly. The entire shed and everything in it looked shiny and brand new, including the tractor which had seen better days and the various old lawn mowers and gardening tools, which seemed as if they'd been delivered from the shop that same day.

'The usual side effects,' the pencil said, responding to Andy's astonishment.

'Just like what happened at the pencil factory last year,' Andy remarked.

'Exactly,' the pencil said. 'And they aren't the only things that have been transformed, Andy ... you look better as a girl.'

'Ha, ha, good joke,' Andy started to laugh then stopped, realising his voice sounded different.

'No joke, Andy.'

'What?' Andy shrieked, suddenly aware of the long blonde hair hanging down to his shoulders. 'Nooooooo!' he cried out, looking down at the frilly dress he was wearing. 'How could you do this to me? I'm a boy—being a boy is my brand! My unruly blond hair, that's part of my boy brand. So is wearing trousers, not dresses! And doing boy stuff with my friends who are also boys! I thought you were going to just *disguise* me as a girl, with makeup and a wig, not actually turn me into one!'

'That wouldn't have worked,' the pencil said calmly.

'Why not?' Andy squeaked—he was so upset he could barely talk.

'Kunnikunde thinks you are dead. And all the other foes are looking for a boy. Makeup and a wig might have fooled some of them but not all—and not for long. So, I had to make sure no one would recognise you, not even your friends. And just to help you calm down, the spell will only last for five days.'

'That'll seem like a lifetime,' Andy mumbled.

'There's a mirror on the wall over near the generator—see if you recognise who you temporarily are.'

Andy trudged over to the mirror.

'Oh my God!' he cried. 'I look exactly like my cousin, Belle!'

'At least I made you a very pretty girl,' the pencil said with a rare chuckle.

'Oh, great—thanks for nothing! What if Belle visits us in the next five days?'

'She won't,' the pencil assured him. 'She's a long way away on holidays with her family.'

Slightly calmer, but still very hot under the collar, Andy started back for the house. He hesitated at the back door, took a deep breath and went inside, heading straight for the kitchen. I *need a cold drink*, he told himself. Anna was at the bench unpacking several shopping bags.

'Oh, hello, Belle,' she said with a broad smile. She expected to see her own sister come in as well. 'Where's your mother?'

'Right in front of me!' Andy Belle growled. He took a lemonade from the fridge and walked off into the entrance hall.

Anna followed him, looking totally baffled. 'What do you mean? Where's Andy?'

'Andy is now going up these stairs to his room, Mum,' Andy Belle muttered.

Anna stood like a stunned mullet watching him go. When Andy's bedroom door slammed shortly afterwards, it snapped her out of her stupor.

'Andy,' she exclaimed, 'is that really you?' Recovering her composure a little, Anna hesitantly climbed the stairs after him. She was about to knock on his bedroom door when she heard the pencil's voice in her head.

'It's not a disguise,' he said. 'I've turned him into a girl, temporarily. Can you please calm him down? We have to focus on the job at hand—there's no room for drama queen behaviour.'

'I wouldn't call it drama queen behaviour,' Anna retorted, jumping to her son's defence. 'You've turned him from a boy into a girl—and without warning him first. That must be a hugely traumatic experience for him.'

'I'm this boy's guardian angel,' the pencil replied, unperturbed. 'It was necessary to ensure his safety, simple as that. Besides, I told him it's only for five days. I don't see a problem with it. He knows what's at stake.'

'OK, I'll try,' Anna whispered as she knocked on the door. 'Andy, it's me.'

'Come in, Mum,' she heard Andy Belle call out grumpily.

Anna's heart went out to her son when she saw him, as a girl, sitting on the side of the bed looking deeply depressed. She sat beside him and pretended to be amazed.

'Andy ... what a fantastic disguise! It really fooled me!' she said. 'If it fools your own mother, it will certainly fool all those enemies who are trying to hurt us.'

Andy Belle reluctantly accepted the sense of that. He was also relieved that his mother thought it was just a disguise, so everyone else would too and he wouldn't have to admit that he actually *was* a girl.

'Yeah, Mum,' Andy Belle said, sounding happier, 'the pencil has done a convincing job making me look like a girl.'

'He sure has,' Anna agreed. 'Imagine what fun it will be looking into your enemies' eyes and them not having a clue it's really you.'

'Oh, yeah!' Andy Belle cried with a huge grin.

Confident that her son was now more relaxed about the whole thing, Anna went back downstairs to finish unpacking the shopping bags.

'I've just added a little fine-tuning to make your "disguise" even more convincing,' the pencil told Andy Belle. 'You can use your own boy's voice when talking to people who think you're in disguise, like your parents and your friends, Jurgen, Hans and Hartmuth—but only them.'

'That's great!' Andy Belle cried. 'Now I won't be embarrassed to see them.'

'That's good,' the pencil replied, 'because I want you to go and get them and bring them here—well, Jurgen and Hans anyway, I know Hartmuth is away on holiday. I need them both. They can play an important role—as decoys.'

Just before he rushed off to find his friends, Andy Belle asked, 'Can I telehop?'

'Yes, of course. And if you picture Sassy arriving at your destination point with you, she will telehop as well.'

'Yay!' Andy Belle cried. Then he was gone.

12

When Andy Belle reached the forest seconds later, Sassy was right beside him. 'Wow!' he cried. 'I have an invincible dog too!'

He knew roughly where Hans and Jurgen would most likely be and it didn't take him long to find them.

Both boys were shocked to see a blonde girl they didn't know calling out to them with Andy's voice. Hansi was the quickest to recover. 'Why are you dressed as a girl, Andy?'

'And your face doesn't look like you either,' Jurgen added.

Andy Belle replied in his own voice: 'Sit down and I'll explain everything ... *except the part about actually being a real girl*, he reminded himself.

Once Hansi and Jurgen knew the pencil had used its magic to make Andy look like a girl, they were cool with it. And when they heard about the plan, they were both excited to be involved.

'We're in!' they cried in unison.

With that, the three friends and Sassy raced off to Andy's house—without the aid of teleportation.

'It seems your dog has two new best friends,' Hansi said, pointing back at Sassy and the two Dobermans running beside her.

When they got to Andy's house, Andy Belle was surprised to see a most beautiful and expensive-looking car parked in the driveway right outside the front door. It looked like it was made entirely of highly polished silver and glistened brightly in the sun.

Andy Belle was so fascinated by this magnificent machine that he couldn't resist touching it. As his fingers came in contact with the glossy surface, the car turned from silver to a light blue colour.

'The colour of innocence,' he heard a voice call out. He turned to see a tall elegant-looking man walking down the verandah steps towards him with his father Johann following close behind.

'If you touch this magic car and it likes you it will turn a nice colour,' the man said to Andy in a rather posh voice. 'Sir,' he said to Andy's father, 'have a go.'

When Johann touched the car, it turned a beautiful shade of green.

'Fantastic!' the stranger said. 'It means you are a good man.'

At that moment two large black limousines appeared in the driveway and made their way slowly towards the house.

'Everyone in the house!' Johann shouted.

Andy Belle responded immediately and went inside, taking Hansi and Jurgen with him.

'Sir, allow me to stay. No one knows me here,' the stranger said, calmly lighting a pipe.

Johann was already on the verandah with his hand on the front doorknob. 'OK,' he called out. With that he went inside and closed the door behind him, leaving the stranger standing in the driveway alone. Everyone in the house immediately went to a front window and peered out.

'Who is that posh-sounding man, Dad?' Andy Belle asked.

'His name is Roger Less,' Johann replied. 'He works for Her Majesty of Britonnia's Secret Service. He said he would help protect us. I don't know why or how, but I'm sure we'll find out soon enough.'

Outside, the two black limousines pulled up behind Roger Less's gleaming machine, crouched like a silver panther on the driveway. At some point, it had reverted from its temporary shade of green to its original colour.

When one of the limousine's doors opened, the first person to emerge seemed to be forcibly ejected. It was poor Werner Little Werner; he landed face down in the gravel.

'You can go home now, little man!' a gruff voice called out from the back seat. That seemed to be a signal for five people to get out of the limousines, all looking sinister and threatening. They were dressed in black with matching headbands, except for the tallest of them who was draped in a long white robe with a hood that partly covered his face.

Inside the house, Andy Belle, who had just received instructions from the pencil, rushed out of the house through the back door to his father's machinery shed.

In the meantime, outside in the driveway, Roger Less appeared nervous, erratically shuffling around as if uncertain what to do next. The pencil quickly intervened in the Secret Service man's thoughts: 'Stand still, you idiot,' it said. 'And please listen to what I tell you to say.'

This sudden, strange, somewhat rude and abrupt voice in his head seemed to settle Roger down and he regained his composure somewhat. Then another voice spoke to him, only this one wasn't in his head. 'Sir,' the tall man in the white robe and hood said, 'are you Count Johann Ritter von Krumm?'

'No, sir, I am not,' Roger Less replied, using the words the pencil was giving him. 'I'm a relative from Britonnia here on a short visit. Johann and his family are away on holiday, and I'm house-sitting for them. They will be back tomorrow.'

Hearing this, the man in white gave an almost imperceptible hand signal to the four men in black, who all began approaching the house simultaneously.

They'd only taken a few steps when a girl's voice rang out, yelling, 'Uncle Roger! Uncle Roger! I've found Andy's alien gun!'

A second later everyone saw a blonde girl appear from around the side of the house and run towards them, still shouting 'Look, Uncle! Here it is—it's amazing!'

Andy Belle stopped short of them, pretending to be shocked at the presence of the strangers. He made a show of trying to hide the large gun behind his back.

The tall man in white rapidly approached him. 'I'm Prince Ulla Dulla Bulla,' he declared loudly, 'Please, my little princess, let me have this amazing gun.'

'Stop right there!' Andy Belle cried. 'This is my cousin Andy's gun—I can't give it away!'

Andy Belle suddenly found himself surrounded by the four men in black who had spread out around him. 'And Andy's already going to be angry with me because the gun won't work without the firing chip.' He showed Prince Ulla an empty chamber in the side of the gun. 'The chip should be in there,' he said.

Prince Ulla knelt on one knee for a closer look. He nodded. 'And where is this firing chip ... did you lose it?'

'No! I didn't lose it! It was stolen by that nasty gangster Gusto Calamari.'

'And where is this very nasty man now?' Prince Ulla asked.

'He is staying at the big hotel in Stone,' Andy Belle replied. 'He has given Andy an ultimatum; if he doesn't bring this gun to him at Miss Heger's wedding reception, he will harm our family.'

'And when is this wedding reception?' the prince asked.

'In two days,' Andy Belle replied.

'Oh, sweet little girl ... beautiful princess,' Prince Ulla cooed, now at eye level with Andy Belle. He gestured to his white robes. 'I wear all white because I am a pure, kind and honest person ... sort of an angel, you could say. I'm the only one in this whole world who can, and will, help you get this firing chip back and have this nasty Mr Calamari arrested.'

Prince Ulla paused, tapped his forefinger on the gun and put on the sweetest voice he could manage: 'But I will need this gun to make sure I have the right chip.'

'OK ... that sounds reasonable,' Andy Belle replied. He handed the gun to the clearly surprised but delighted prince and then, with a happy smile, rushed over to Roger.

'That was easy,' murmured the prince to one of his men. 'Let's go.'

The five of them headed back to the black limousines. On the way past Roger's car, the prince gave it a gentle pat. 'Nice car!' he said cheerily, very happy and excited about getting hold of the gun. He climbed into the back seat and nursed his newfound treasure as if it were a baby.

13

As the two limousines drove off, Andy Belle and Roger noticed that his magnificent silver machine had turned pitch black.

'That pure white prince must in fact be a very bad man,' Roger remarked.

'Come up,' Johann called out from the verandah. 'I think you need another drink, sir!'

'I need more than a drink,' Roger responded, putting both hands on his head, 'I'm hearing voices in my head.'

'Welcome to the Addams Family—this is a normal occurrence here,' laughed Johann.

They sat down at an outdoor setting on the verandah as Anna appeared with a tray holding three large, very dry martinis in authentic cocktail glasses.

'We have prepared these in honour of our special guest from Britonnia,' Johann declared as they all clinked glasses.

'How are you feeling after your encounter with Prince Ulla Dulla Bulla and his assassins?' Johann asked.

'Shaken *and* stirred,' Roger quipped, holding up his martini. Johann laughed uproariously, and Roger looked delighted.

Anna was very pleased to see that her husband and Her Majesty's Secret Service man hit it off so well. They gave the impression they had known each other for a long time rather than less than an hour.

It suddenly occurred to Johann that his son was nowhere to be seen, but his niece Belle had joined them. 'Hello, Belle,' he said, 'what are you doing here?' He turned to Anna. 'And where's Andy?'

'I'm replacing Andy,' Andy Belle said.

'So, Andy is with your sister?' Johann said.

'No, not quite,' Anna replied, smiling. 'But he is very well hidden away, Johann.'

'Where?' Johann retorted, a little sharply. He was quickly getting the feeling something was being kept from him.

'You will find out soon,' Anna giggled, glancing at the young blonde girl sitting opposite.

Johann let it go at that but almost immediately another thought popped into his mind. 'Um,' he said, looking at the magic pencil Andy Belle had placed on the table in front of him. 'I should apologise to you, pencil. You were right and I was wrong to doubt you.'

'Apology accepted, sir,' the pencil responded. His reply was also heard in Roger's head. He nearly dropped his glass. 'Sir!' he cried, 'did you hear that?'

'Yes, of course,' Johann nodded with a broad smile. 'That's the naughty little spirit inside that pencil who's been driving me bananas recently. Although now I'm used to him—not to mention very grateful to him. When he first appeared in my brain, I thought I was hallucinating.'

'My God!' gasped Roger. 'I've never heard a dead person's voice in my brain before!'

'I'm not dead, you idiot!' the pencil retorted. 'I'm alive! More alive than you'll ever be in your present primitive physical form! There is no death! There is only life! Get that into your empty head!'

'OK! OK! I get it,' Roger cried, holding his head. 'Stop abusing me!'

'Good,' the pencil said, instantly calming down. 'Now we can go back to discussing the plan.'

As the pencil had requested, Hansi and Jurgen came out onto the verandah to join the discussion. Like the others, they listened as the pencil spoke at length. It seemed he might go on forever, but his discourse was finally interrupted by a disturbance in the bushes at the edge of the garden. The two Dobermans were immediately on the alert and sat up with their ears pricked. Sassy, however, didn't hesitate and shot off like a bolt of white lightning towards the disturbance, disappearing into the shrubbery. The two guard dogs quickly followed. After a brief commotion of growling, barking and yelling, a distressed and dishevelled Werner Little Werner burst from the bushes like a fox being flushed out by the hounds.

'Count Johann,' he wailed, 'please call the dogs off me!'

'Werner!' Andy Belle exclaimed. 'He's been spying on us!'

'No! No!' Werner cried. 'I have seen nothing. I have heard nothing. I promise you. I was kidnapped by the terrorist Ohama Bin Schaden, who calls himself Prince Ulla Dulla Bulla. I just managed to escape.'

'Would he have heard any of our plans?' Andy asked the pencil.

'No, not much. But he saw and heard everything that went on with Ohama Bin Schaden in the driveway earlier when you handed over the fake gun. Andy, go over and hold Werner's hand for three seconds—I'll try to manipulate his recollection of it for our benefit.'

Andy Belle went across to Werner, grabbed his hand and led him through the garden shrubbery to the verandah. 'This way, sir,' Andy Belle said kindly. 'Uncle Johann has called the dogs off.'

'Thank you, little girl,' a relieved Werner replied.

'You can let go of his hand, Andy,' the pencil said, 'I've finished with him.'

'Count Johann,' Werner Little Werner pleaded. 'Can you drive me into town?'

'Unfortunately, not,' Johann replied. 'However, there is an unlocked car parked just around the corner, probably stolen and abandoned. You could use that. Obviously, I don't have the keys to it. Do you know how to hot-wire the ignition, Werner?'

'Yes, yes I do,' Werner cried. 'Thank you, Count Johann!'

The little man rushed off to find the car. Everyone on the verandah watched him go.

'I think that was a little mean, Johann,' Anna said.

'He deserves it,' Johann retorted. 'There is no one meaner than that nasty little weasel of a man.'

14

Werner Little Werner found the abandoned car unlocked, as Johann had promised. He eagerly jumped into the driver's seat and started feeling around for wires under the ignition. He had just found the two he needed when he heard a sharp knocking on the glass. Werner looked up to see the angry face of Gusto Calamari, who was tapping on the window with the barrel of a pistol.

The next thing Werner was aware of was waking up in the local hospital heavily bandaged and hurting all over. 'I have been tricked by Count Johann,' he growled and groaned at the same time. 'The pleasure of blowing up his factory will be my greatest satisfaction!' An evil grin spread over his face, and he tried to laugh, but it was too painful. Several hours later he hobbled into his hotel room vowing to also blow Johann's house up, preferably with him in it.

Meanwhile, back at the house Werner was picturing blowing to pieces, the magic pencil finished outlining his plan for the next few days. 'Beyond that,' he said, 'we have to be prepared for the unexpected and may have to do some contingency planning.'

He had given everyone a role to play, including Hermann the plumber and Fritz the painter, who arrived suddenly and unexpectedly; only the pencil had known they were coming.

'Count Johann! Count Johann!' Hermann called out. 'Fritz and I are here. You called for us to come urgently!'

Johann was about to say he had done nothing of the sort when he heard the pencil say to him, confidentially, 'Yes, you did. That is, I did. They are both in danger of being arrested tomorrow. So, we have to hide them ... and also use their professional skills. Please ask them to stay the night here while you check into the big hotel in town.'

'Gentlemen,' Johann said, 'thank you for responding so promptly. I could use your help. I'll explain how later, but would you please stay here tonight? Countess Anna, Andy and I have to stay at the hotel.'

'Of course, Count Johann,' Hermann exclaimed while Fritz nodded enthusiastically, 'we would be delighted to help.'

'Wonderful. Thank you,' Johann said.

Suddenly, everyone seemed to have things to do. Anna started packing and Johann showed Fritz and Hermann to their rooms, while Hansi and Jurgen followed Andy Belle upstairs to his room and slammed the door shut after them. If anyone else in the house had been upstairs an instant later, they would have noticed a mighty flash through the gap under the bedroom door.

At that moment downstairs, Roger Less was in the living room distractedly puffing on his pipe, still trying to understand and accept the idea of a spirit talking to him in his head. His pondering was intruded upon by Anna calling out, 'I believe I'm finished! We can go now!'

'Where is Andy?' Johann asked. 'And is it wise to be taking Belle with us?'

Before Johann could add words to go with his bewildered expression, the door to Andy's bedroom opened and the three occupants raced downstairs and into the living room. Johann was about to become even more bewildered. Standing before him were his niece Belle and two Andys. *Two Andys?* Johann's head was spinning. 'What in God's name is going on?' he bleated.

'I'm Jurgen,' stammered the Andy standing directly in front of Johann.

'And I'm Hansi,' said the other Andy.

'And I'm the real Andy, Dad!' Andy Belle said.

'What?' Johann began swaying on his feet and felt his legs start to wobble beneath him. Roger caught him before he toppled over and helped him to a chair. The two men looked at one another and nodded, which was a cue for Roger to rush to the bar and fix a couple of stiff drinks.

Johann stayed seated and simply stared in astonishment at the three children. *Unbelievable!* he thought. *They could be clones.*

As Roger returned and handed Johann a large scotch, the pencil spoke up.

'It is the art of disguise, sir,' he said, 'spirit style. I learnt this skill on my recent trip back. I thought it would come in very handy—particularly for confusing our enemies.'

'I'm sure it will,' Johann said, the effect of the scotch beginning to calm him somewhat. *It's certainly baffling the living daylights out of me!* he thought.

'Let's not stand around gawking any longer,' the pencil said impatiently. 'We must get to the big hotel.'

Johann and Roger quickly finished the last of their scotches and followed Anna and the three children clones out the front door as Hermann and Fritz waved goodbye.

To his exuberant delight, Andy Belle was allowed to go with Roger in his magnificent silver machine. It was only a two-seater and so there was no room for Hansi and Jurgen.

'Please do not touch any buttons in this car,' Roger warned Andy Belle as he buckled up. 'And don't pull any levers.'

'No, sir,' Andy Belle assured him.

'Just sit back and enjoy the ride!' Roger said.

As the car moved off with a deep-throated growl, Andy Belle was immediately fascinated by the many buttons and levers he was forbidden to touch.

'What are they all for, Roger?' he asked.

'They are all classified top-secret devices,' Roger replied. 'But I'm sure I can trust you not to tell anyone about them.'

'Oh, yes!' Andy Belle said.

'If I push this red one here,' Roger said,' it will electrocute whoever's in the passenger seat ... which at present is you. Pulling this green lever here will knock you out. And pushing this pink button here will eject your seat and you out of the car.'

Andy was so fidgety with excitement that the seat belt was having trouble restraining him.

'Actually,' Roger said,' see this blue button here? I'm going to let you push it—but only that one!'

'All right!' Andy Belle cried and without hesitation pushed the blue button. A fraction of a second later Andy Belle found himself securely tied to the seat with various straps. He could move his legs a little and wiggle his fingers, but that was about all.

'Now, let's have a calm and relaxed drive,' Roger chuckled.

15

A short time later Roger turned his magnificent silver machine into the impressive circular driveway of the big hotel and parked in a specially reserved bay.

'OK, Andy,' Roger said, 'I'll untie you.'

'No need, thanks,' Andy Belle said. 'I'm already untied.'

Roger's usual calm and collected demeanour deserted him momentarily. 'What the—? How did you do that? These functions are supposed to be infallible. There must be a fault with that one!'

'Not at all,' Andy Belle replied casually. 'It's just that it doesn't work on me. I can telehop.'

'Oh my goodness!' Roger exclaimed, flabbergasted. This place is destroying all my guiding principles! I can't believe it ... I can't believe it,' he kept muttering as he got out of the car and ushered Andy Belle towards the big hotel's front entrance.

Even for someone like Roger, who had travelled all over the world, the Stone hotel was an impressive building. It was a massive and elaborate relic of a bygone era. The wide entrance doors opened into a vast polished oak lobby filled with precious antique furniture and a profusion of plants and flowers; hanging from the centre of its soaring domed ceiling was a spectacular and dazzling crystal chandelier.

While it was beginning to date, it still maintained the aura of a true luxury hotel. At this time, it was unusually busy, and the lobby had a long queue of guests checking in and out. The hotel manager was animated with delight and excitement, scampering hither and thither, greeting and bowing; he had never seen the place so busy. It seemed most of Stone's population were staying in his hotel for the huge wedding the following day. And with all the visiting guests as well, Stone's big hotel was packed to the gunwales.

When Roger saw the long lines at the check-in counter, he set Andy Belle on a little mission: 'Go and sit in the lounge area and start observing the people coming and going. We have to figure out who's who.' Suddenly, a better idea occurred to him. 'Actually, what we really need to do is get our hands on their guest book.'

'That's easy!' Andy Belle said. Before Roger could stop him, Andy Belle jumped up and headed off to the reception desk, taking the magic pencil from his pocket as he went. Once there, he greeted the person manning the desk with a cheery smile, touched the pencil on the large guest book and returned to Roger empty-handed.

'Well, that was a non-event,' Roger chirped, a little too gleefully Andy Belle thought.

'No, it wasn't,' the pencil piped up.

Andy touched Roger's hand with the pencil, creating a tiny blue spark at the tip of one of his fingers. Again, Roger briefly lost his elegant demeanour. 'You are the freakiest family I've ever met in my life! Your father was wrong—the Addams Family has nothing on you lot!'

'You'd better start reading,' the pencil said curtly.

Roger realised he had the entire guest book in his head. 'Good God!' he wailed. 'I'll need a long holiday after this!'

Just then, something caught his attention. A strikingly beautiful and stylishly dressed young brunette was having trouble managing her large suitcase. As if he'd suddenly been bitten by a snake, Roger leapt up and rushed over to this apparition.

'May I help you?' Roger offered in his most polished and refined Britonnian accent.

'Oh! Thank you, yes,' the stunning young brunette replied with a smile that made Roger tingle all over. The huge guest book filling his head was temporarily forgotten. The brunette introduced herself as Cornelia, explaining that she was a journalist from Helvetia who was on assignment to find out about the strange events in Stone a year ago.

'Strange is an inadequate word for it from what I can gather,' Roger replied as he gallantly lugged her huge suitcase towards the check-in counter. Once there, he handed the case over to the porter and in a most debonair and gentlemanly manner took Cornelia's hand and kissed it.

She recoiled with horror and looked like she might slap him. 'Why did you lick my hand?' she snapped, taking a tissue from her handbag and wiping the back of her hand. 'Weirdo!'

Roger was indignant. 'In Britonnia it is a gesture of admiration and respect! I even do it to our queen!'

'Well, I'm not your queen, sir! ... And I find your behaviour disgusting! Men don't lick women's hands in Helvetia!'

'Kissing! It's kissing not licking!' Roger retorted, deeply insulted and embarrassed. He turned on his heel and went back to his seat. 'That is the first woman who did not swoon when I kissed her hand,' he lamented to Andy Belle.

'Helvetian ladies are obviously not as romantic as those in Britonnia,' Andy Belle answered, trying not to grin. He wasn't totally successful.

'It wasn't funny!' Roger barked. 'It was humiliating! Those Helvetian women must be a—' He cut himself off when something else caught his eye. Five men in black suits with red ties marched purposefully through the lobby in tandem and advanced on the reception desk. The man in front was considerably shorter than the others. He continuously rubbed his hands together.

'Out of the way!' a voice demanded of those standing in the queue. 'We are the Teutonian Secret Police!'

The front man swung around angrily. 'Heiner,' he hissed to the man directly behind him, 'give that idiot Friederich a slap! We are *secret* police; we're supposed to act inconspicuously!' Then, in a loud voice, he said, 'That is my friend Dieter's idea of a joke. Ha ha ha. We are members of the Red Tie Jazz Band; we are here as tourists, yah! We can wait our turn like everyone else, yah! But I think those behind the reception desk could work a bit faster, yah! And I would like to see the manager now, yah!'

The sharp 'yah!' at the end of every sentence gave Dr Folterknecht away. Mr Vogelfutter, the hotel manager knew exactly who he was and hurried over to him, arriving with a bow, which he repeated several times, like a bird feeding.

'Dr Folterknecht!' he sang. 'What a pure pleasure to see you again!' He lowered his voice. 'Your suites are ready. And this morning I received your special equipment and set it up in the cellar.' He bowed again.

'Very good, Vogelfutter. I shall inspect it immediately, yah!' He turned to his colleagues. 'Manfred and Karl-Otto, you will scrutinise the guestbook and compile a list of any ten-year-old boys who are staying here and their parents' names and addresses. Add them to the list we've already compiled of all the ten-year-old boys who live in Stone. Now, hurry up, yah! We will meet in two hours in my suite, yah! Heiner and Friederich ... come with me, yah!'

With that, the Secret Police officers dispersed.

16

From the moment he first spotted the secret police chief, Roger had kept a newspaper concealing his face, occasionally peering over it to see what was happening. He lowered it and stared after the departing Dr Folterknecht.

'Do you know that man?' Andy Belle asked.

'Oh yes ... indeed, most definitely. He is Dr Folterknecht ... a nasty piece of work. And I never expected, or wanted, to see him again!'

As he spoke, Roger casually looked towards the front door and gasped with shock. 'My God!' he muttered. 'Moses Clay!' The newspaper returned, blocking his face. 'I haven't seen *him* for a while.'

'Which one is he?' Andy Belle asked.

'The sinister one with the slicked-back hair and pencil-thin moustache,' Roger answered from behind the newspaper.

'The one who looks like Mandrake the Magician?' Andy Belle asked.

'Exactly, that's him. There must be something big going on here if he's involved ... and we'd better find out what.'

'Isn't it time to explain to Roger the events in Stone last year?' Andy Belle asked the pencil.

The pencil agreed and gave Roger a detailed account of everything that had happened and the subsequent fallout. Her Majesty's Secret Service agent was astonished and also angry.

'Prince Ulla Dulla Bulla and Ohama Bin Schaden are one and the same? Why didn't you tell me? I could have apprehended him on the spot. And you had Gusto Calamari locked up and let him go? This is insane! I'm the professional—let me handle these people from now on, please! Both of these men are on my target list. However, I wouldn't recognise them; I've never seen their faces. 'Actually, it's said that anyone who sees the faces of Gusto Calamari and Ohama Bin Schaden and recognises who they really are doesn't live to tell the tale.'

'Well, that's just stupid!' Andy Belle cried. 'I've seen both their faces and I'm still living!'

'Maybe it doesn't work on you, Miss Smartypants,' Roger remarked sarcastically. 'Like the functions in my car.'

The pencil ignored their exchange. 'You saw Prince Ulla—Bin Schaden's—face at the house. Now I'll show you Gusto Calamari's … on one condition.'

'And that would be?' Roger enquired irritably.

'That you follow my plan for the next two days—to the letter,' the pencil insisted. 'After that, you can arrest whoever you want to.'

'OK! OK!' Roger begrudgingly agreed. 'It'll make my job easier if I know what the person I'm arresting looks like.'

Andy Belle touched Roger with the pencil and the secret agent suddenly had a clear picture of Gusto Calamari in his mind. 'I know that man!' he exclaimed. 'I've met him in various casinos around the world. I've actually sat next to him at a gaming table without knowing who he was. Oh my God! Anna and Johann saw his face and know who he is. They're in grave danger … I have to protect them!'

'Well, that *was* the plan,' the pencil remarked sharply.

Roger didn't respond. Instead, he rose from his seat and asked Andy Belle to help him unload his car. Between them, they transferred two heavy large duffel bags and two smaller rolling suitcases from the silver machine to the hotel lobby. A porter immediately loaded them onto a trolley and delivered them to Johann's palatial suite and deposited them in one of the spare bedrooms.

When Roger started to unpack his bags, Andy Belle couldn't believe his eyes. He saw numerous weapons, including guns, knives and grenades, as well as various expensive-looking fountain pens, sunglasses and all sorts of fancy wristwatches. Her Majesty's secret agent also unpacked several black suits.

'One of these is for your father,' he said.

'He has plenty of suits of his own,' Andy Belle replied.

Roger laughed. 'I doubt that any of them are bullet-proof.'

'Bullet-proof?' Andy Belle exclaimed. 'Wow!'

If the suits excited him, the next item Roger produced from his suitcase mystified him. 'What are *they* for?' Andy asked, pointing at a small glass case that contained four flies. 'They look disgusting!'

Roger roared with laughter. He opened the case and carefully withdrew one of the flies. 'These are the very latest spy tools that have only been issued to a very few of our secret agents. They are tiny drones—the ultimate in nanotechnology. They require a great deal of training to master. I operate them with my mind using these.' He held up an unusual pair of spectacles. 'Electronic glasses that connect the electrical impulses in my brain to the power circuits in the drones. My brain is the control centre.'

The pencil couldn't resist: 'It's a wonder it works—your control centre is smaller than the drones themselves.'

Roger took instant exception to this facetious remark and became visibly upset. 'My brain is more than big enough to control these drones. At least I have a brain! You're just a disembodied voice inside it—you couldn't control those drones—or me, for that matter!'

While Roger got more and more wound-up defending himself, the pencil spoke so that only Andy Belle could hear. 'Let me touch him,' he said.

Andy Belle managed to surreptitiously touch Roger with the tip of the pencil. A second later the secret agent stuck a finger up his nose. At that point, Anna walked in and saw what Roger was doing. She immediately turned around to go and fetch some tissues for him. When she returned with a box of them, she noticed Roger now had his finger halfway down his throat. Anna just shook her head in disgust and walked out.

Andy Belle observed a pronounced change in Roger's facial complexion—the agent's naturally pale Britonnian skin turned a bright pink and then a vivid red. His eyes had a glazed, puzzled look and his body was as rigid as an iron rod.

'If you don't admit that there are higher powers that can control you,' the pencil demanded of Roger, 'I will make you bite into your finger ... very hard!'

'No! No! Don't!' Roger tried to yell, which sounded more like a choking sound with his finger jammed into his mouth. He felt his teeth tighten on his finger. 'OK! OK! ... I admit! I admit!'

True to his word, the pencil released his control over him. Roger removed his finger from his mouth and emitted a huge groan of relief.

'Oh my God!' he said. 'That was ghastly—not to mention disgusting and embarrassing!'

He soon recovered his composure and continued expounding on the drones. 'They are all equipped with highly toxic microscopic darts, each one capable of knocking out even the strongest person for at least five minutes.'

'They will come in very handy,' the pencil said. 'Thank you, sir!'

The pencil's positive comment seemed to mollify Roger, and he smiled with appreciation.

'Now, let's all get together and fine-tune our plan,' the pencil said.

The meeting went on for several hours and they all went to bed late, except for Jurgen and Hansi who were too tired to see the meeting through and crashed on a comfortable sofa. It was a bizarre sight for Andy seeing his two identical twins sound asleep together.

17

At the same time, in a different suite, another meeting was just concluding. Dr Folterknecht finished by naming all those he intended to arrest. It was a long list that included all ten-year-old boys and girls in Stone, as well as Anna and Johann, Hermann and Fritz, Countess Kunnikunde, Werner Little Werner, and even the head of the local police, Commander Wurstling.

'A very comprehensive list, yah!' Dr Folterknecht said to his second-in-command, Horst Heiner. 'It covers all possible suspects, yah! We will have a very busy day tomorrow, Heiner, yah! By infiltrating the wedding as guests, we will be able to arrest most of them in one fell swoop, yah!'

At that moment in yet another suite, Mr Werner Little Werner was frantically composing an email to send to Countess Kunnikunde, whom he was expecting to appear sometime the next day. It was a full report of the false recollections the magic pencil had put into Werner's head without him knowing just after the three dogs had flushed him out of the bushes near the house.

Gusto Calamari and Ohama Bin Schaden were also ensconced at the hotel. In a secluded meeting room, they were in a deep and tense discussion about securing the crucial thing they both needed but which the other possessed: Ohama had the gun, but it was useless without the firing chip which Gusto had. It was a stalemate with little chance of being resolved anytime soon.

As Roger had observed, the man he called Moses Clay was a guest at the big hotel as well. Clay, in turn, had recognised Roger. Now, Clay was in his room trying to make sense of some papers laid out before him, but they didn't tell him anything. The only thing he did know for sure was that if the secret agent Roger Less was there, then something very big was going down. Moses Clay was an opportunist, and he didn't want to miss out on whatever that something big was.

In the meantime, in a room across the corridor from Clay, Cornelia from Helvetia was compiling a list of the people she wanted to interview about last year's event.

Everyone, it seemed, was well prepared for the big day—everyone, that is, except for the not-so-blushing bride-to-be Miss Heger and her future husband, Jim Steel, who were at Miss Heger's house going through the procedures for their wedding. Jim, who thought they had it pretty much down pat, was trying to calm his bride-to-be, who insisted on going through things over and over again.

'Don't worry, sugar bum,' he chirped, 'everything will be fine.'

'Jim!' shrieked Miss Heger. 'Come here!' Slap! Slap! 'How many times do I have to tell you? ... It is sugar *doll* ... NOT *bum*. Sugar doll! Sugar doll—got it? If you call me sugar bum once more, I will divorce you before we even get married. Is that clear?'

'Of course, sugar bu—I mean doll. Yes, doll! Sugar doll! I have it! Sugar doll!' Jim sang out as he danced out of the room.

Ten minutes later they were both lying in bed in separate rooms wide awake with excitement about the next day.

The church bells rang out at dawn as the pink glow on the horizon heralded a beautiful day in Stone for the big wedding. In the streets, the hustle and bustle increased rapidly as the morning progressed and the festive air of celebration drew everyone out into the sunshine. Few could resist checking out the magnificently decorated big wedding tent set majestically on the lawn beside the church.

Another big tent was also creating great excitement among the residents and visitors in Stone. The famous Circus Elbow had come to town and had set up its big top on the outskirts of town.

Soon after the sun came up, the circus displayed its attractions in a spectacular parade through the centre of the village with colourful floats, acrobats, clowns and a vast array of animals, including elephants, camels, horses, lions and tigers in cages carried on wagons.

Watching the great spectacle with mounting excitement, Andy Belle couldn't wait to see the circus the next day, but at the same time, he felt sorry for the captive animals and wished the circus were more about the clowns and acrobats than the taming of wild animals.

Hansi, Jurgen and I will be captives too if all goes to plan, he told himself. The boys' mission for the morning was to be arrested by Dr Folterknecht and his secret police as soon as possible.

For Jurgen and Hansi, disguised as twin Andys, that was easier than they expected because they ran straight into the arms of the two secret police officers, Karl-Otto and Manfred. They offered the twins hot chocolate and cake if they would help them with their secret investigation and join them in the cellar.

Jurgen and Hansi pretended to be excited about that and willingly went with the two officers. In the meantime, Andy Belle had spotted Dr Folterknecht standing out front of the big hotel observing the people. Safe in his perfect disguise as a girl, Andy went straight up to the secret police chief. 'Excuse me, sir,' he said, 'but I have to say what a beautiful red tie you are wearing.'

'Yes, yah,' Dr Folterknecht replied curtly. 'But I'm busy, little girl. Go away, yah!'

'Are you one of the men who are looking for the boy with the alien laser gun?' Andy Belle asked boldly.

Dr Folterknecht was startled. 'How did you know that, yah?'

Andy Belle suddenly pretended to look nervous. 'I didn't know, sir,' he stammered. 'I don't know anything … it was just a guess.

It just slipped out.' Andy Belle glanced around anxiously as if looking for the best way to run.

'Wait, little girl, yah!' Dr Folterknecht said, rubbing his hands together. 'Let me at least offer you a cup of delicious hot chocolate,' he coaxed, trying to ooze charm but only coming across as oily and slimy. 'I also have some chocolate cake, yah.'

'I prefer strawberry cake,' Andy Belle said.

'Of course! Of course!' oozed Dr Folterknecht. 'I happen to have strawberry cake as well, yah!'

'Oh, lovely!' Andy Belle cried. He took Dr Folterknecht's proffered hand and allowed himself to be led into the hotel and down to the cellar. At the bottom of the steps, they were greeted by an excited Karl-Otto.

'Doctor!' he called out, 'we caught the boys!'

'Boys?' Dr Folterknecht countered. 'We are looking for *one* boy, you fool, yah!'

'But they are twins and fit the image you gave us exactly!'

'We shall see, yah!' Dr Folterknecht growled. 'Bring me my blood pressure pills immediately. I think I'm going to need them, yah.'

'Sir!' Andy Belle complained, 'you are squeezing my hand—it hurts!'

'I'm sorry, my sweet little girl,' Dr Folterknecht oozed, as he gently shepherded Andy Belle through the door that Karl-Otto had opened. 'Just go in through this door.'

18

What Andy Belle stepped into on the other side of the door was no cellar. From the warm, subdued lighting of the hotel corridor, he had walked into a bright, stark fluorescent glare more befitting a hospital operating theatre than a luxury hotel room.

Andy Belle looked around with mounting alarm. He saw an array of strange-looking instruments hanging on the walls that didn't seem to have any place in a hotel. He gasped audibly when he noticed the bench in the centre of the room was covered with black straps and had handcuffs and leg restraints attached to it.

What really shocked Andy was the sight of his identical twins strapped firmly in two high-backed chairs on the far side of the room. It was clear from Jurgen and Hansi's facial expressions that they would much rather be themselves again and out playing in the forest.

Dr Folterknecht put on a white lab coat and placed what looked like some sort of helmet on his head with a combined magnifying lens and bright light attached to it, which he pulled down over his eyes.

'I will examine the boys, yah!' he said.

His four colleagues were all now in the room and pressed in close to observe what their chief was doing.

'Get back!' Dr Folterknecht shouted, shooing them away with his arms. 'Give me room, yah!'

The four men fell back to a respectable distance and watched Dr Folterknecht analyse the two boys' heads, much like a forensic anthropologist would an ancient skull from an Egyptian tomb. He took measurements of their heads, noses, eyes, ears and teeth. Jurgen's gaping mouth inspired Andy Belle to pipe up, 'Where's my hot chocolate and strawberry cake?' This was pure cheek; he didn't really expect to be getting the promised delights.

'Shut up, little girl!' Dr Folterknecht shouted. 'I'm busy right now, yah!' Then he paused, as a thought occurred to him. He glared at Andy Belle ferociously and pointed to the bench in the centre of the room. 'Karl-Otto! Manfred! Tie the girl onto the operating table, yah!'

Andy Belle was grabbed roughly by the two men, lifted off his feet and dumped unceremoniously onto the bench. They cuffed his hands and legs and strapped his body firmly to the table. 'Ahhhhhhh!' Andy Belle screamed in the highest pitched girl's voice he could manage. 'That's not fair!'

'The world is not fair! Life is not fair!' cried Dr Folterknecht as an evil grin spread over his face and he began laughing like a crazy man.

Just as the time he was briefly restrained in Roger's car seat, Andy could hardly move, except to wiggle his fingers. But again, these restraints would be very temporary ones.

When Dr Folterknecht finally stopped his maniacal laughter, he shouted at his men, 'I want everybody out! Yah! I have further examinations to do! Out! Out! Out! Lock the door and wait for me outside! Yah!'

The loud click of the door being locked hung in the air because nobody spoke for almost ten seconds. The eerie silence was eventually broken by Dr Folterknecht's menacing voice. 'Children,' he snarled, 'it's show time, yah! And because I'm a lovely and polite person ... ha ha ha ... I will start with the torture—I mean, the *examination* of the girl first, yah!'

He stood at a desk and began preparing several injections involving large, scary-looking needles with syringes filled with bright yellow and green liquid.

'Ask him what they are,' the magic pencil said, telling Andy why he wanted to know.

'What are those for?' Andy Belle enquired cheekily.

Dr Folterknecht had his back to the examination table where Andy Belle had been strapped down and didn't bother to turn around when he answered the question.

'Oh, you will find out soon enough, yah! But I'll tell you anyway. The yellow one is a truth serum, but it will also relax you so much that you will be almost paralyzed and only able to whisper—but you will whisper the truth! Yah! The green one is the antidote so that you will become fully awake again and feel the pain of my ... *examination!* Yah!'

When Dr Folterknecht threw his head back and started laughing maniacally again, the pencil said, 'Now Andy—do it!' Employing his newfound skill, Andy Belle telehopped from his restraints on the examination table, grabbed a syringe filled with yellow liquid and jabbed it into the mad doctor's backside, delivering a full dose.

'Yeeeeeaaaaaahh!' squealed Dr Folterknecht like a stuck pig. He swung round to face his attacker and was stunned to see the girl standing there holding the empty syringe. He glanced back and forth from Andy Belle to the empty examination table several times, his eyes wide with disbelief. He tried to say something, but it was barely a whisper—the yellow sedative was already taking effect and Dr Folterknecht started to wobble on his feet.

Fortunately, the mad doctor was a small man and Andy Belle managed to grab him before his legs gave way and manoeuvre him to the edge of the examination table, which the doctor clung onto desperately for about thirty seconds before gradually collapsing to the floor. It gave Andy Belle time to get the key to the handcuffs from the desk drawer and secure Dr Folterknecht's right arm to the examination table. Andy then freed his two lookalikes from the straps tying them to their chairs.

'About time, Andy!' Hansi cried, 'We were getting worried! But thanks ... that was brilliant!'

'Yeah!' Jurgen said. 'How did you do that?'

'I'll explain later.' He lowered his voice to a whisper. 'Don't believe everything I'm about to tell Dr Folterknecht.'

The stricken man was still very groggy, lying face down on the floor. The three friends managed to turn him over and sit him up against a leg of the examination table. They all stood staring down at him with very angry expressions.

'Dr Evil,' Andy Belle said. 'Sorry .... *Folterknecht*. You are a very nasty and bad man! This has to stop! I will now admit to you that I am an alien.'

Dr Folterknecht made a strange gurgling sound.

'Your evil cannot work on me!' Andy Belle said fiercely. The doctor simply stared up at him in wide-eyed disbelief and alarm. 'Mere straps and locked doors cannot hold us!' Andy Belle cried out melodramatically.

With that, the three friends held each other's hands and stood with their backs close to the wall, facing the dumbstruck glassy-eyed doctor. Dr Folterknecht blinked once, and they were gone.

19

Andy Belle telejumped along the corridor a short distance and around a corner to be out of sight of Folterknecht's four men still guarding the door. On instruction from the pencil, the twin Andys, Jurgen and Hansi, went straight up to their suite. Also on the pencil's orders, Andy Belle had brought one of the green antidote syringes with him. He went immediately to confront Folterknecht's four men, who were sitting on four small chairs outside the locked door waiting patiently for a signal from their chief.

When Andy Belle appeared, striding towards them, all four leapt up from their chairs in such perfect unison it would have impressed a synchronised swimming team. Their animated astonishment was so extravagant it looked like bad overacting. They all gawped at him, totally lost for words, until Folterknecht's second-in-command, Horst Heiner, gasped, 'What? No way! How did you—'

Andy Belle cut him off. 'The doctor let me go ... through a small service door I thought was a cupboard. He wanted me to pass on a message to you. He doesn't want to be disturbed for at least one hour. He wants you to know he found some alien tissue in the two boys, and he has to examine it carefully without any interruptions. He said it could be a very dangerous process because the properties of alien tissue are totally unknown.' He held out the green liquid-filled syringe. 'However, if his examination goes wrong and you find him semi-conscious, he said to just inject this deep in his nose and it will revive him.'

'There's no way Dr Folterknecht would let you go!' Karl-Otto bellowed. 'I don't believe it!'

'I couldn't believe it either!' Andy retorted. 'He promised me hot chocolate and strawberry cake! But instead, he took me prisoner. Then he suddenly unstrapped me, unlocked the cuffs and started yelling at me, "Out! Out! Out! You are not important! I need this table for the boys! Get out!"'

Heiner took the syringe from Andy Belle's outstretched hand. 'Now go, little girl!' he ordered. 'Go! Go! Go!'

As Andy Belle walked away very slowly down the corridor, Heiner said, 'Yes, that is Dr Folterknecht through and through—erratic and unpredictable. We shall wait for an hour.'

Once Andy Belle was out of sight of the men, he rushed upstairs to join Jurgen and Hansi in the suite.

'Well done, Andy!' the pencil applauded. 'Very convincing. But there is still a lot more work to be done. We must monitor the movements of Gusto and Ohama, but that will be easy enough because the one with the chip will be sticking like glue to the one with the gun and vice versa. Keeping an eye on Werner Little Werner and Countess Kunnikunde will be more difficult.

'Werner is at this moment here, in the hotel, waiting for her to arrive—which she will definitely do after reading his report. The minute she arrives, Andy, you will have to make an important phone call.'

'What phone call?' Andy Belle asked.

'Never mind,' the pencil said, 'you will know once it's happening.'

Andy Belle shrugged at his identical twins. Hansi and Jurgen were sitting quietly together taking no part in the conversation because they couldn't hear what the pencil was saying to Andy. That suddenly changed.

'Hansi and Jurgen,' they heard the pencil say. 'You have a part to play helping Andy.'

'Yes, sir!' they said as one. 'We're listening!'

'Good!' the pencil replied. 'And listen carefully! The marriage ceremony in the church will commence in two hours. Half an hour after that, the guests will start taking their seats in the celebration tent. It is your job, with Andy, to ensure our enemies are seated in their correct places at the table. And Andy, you must ring your father and ask him to tell Hermann and Fritz that it's now OK for them to join the wedding party—otherwise Jim will be without his best men!'

When Hermann and Fritz arrived, they presented quite a picture. Without any clothes of their own suitable for a wedding, they had chosen an outfit each from Johann's wardrobe. Hermann wore a grey suit that fitted rather too snugly with the sleeves and trouser length comically short. Fritz on the other hand had taken the description "loose-fitting" to a new extreme; he seemed almost consumed by his suit and shirt. Hermann's shirt was something else again. The only shirt of Johann's he could get into was a nightshirt, without a collar, which made a strikingly bizarre fashion statement when worn with a tie.

Anna had to summon superhuman self-discipline not to laugh out loud when she saw them walk into the hotel suite together. She helped disguise it by immediately rushing off to get her sewing kit, which she always had on hand at weddings, usually for last-minute adjustments to bridal gowns and bridesmaid ensembles.

She worked wonders with needle and thread and by the time Hermann and Fritz left for the church a while later they at least looked presentable and wouldn't draw attention away from the bride.

When Andy Belle announced he would go with them just to check out the wedding tent, the pencil stopped him. 'This is not the time to be distracted!' it scolded. 'Kunnikunde could arrive at any moment.'

As if on cue, Kunnikunde arrived at that precise moment, accompanied by a repetitive high-pitched screeching as she moved along the corridor towards her suite. Now a fully-fledged fire witch, Kunnikunde set off every smoke detector alarm as she passed under it. When Werner Little Werner let her into their suite, several alarms inside went off as well.

The hotel manager, Mr Vogelfutter, who had personally shown the countess to her suite, had the door slammed in his face and was left standing in the corridor. He hastily grabbed a fire extinguisher mounted on the wall close by and banged frantically on the door of Kunnikunde's suite. When Werner opened the door, the panic-stricken manager instantly triggered the extinguisher, covering Little Werner from head to toe with fire retardant foam. A large amount of the foam missed Werner and landed behind him ... on the elaborately coiffed hair of the countess.

The substances in the fire retardant and those in Kunnikunde's hair gels were chemically incompatible and the volatile reaction that followed turned the countess's coiffure into a gooey bird's nest.

'This is outrageous!' screamed Werner, spurting a mouthful of foam and wiping the stuff from his eyes.

The mortified Mr Vogelfutter apologised profusely as he slowly backed his way out of the room, bowing continually as he went.

'Get me out of here at once!' Kunnikunde screeched at Werner. 'I need to change! Drive me to my castle, now!'

20

In Johann's suite, meanwhile, the pencil was issuing orders to Andy Belle.

'It's now time to make our crucial phone call, Andy—much depends on it. I'm going to have to take control of your body for a few minutes. You'll need this phone number—it's Kunnikunde's home number at Snobtown in the new colonies.'

'But she's here in Stone!' Andy Belle objected. 'What's the point of—'

Before he could finish the sentence, he was engulfed in a blue flame then felt himself rushing to the phone and dialling Kunnikunde's number.

'The Ritter von Krumm residence,' a girl's voice answered. 'Pink speaking.'

The magic pencil, speaking through Andy Belle, put on a perfect impersonation of Kunnikunde's voice. 'Pink, sweety,' it cooed.

'Mum, is that you?'

'Of course, darling.'

'Where are you? When will you be back?'

'Never mind, Pink, darling. I'll be back in a couple of hours. I want you to do me a big favour.'

'Sure, Mum, what is it?'

'You know the big black chair in my office?'

'The one you went ballistic at me for touching?'

'Sorry about that, sweety—but yes, that's the one. Listen carefully ... I want you to get the gardener and Rose to help you hide the chair in the deep end of the swimming pool.'

'But, Mum, that could ruin the chair!'

'Not for the short time it'll be in the water. Attach a strap to it so we can easily pull it out when I get back. But do it straightaway! Understood? It's very important—and urgent! There are some bad people after that chair. Now, get off the phone and do it!'

'Yes, Mum!'

'Good girl.'

The pencil had Andy Belle hang up. 'That should work,' it remarked. 'Hopefully.'

'Why do you want the chair in the pool?' Andy Belle asked.

'Whenever Kunnikunde returns to Snobtown from a stint as a fire witch she has to teleport herself back, and that big black chair is her homing device; she will always reappear in that chair. Lucifer has given her the power of fire and the only way to take that gift away is to fully submerge such a person in water for at least one second. When she returns to the chair this time, she'll be completely underwater for about three seconds, according to my calculations. That will destroy ninety-five percent of her power and make it impossible for her to kill anybody by striking them with fire missiles.'

'But right now, she can still kill people with them, and she's here now ... in this hotel!' Andy Belle said.

'That's why I put some false recollections and ideas into Werner's head—remember when I got you to hold his hand at the house when he was trying to escape the dogs? We'll be giving Kunnikunde what she wants, briefly, before we persuade her to leave Stone and return to the new colonies as soon as possible. But to do that we need everyone to perform their roles—to the letter! That's the only way my plan will work.'

'We don't want an adventure, right?' Andy Belle remarked with a grin.

'What?' the pencil replied, uncharacteristically caught off guard.

'What you told me before ... about an adventure being what happens when you don't have a plan.'

'What? Oh! ... Yes, I see. Very good, Andy. It's gratifying to know you occasionally pay attention to what I tell you.'

Andy Belle just grinned.

People began to file out of the church the moment the marriage service had finished. All were keen to see the bridal entourage parade from the church to the big tent close by.

Cornelia, the journalist from Helvetia, had hired a cameraman and began interviewing various people about the extraordinary events of a year before. Everyone had a different story. Sergeant Fritzel's was probably the most colourful. He claimed that he was the one who had fired the cannon straight into Commander Wurstling's car. 'The car took off like a rocket or a shooting star and flew through the clouds straight into car heaven. Minutes later it came back to Earth like brand new! I believe my cannon is magic, and I polish it every day.'

Cornelia heard many crazy and contradictory stories and soon became totally confused with no idea of what really happened. But she was determined to find out the truth and had a good idea about where to find it.

Meanwhile, Roger Less, Her Majesty's secret agent had hidden under the stage where the band was playing. From there he could launch his drones on the magic pencil's instructions. He needed earplugs to minimise the loud noise of the Oompa brass band above him being proudly and exuberantly conducted by the police chief, Commander Wurstling.

The first of the enemies to appear at the tent was Gusto Calamari, who loudly announced himself with the pseudonym Arturo Pastadelli. Andy led the gangster boss to the seat the pencil had assigned him.

Gusto whispered to Andy Belle, 'A boy called Andy told me to tell you to seat me near the man with the gun.'

'Of course, Mr Pastadelli,' Andy Belle whispered back, indicating the seat one along from Gusto's, 'that's where Prince Ulla Dulla Bulla will be sitting. In fact, here he is now!'

Andy Belle rushed off to greet the prince, aka Ohama Bin Schaden. Ohama immediately recognised Andy Belle as the girl who had handed the gun over to him.

'Hello, my little princess,' Ohama whispered. 'You promised you'd seat me very close to the man with the gun's firing chip.'

'The closest I could get you was two seats away on his left,' Andy Belle whispered back. 'Your men are seated in a row next to you on the other side.'

'Excellent!' Ohama exclaimed, forgetting to whisper.

Following the pencil's explicit instructions, the enemy sitting between Gusto and Ohama was Mr Broombridge, Countess Kunnikunde's new head of the advisory board of her new pencil factory. In complete contrast to the last time Andy Belle saw Ohama, he was now dressed all in black robes, but again his face was half-covered by a hood. The black prince sat down looking very pleased with himself.

At that moment, the church bells rang out signalling that the church marriage service was over, and the happy couple would be making their way to the wedding tent. According to those who had snuck out of the church early, Miss Heger, now Lady Heger-Steel, looked radiant in her magnificent bridal gown and was glowing with joy. Her new husband, Jim, was all smiles and looking like the happiest man in town.

21

Things started to heat up in the wedding tent well before the bride and groom appeared. Andy Belle leant over Gusto Calamari's shoulder and whispered that the man in the black robes two seats down on his left was the terrorist leader Ohama Bin Schaden, the man who had stolen the gun from him.

Gusto Calamari reacted instantly. He signalled to his thugs sitting on his right to be ready to move at a split second's notice. With that, he leant forward as far as possible and craned his neck towards Ohama Bin Schaden, his head virtually over poor Mr Broombridge's place setting.

'Excuse me, sir!' Mr Broombridge objected. 'Do you mind?'

Gusto ignored him as he snarled at Ohama, 'Listen, you camel-dung-eating sand rat, hand over my gun now!'

Ohama snarled back, 'If you don't hand over the chip to *my* gun, I will pull the beard off your grandmother—hair by hair!'

Gusto jabbed an elbow into Umberto sitting beside him, who jumped to his feet. Ohama's man, Omar, did the same.

Poor Mr Broombridge suddenly felt the hard steel of Gusto's pistol barrel pressed firmly into his right rib cage, and the larger but equally hard steel of Ohama's sawn-off double-barrelled shotgun pressed into his left rib cage. Finding himself in the middle of a deadly argument between two criminal maniacs, Mr Broombridge had trouble breathing; he seemed to be involuntarily holding his breath.

'For the last time, camel dung,' Gusto snarled at Ohama, 'if you don't give me the gun in three seconds, I'm going to blow Mr Broombridge's guts all over that fancy nun's habit you're wearing.'

'If you don't give me the chip now, garlic muncher,' Ohama snarled back, 'you'll be having Mr Broombridge's liver for lunch.'

Mercifully, at that point poor Mr Broombridge passed out, slid off his chair and disappeared under the table.

This prompted the pencil to intervene. 'Roger,' he ordered, 'please have your nano-drones knock out Gusto and Ohama's men, otherwise there will be a gunfight and it won't just be the bad men who'll be hurt.'

'Roger!' Roger replied. 'Remember, each drone has only five tranquilliser darts.'

'OK,' the pencil said. 'To begin, just take out the five thugs who are still seated—two of Gusto's and three of Ohama's.'

'Roger!' Roger said again.

Seconds later, a tiny drone, like an electronic fly, hovered over the table and released its five darts with precision accuracy. Almost instantly, Alberto, Rudolfo, Qadir, Aashiq and Mahfouz slumped forward in their seats, their heads thumping face-first onto their place settings, knocking over innumerable wine glasses and champagne flutes. Some shocked guests wondered how five men could get so drunk so quickly.

A Mexican standoff ensued. Gusto had his pistol pointed at Ohama's head while Ohama and Omar had their guns pointed at Gusto's head. So did a confused Umberto, until Gusto threatened to shoot him first.

With neither side able to gain an advantage, Gusto decided to taunt Ohama by waving the precious firing chip in his face. 'You want this? You want this?' he yelled.

Ohama made a lunge for the chip. His hand moved like a striking snake—its speed startling Gusto. He pulled his hand back in a flash, just avoiding Ohama's strike, but lost his grip on the chip, which flew over his shoulder.

At that precise moment, the huge wedding cake was being paraded through the tent on its way to the bridal table. It passed along the row behind Gusto as he let go of the chip, which flew into the cake like a bullet. The soft, thick icing closed over the projectile, leaving no hole or mark whatsoever.

Gusto swung round just in time to see where the chip had gone. Only two other people saw the chip disappear into the wedding cake—Andy Belle and Ohama. Ohama hadn't taken his eyes off it from the time Gusto started waving it under his nose.

'You'll have to wait till after the cutting of the cake before you can make a move,' Andy Belle whispered to Gusto.

The gangster boss was wide-eyed with disbelief and frustration but managed to nod his reluctant agreement. Ohama too had decided to wait before he made his move. But, unlike Gusto, he had a plan. Once the cake cutting ceremony finished, he would go quietly up on stage while his men maintained the Mexican standoff with Gusto's men. He would then present the laser gun and announce that, with it, he could destroy the whole town—and that that was exactly what he would do if they didn't sit down quietly and not move from their seats. Then his man Omar would retrieve the chip from the wedding cake and he and his men would rush to the airport and fly away. He would simply shoot Gusto if he attempted to interfere.

Ohama closed his eyes and smiled with satisfaction, convinced that it was a simple but good plan. He failed to notice both Omar and Umberto sit down at the table simultaneously and, seconds later, slump forward in their seats: two more victims of Roger's nano-drone tranquilliser darts.

Their heads had only just thumped onto their place settings when the master of ceremonies announced that the bridal entourage had arrived at the hotel and was about to make its grand entrance into the tent.

Everyone looked up expectantly, except the five unconscious thugs, of course, and poor panic-stricken Mr Broombridge, who had regained consciousness and was crawling frantically under the table to escape the lunatics above him. He emerged at the far end of the table, close to the tent entrance, staggered to his feet and ran across the small patch of lawn between the tent and the hotel, yelping, 'Help! Help!' as he went.

22

Mr Broombridge's ordeal had given him a sudden, irrepressible urge to go to the toilet. He hurtled through the lobby towards the men's room just seconds after the radiant bride had rushed off to the ladies' room to powder her nose before her grand entrance into the tent.

Mr Broombridge moved so fast he almost foiled the pencil's little diversionary tactic, but the pencil saw him coming just in time.

'Hansi! Jurgen!' the pencil cried. 'Switch the toilet signs now!'

The two boys reacted instantly and did as commanded with only seconds to spare. When Mr Broombridge reached the toilet the "Men's" sign was on the ladies' room door. He burst in and ran straight into the large bottom of the blushing bride, Lady Heger-Steel, who was leaning forward in front of the mirror applying her lipstick. The jolt from behind by Mr Broombridge shoved the lipstick up her nose, where half of it broke off and the other half, still in her hand, smeared her face from nostril to forehead.

The former Miss Heger was no less ferocious in her new persona as Lady Heger-Steel. She swung round on her assailant like an enraged lioness.

'You, again!' she screeched, recognising Mr Broombridge. 'You pervert!'

Recollection of the pervert's last assault on her broad backside with the sharp point of a pencil turned her into a human slapping machine. Lady Heger-Steel's mighty slaps were so loud and repetitive that from outside the toilet it seemed that some miscreant had thrown a string of lit firecrackers into the ladies' toilet.

Half a minute later a battered and bruised Mr Broombridge burst out of the ladies' toilet and ran like a lunatic through the lobby, crashing into Dr Folterknecht as he stepped out of the lift with his henchmen, knocking the secret police chief to the ground.

'Maniac!' the doctor screamed as he got to his feet, waving a fist at the fast-disappearing Mr Broombridge. He noted the maniac's puffy red face as he crashed into him, perhaps because he himself had a very red and swollen nose. Most of his men too looked a little worse for wear with various cuts and bruises on their faces.

But one of them, Karl-Otto, looked like he'd been in a war and had his head almost completely wrapped in bandages. Apparently, things had taken a violent turn when he injected the syringe full of green antidote deep into the still groggy Dr Folterknecht's nose as he sat handcuffed to the examination table. Initially, the doctor very calmly and politely requested that his handcuffs be removed, took a deep breath ... and then flew into a psychotic rage as he tried to kill Karl-Otto with his bare hands and any hard or sharp object within his reach. His men ultimately subdued him, sustaining flesh wounds themselves, but probably saving Karl-Otto's life. They now all had serious concerns about their chief's mental state.

'Act inconspicuously,' Dr Folterknecht demanded as he recovered from the collision with Mr Broombridge. This was an unrealistic expectation, considering his own distinctive red swollen nose, his men's facial wounds and Karl-Otto's bandaged head.

'I have the list of people to be arrested,' Karl-Otto mumbled through his bandages, as they all started marching across the lawn towards the wedding tent.

'Forget that list, you carrot brain!' Dr Folterknecht snarled. 'We are now only after that alien, disguised as a human girl, who attacked me with the syringe. Have your tranquilliser guns ready and take out any little girls in the wedding tent! Understood?'

'But Doctor,' Karl-Otto protested, 'you always told us that aliens don't exist!'

'Never mind that, you noodle head! It seems they do exist after all! And I will catch this one and dissect it for science! Yah! I will be famous and will finally become a professor! Ha ha ha!'

His men noticed that their chief had developed a new mannerism. Rather than continually rubbing his hands together, he now made a fist of his left hand and constantly punched it into his open right hand. He had also developed a constant twitch in his left eye.

It seemed the doctor wasn't the only one becoming mentally unhinged. In his confused panic to escape the human slapping machine in the ladies' toilet, the hysterical Mr Broombridge ran back through the lobby yelling, 'Help! Help!' at the top of his voice. He continued across the lawn towards the wedding tent. Dr Folterknecht heard him coming, stopped and turned around. As Mr Broombridge hurtled past, the doctor stuck his foot out bringing him to the ground.

A dazed Mr Broombridge somehow saw the secret police chief as his saviour and grabbed hold of him by his trousers. With the vice-like grip of a man in a state of extreme panic, Mr Broombridge tried to pull himself to his feet using Dr Folterknecht's trousers for leverage. Perhaps the doctor's trousers were a little loose around the waist, or his belt snapped under the pressure, but a split second later his trousers were down around his ankles.

An ear-piercing sound issued forth from the doctor as he stood in the middle of the small patch of lawn in his underwear. 'SCHWEINEHUND!' he shrieked.

He quickly pulled up his trousers and proceeded to vehemently kick Mr Broombridge, keeping him down on the ground, as a couple of his men joined in. Finally tiring of it, they desisted and continued to the tent.

Andy Belle, watching all this with Jurgen and Hansi from their hiding spot behind the large flowerpots, wondered how he could get back to the tent without being seen by Dr Folterknecht and his henchmen. Fortune smiles on the brave because at that moment old Mrs Rottweiler emerged from the ladies' toilet with her four-wheeled walker. Fortunately, the patch of lawn was as smooth as a bowling green and she made good pace for an old lady, almost at a trot. Andy grabbed his opportunity and, hiding behind her as she went, was able to keep out of sight of the doctor and his men.

Even though Mrs Rottweiler wasn't dawdling, Dr Folterknecht and his men were on a mission and marching at a brisk pace behind her.

'Get out of my way, old woman!' Dr Folterknecht arrogantly shouted at her, obviously assuming she was deaf.

'Andy, touch me to Mrs Rottweiler,' the pencil ordered.

An almost invisible blue flash engulfed the old lady, turning her into a kind of fierce ninja warrior grandma. Suddenly she was whirling her walker above her head as if it were light as a feather. Out of her mouth came a blood-curdling scream: 'AAAIIEEEEYYAAHHH!' What also came out of her mouth were her dentures, which catapulted forward at speed and clamped themselves firmly onto Dr Folterknecht's swollen nose.

Mrs Rottweiler's whirling walker became a lethal weapon. The doctor, still coping with the disembodied set of teeth biting painfully on his nose, was the flailing walker's first victim. One of its legs struck him on the temple, knocking him unconscious. Seconds later his four henchmen joined him unconscious on the lawn. With ninja-like agility, Mrs Rottweiler retrieved her dentures from Dr Folterknecht's nose, a nose which, already very swollen, now had visible teeth marks on it.

The moment Mrs Rottweiler put her false teeth back in she reverted to her old non-ninja self and made it safely back to her seat in the tent.

23

'One should always treat old people with respect!' Cornelia heard Mrs Rottweiler shout as she passed her by. The journalist and her cameraman had fortuitously arrived on the scene just as the old lady had sprung into action.

Cornelia had been too astonished to speak while it was happening but afterwards kept asking her cameraman, 'Did you get that? Did you get that?' Just as shocked as Cornelia, all he could do was keep nodding his head. They were both in a daze.

The sound of the band starting up on stage in the tent snapped them out of it. It meant that the happy couple was about to make their grand entrance. Cornelia and her cameraman rushed inside the tent to ensure they got the big arrival on camera.

They just made it as Lady Heger-Steel and Jim Steel proudly walked into the tent to loud, rapturous applause from everyone present, except for the unconscious Gusto, Ohama and their men.

'Andy,' the pencil commanded, 'touch me to Gusto and Ohama's men. We need them to stay sleeping for longer. But not their two bosses; they should be waking up any minute now.'

Andy Belle obliged, but he had to be very sneaky and subtle about it because he was aware that Cornelia's cameraman seemed to be more interested in filming him than the speeches, which were taking place at the bridal table. The cameraman had already noticed that any time something filmable happened, this same blonde girl was somewhere in the shot, even if he happened to suddenly point the camera in a different direction.

'There's something weird going on here!' the cameraman said, getting agitated. 'Even the fastest person on Earth couldn't cover that distance in a split second. She's freaking me out!'

'Just calm down, will you!' Cornelia demanded. 'Maybe she's one of twins.'

'Or triplets ... or even quadruplets!'

'Just calm down,' Cornelia repeated. 'We have a lot of filming to do.'

'And those twin boys she's always talking to—they seem to be everywhere at once too!'

'Forget them!' Cornelia demanded. 'Just focus on what I've hired you for—to film anything interesting or dramatic that happens—not little kids making a nuisance of themselves.'

'Like the ninja grandma—I got her!'

'Exactly!' Cornelia said. 'We want more of that kind of stuff.'

One of the kids making a nuisance of himself was arguing with the magic pencil.

'Andy,' the pencil ordered, 'telehop yourself to a position five metres behind the main table.'

'But I don't think that's—'

The pencil cut him off. 'Just do it!'

'But,' Andy Belle cried, 'that cameraman is watching me like a hawk! He's filming me right now!'

'Don't worry about him!' the pencil retorted. 'If he ever shows it to anyone, they'll think it's just special effects or some kind of trick filming. Now go!'

Andy Belle did as he was told and telehopped about ten metres in a split second.

The poor cameraman nearly fainted when the girl he was filming instantly disappeared from the frame. He looked around frantically and finally spotted her way over behind the main bridal table.

'Impossible!' he cried, startling a waitress standing close by with a tray of champagne glasses, which she almost dropped.

Embarrassed, the cameraman cleared his throat and turned his attention to his camera. 'The retrofocus or the zoom lens must be malfunctioning,' he muttered to himself. He didn't have time to think any more about it because a sudden burst of clapping and cheering from the main table meant the cake cutting ceremony had begun; he leapt into action with his camera.

Gusto and Ohama woke up together on cue. Each was desperately trying to wake up his respective key man so they could make their move to get hold of the precious chip.

'Wake up, you lazy ape!' Gusto shouted at Umberto, while he slapped him repeatedly about the head. 'This is not-a the time for sleeping!'

Ohama too was cursing Omar while shaking him violently. But his efforts, like Gusto's, were to no avail. Both bosses gave up and rushed towards the stage. They found this no easy task as almost everyone in the tent was on their feet brandishing cameras or phones to capture the great event.

'Roger,' the pencil said, 'would you please put a dart into Lady Heger-Steel's butt?'

'Roger!' Roger responded.

'Then launch another drone,' the pencil went on, 'armed with all five darts. We'll need them all because they are for Kunnikunde.'

'Understood!' Roger said. 'But can you identify this target for me? I don't know her.'

'She's the woman standing near the entrance in bright purple with a green scarf over her head; she obviously doesn't want to be recognised.'

'Got her!' Roger said. 'She's just started heading towards the bridal table. I see her clearly.' He launched the next drone, just as the first one shot its tranquilliser dart into the backside of Lady Heger-Steel, who, with her husband Jim, was about to make the first cut into the cake. Jim also had a grip on the knife. The dart took effect immediately and Lady Heger-Steel slumped forward face-first into the huge wedding cake, dragging Jim with her.

'They are cutting the cake with their heads!' some people gasped. 'Is this a new tradition?'

24

Roger's drone darts, which usually knocked people out for half an hour, had only a very temporary effect on Lady Heger-Steel. After just ten seconds she wrenched her head out of the cake. Amidst all the whipped cream and icing covering her face, a glittering object protruded from the area where her mouth was. When Lady Heger-Steel removed the obstruction from her mouth it allowed an ear-splitting screech to escape her lips that almost shattered the glasses on the bridal table. Quite a few glasses vibrated dangerously but remained intact.

Her second screech seemed even louder. 'Who pushed me?' she demanded to know at the top of her lungs.

Seeing the chip in her hand, Gusto rushed at her shouting, 'That-a belongs to me! Me! Me!'

Lady Heger-Steel seemed to have heard only the 'Me! Me!' which she took to be the answer to her question and an admission of guilt. Poor Gusto met the full force of Teutonia's fastest and hardest hitting hand. SLAP! SLAP! SLAP! The gangster boss fell to the floor in a daze.

Grateful for this distraction, Ohama started to make his move. He leapt onto the stage, pushed the master of ceremonies away from his microphone, then slowly withdrew the laser gun from under his black robes.

Before the terrorist leader could talk into the microphone and make his demands, Kunnikunde made *her* move.

Her lightning-fast extendable arm seemed even more effective than ever. Quicker than the eye could see, she snatched the chip from Lady Heger-Steel's hand. A second or two later, Ohama was shocked and horrified to find himself standing at the microphone in his underwear. Kunnikunde had snatched the laser gun from him, as well as his fine black robes and other weapons he had concealed under them.

With the big bag she'd bought with her now almost full, Kunnikunde threw off the scarf covering her head.

'Countess Kunnikunde!' the people cried with a mixture of disbelief and terror.

'You are right to be afraid of me!' Kunnikunde shrieked, her face full of hate. 'So, you think you can all live a life of happiness while I am miserable and depressed? Think again, you lousy peasants! That won't happen because I'm sending you all to meet your maker!'

'Roger!' the pencil ordered. 'Fire the darts straight into her neck now!'

Kunnikunde threw her head back and raised her arms in the air ready to unleash a barrage of fire bolts and turn the wedding guests to ashes when she felt something cold and hard press against her neck.

It was the barrel of Gusto's pistol. 'Lady,' he mumbled, through battered and swollen lips, courtesy of Lady Heger-Steel, 'you have something that belongs to me. Hand over your bag now!'

Kunnikunde wondered how a cold gun barrel pressed against her neck could cause a burning sensation and make her feel dizzy.

'She's got five darts in her neck,' complained an astonished Roger. 'Will this woman ever fall?'

'Probably not,' the pencil said. 'But she should leave now—which was the idea all along.'

And so, she did. With a gun to her head, a painful, burning neck and the 'alien gun' in her bag, the startled Kunnikunde teleported herself back home to Snobtown. The whirling force of the small hurricane she created with her disappearance flung Gusto to the floor holding just the handle of his pistol—with its barrel touching Kunnikunde's head most of the weapon had been teleported with her.

The gangster boss looked like he'd seen the ghost of Al Capone and ran screaming back to the hotel.

In Snobtown, a shocked Kunnikunde emerged from her teleportation in her big office chair two metres under water. She climbed out of the pool coughing and spluttering, screaming out for her daughters. In a fury, she marched towards the house, her clothes drying instantly.

'Pink! Rose!' she shrieked. 'Where are you?'

'Up here, Mum!' Rose called from the second-storey balcony.

'Come down here immediately!'

The two girls got down almost as fast as if they'd teleported themselves.

'What is it, Mum?' Pink asked, anxious. 'Why are you so angry?'

'Get that chair out of the pool now! Who put it there?'

'We did.'

'What possessed you to do such a stupid thing, you naughty, nasty girls!'

'You asked us too,' Rose cried. 'On the phone ... yesterday.'

'What?' Kunnikunde exclaimed. 'I didn't call you yester—' She cut herself off.

'You didn't?' Pink said. 'But I spoke to you.'

'Never mind,' Kunnikunde snapped. 'Just get that chair out of the pool and put it back exactly where you took it from!' With that, she disappeared into her study. She locked the door behind her and began to unpack her big bag—it was quite a haul, even by her standards. Apart from seventy-five stolen wallets and purses, there was also Ohama's black robe, his knives and handguns, and of course the prize piece, the shiny silvery laser gun—with its precious firing chip.

'Such fools!' she squawked. 'Ha ha ha! Like taking candy from babies! Ha ha ha!'

Kunnikunde cradled the laser gun in her arms like a puppy. She stroked it and hugged it. Eventually, she put the gun down then cleaned the wedding cake residue from the chip so meticulously that it sparkled like a jewel in the sun.

'This incredible gun will make me rich! Very, very rich!' she sang ecstatically. 'It could be more valuable even than Lucifer's powers! I need lots of money! I *want* lots of money—and this gun will get it for me. All the money I could possibly want will be mine! Mine! Mine! All mine!'

After spending a couple of hours drying the chair as best they could, Pink, Rose and the gardener returned it to Kunnikunde's study and placed it in its original spot.

Kunnikunde suddenly turned on the poor gardener like a rabid dog. 'Get out! Out! Out!' she screamed at him. 'You're fired! Get out now or I'll call the police!'

The intimidated gardener knew better than to argue with Kunnikunde and scurried away without a word.

Pink and Rose were visibly shocked and horrified by their mother's brutal behaviour.

'I had no choice, my darlings,' Kunnikunde explained. 'He's been working here for three months and tomorrow's his last day anyway. By firing him now, I won't have to pay him. I would have had to pay him with my own money—*my* money! He's like everyone else—he was after my money. They all are. Everyone wants my money! Why? Why? Is it fair? Is it fair?' She choked on the last word and tears filled her eyes. It was an extraordinarily convincing performance that even her two daughters were taken in by. But if they had looked very closely at their mother's weeping eyes, they'd have seen that behind the veil of tears, her eyes were as hard and cold as steel.

25

Lady Heger-Steel had some steel about her too, and not just in her new surname. There was plenty of it in her backbone as well; she wasn't going to let the demented acts of violent lunatics ruin the biggest day of her life. She took her bridesmaids back to the hotel to help her get cleaned up after the cake-cutting fiasco. It was the second time that day she'd had to clean herself up after a surprise attack by a savage maniac. Her fortitude in coping with such adversity on her wedding day was admirable, to say the least.

The mutilated wedding cake, however, had no steel in it and was a collapsed mess. The caterers rushed desperately to try and restore it to its former glory.

Unaware of the crisis with the cake restoration on the stage above him, Roger began to climb out from his hiding place. As he emerged his feet became caught up in some electrical leads and he stumbled as he stepped out, almost knocking down a woman who was standing beside the stage.

'Excuse me!' Cornelia cried. 'Clumsy oaf—you nearly knocked me down!'

'Oh, my lord!' Roger exclaimed. 'Ms Cornelia—frightfully sorry! Listen, I'm in a rush trying to catch a terrorist but how about a drink tonight at the hotel? I'd be delighted. My room number is 155—let me know. Must dash!'

Roger headed off across the small patch of lawn at a run, but he didn't get far; the terrorist caught him first. Ohama Bin Schaden bailed up the head of Her Majesty's Secret Service and held a gun to his head.

'Just walk slowly back to the tent, Mr Secret Agent,' Ohama snarled, 'or I will blow your head off.'

This unwelcome change to Roger's plans coincided with a welcome change in the condition of Dr Folterknecht and his henchmen—they had all regained consciousness after their violent encounter with Mrs Rottweiler.

'We have to find the alien!' hissed the doctor, his mind immediately focused on their mission. He was about to dash off when he saw Roger walking slowly towards the big tent, closely followed by a man in a loose-fitting white robe and hood, who was holding a gun at Roger's head.

'Roger Less!' Dr Folterknecht called out excitedly. 'What a pleasure to see you here! What a total pleasure!'

The doctor and his men marched towards Roger and Ohama.

'You remember the last time we met, I'm sure, Mr Less,' Dr Folterknecht shouted, 'when I ended up in hospital for six weeks, yah! You tricked me! You tricked me! There was a bomb in the bottle of whiskey, yah! Now I have you!'

The doctor and his men stopped Roger and Ohama just short of the tent and surrounded them.

'You ... pyjama-man,' Dr Folterknecht snarled at Ohama, 'I am the head of the Teutonian Secret Police—hand over your gun immediately, yah!'

'I don't think Ohama Bin Schaden will surrender his gun so easily,' Roger dryly remarked.

'Ha ha ha!' Dr Folterknecht laughed derisively. 'You won't trick me again, yah! You expect me to believe this little clown in the pyjamas is the infamous terrorist leader? Ho ho! No tricks this time Mr Secret Agent ... only gaol time, yah!'

Lady Heger-Steel chose that moment to walk out of the amenities block. When she saw seven men and lots of guns being waved about at her wedding, the biggest day of her life, the red mist descended, transforming her into a human slapping machine once again. She charged the men like an angry rhinoceros. SLAP! SLAP! The first to go down was Ohama. 'Naughty boy!' she screeched.

She then turned her fury on Dr Folterknecht and his henchmen. 'Naughty little boys need a spanking, yes?'

No machine gun could fire faster than the school headmistress's hands could slap. Even if you read the next sentence as fast as you possibly could, it wouldn't match the blurring speed of Lady Heger-Steel's hands of wrath as they dispatched the Secret Police Chief and his men. *SLAP! SLAP! SLAP! SLAP! SLAP! SLAP! SLAP! SLAP!*

The five secret policemen were all knocked to the ground in a daze for the second time in the past hour or so. It just wasn't their day. Roger didn't escape the fury of the human slapping machine either and he, too, ended up half-stunned on the ground.

The commotion caught the attention of Commander Wurstling, who rushed over full of bluster and self-importance. 'There will be no disturbances in my town!' he declared pompously. 'I will handle this myself!' He turned to Sergeant Fritzel. 'Sergeant!' he boomed. 'Get all the handcuffs out of my car and arrest these seven men!'

Moses Clay started to help Roger to his feet but was stopped by Commander Wurstling. 'This man is being arrested!'

Johann quickly intervened. 'He is a friend of mine, Commander. Roger is an innocent party in all this.'

Moses and Roger knelt beside the semi-conscious Ohama.

'My God!' Moses exclaimed as he pulled back Ohama's hood from his face. 'It really is Ohama Bin Schaden!' Moses was shaking his head as he turned to Roger. 'I knew there was something big going on here when I saw you in the lobby but never expected to see one of the world's most notorious terrorists here!' Moses Clay stood up and applauded. 'Congratulations to all of you,' he proclaimed. 'This world is a bit safer now that this savage criminal has been captured.'

Cornelia and her cameraman couldn't believe their luck at getting so much exciting footage. Their camera was now capturing a very proud Commander Wurstling with his foot planted on Ohama's stomach like a big game hunter posing with a wild buffalo he'd just shot. 'No one escapes the eye of the Teutonian Police,' he declared, 'especially in this town, where I'm in charge!'

His pompous performance was being spoiled by an enraged Dr Folterknecht, who was cursing at the top of his voice.

'Sergeant Fritzel!' Commander Wurstling commanded. 'Go tell that noisy little man with the ugly nose to be quiet!'

The sergeant cuffed Ohama before rushing over to the doctor and his men, who were getting back on their feet. Karl-Otto defiantly presented his Secret Police badge, but at the same time pointed to Dr Folterknecht as he struggled to his feet, still cursing profusely. 'Cuff him,' Karl-Otto said to Sergeant Fritzel, 'he's gone mad.' Karl-Otto's colleagues nodded their agreement.

When the handcuffs went on Dr Folterknecht, he seriously 'spat the dummy', reinforcing Karl-Otto's assessment of his chief's mental state. 'You are all under arrest!' the doctor screeched.

At that moment Dr Folterknecht spotted Andy Belle. 'Shoot the alien, Karl-Otto, yah! Shoot! Shoot! Yah!' he screamed. The poor doctor couldn't point at the alien he wanted shot because his hands were cuffed behind his back. Instead, he began nodding his head furiously in Andy Belle's direction, which only added to the impression that he had lost his mind. 'How dare you handcuff the chief of the secret police! Karl-Otto, uncuff me immediately, yah! This whole town is under arrest! For harbouring an alien, yah!' He continued nodding repeatedly in Andy Belle's direction. 'Get the alien! There she is! The alien! The alien, yah!'

'It's OK, Doctor,' Karl-Otto spoke soothingly. 'We are all going up to our rooms to have a nice rest.' With that, Karl-Otto and his colleagues unceremoniously carted their chief off.

'This is sabotage!' shrieked Dr Folterknecht. 'This is mutiny, yah! It's treason! No, high treason, yah!' His cries faded as his men carried him away.

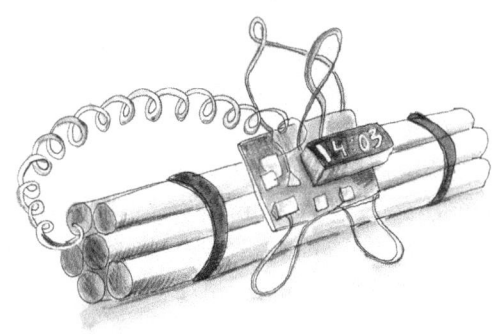

26

'It is interesting,' the magic pencil said, 'to see how human beings can become fixated on a certain belief without being able to conquer their impulsive emotions with calm and logical reasoning.'

Andy Belle could only shrug his shoulders. 'What now?'

'Ohama Bin Schaden is on his way to the big city gaol,' the pencil replied. 'Even if he escapes from prison, he won't come back here. Gusto is still around and hiding with his men. He needs to be caught and locked away as well. As long as he's at large, your family isn't safe. I expect, or hope anyway, that Kunnikunde has lost most of her fire powers. But she is still able to teleport, so she still poses a present and future danger. However, my plan exploits her insatiable greed, so in a couple of days the evil countess should be put out of commission for at least a year.'

'But what about Werner Little Werner?' Andy asked. 'You said he had a bomb.'

'At least two bombs,' the pencil responded. 'Your father has given his factory workers the day off tomorrow to go to the circus with their families. In the morning, Werner will plant the bombs at the factory. Later, sometime that afternoon when Kunnikunde has an advisory board meeting scheduled at her factory next door,

Werner plans to detonate the bombs. However, for most of the day, Kunnikunde and her board members will be at the circus for an alibi so they can't be accused of planting the bombs in your father's factory.'

'And Gusto and his thugs?' Andy Belle asked.

'Gusto is now desperately looking for the lady who stole the laser gun—he has no idea, at this stage, that it was Kunnikunde. I guarantee that Gusto and his men will be at the circus somewhere. Tomorrow will be a very interesting day!'

'I'm worried about those bombs at Dad's factory,' Andy Belle said.

'Don't be,' the pencil replied with an uncharacteristic softness in his voice. 'I have a plan to prevent them from being a problem. But again, Andy, it will take teamwork. Even a great spirit needs an equally great team behind him. I count on you and your many friends to help me bring this to a good end—but especially on you. And I have to say, so far, I am extremely proud of you!'

Andy Belle almost fainted with astonishment at such a compliment from the pencil. Normally he would hear that he had done well but could still do better. He accepted the compliment gladly and proudly. It emboldened him to ask a question: 'Is my disguise as a girl still necessary?'

'Don't worry,' the pencil replied, 'it will fade away tomorrow.'

'Yes!' Andy Belle cried, punching the air. He looked around the tent and saw that all the earlier commotion and disruptions had been forgotten and the wedding festivities were in full swing. Although he wasn't there to see it, they went on until the early hours of the morning. According to all reports, the wedding of Lady Heger-Steel and Jim Steel was a huge success.

The next morning, Andy woke early. His very first thought was the hope that he'd been turned back into a boy overnight. It was dashed the instant he awoke and had to brush the long blonde hair from his face. But he trusted the pencil and knew that sometime today he would be himself again. The thought excited him, and he ran down to the hotel dining room for breakfast full of energy and anticipation.

Andy was surprised to find Roger, Moses Clay, Sergeant Fritzel and Commander Wurstling seated at one of the tables in deep discussion. At that moment, they were joined by a very tired-looking Jim Steel, Hermann and Fritz. Curious, Andy Belle approached the table, only to be stopped in his tracks by Commander Wurstling who told him not to come any closer and tried to wave him away.

'Nothing we discuss at this table is for the ears of a little girl, understood?' the commander said firmly.

Andy Belle started to turn away when Roger spoke up. 'Commander,' he said, 'this little girl has been of great help so far, and she is also one of very few who could recognise the face of Gusto Calamari. I suggest it will be a lot less conspicuous if it is a young girl scouring the faces at the circus than a group of large men.'

Commander Wurstling agreed. 'Well then, little girl, I will tell you where to begin looking for Gusto Calamari and how to signal me if you locate him.'

'If you spot Gusto,' Roger added, 'and signal Commander Wurstling, he will signal me, and I will launch a drone with tranquilliser darts to knock out the gangster boss and his henchmen. Once they are out to it, Sergeant Fritzel will handcuff them. Jim, Moses and Hermann will cover the exits in case any of them try to escape before the tranquillisers take full effect.'

'And I will be watching everything very closely,' Commander Wurstling declared, proudly showing off his big binoculars.

If he had trained them on the castle at that precise moment, he would have seen a miniature hurricane swirling on the front steps and observed Countess Kunnikunde Ritter von Krumm emerging from it and going inside. The dumbfounded commander would have had no idea that this was the evil countess's usual mode of arrival.

Kunnikunde went straight into her meeting room where the four key men of her advisory board were waiting for her. 'Mr

Broombridge!' Kunnikunde cried, startled. 'Have you been hit by a bus?'

The poor man was heavily bandaged and supported on crutches. 'It's a long, ugly story,' Mr Broombridge winced as he sat down. Beside him was Rollover von Cracklingen, and next to him, Farty Ritter von Krumm. Across the table from them sat Mr Werner Little Werner.

'Once and for all,' Kunnikunde snarled, as she took her seat beside Werner, 'we have to put a stop to the treacherous behaviour of my brother-in-law, Johann! His new pencil factory is very successful and drastically reducing our sales ... and profits!' Her snarl became a screech. 'That means it's costing me money! Money! My money! It has to stop! Now!'

As Rollover von Cracklingen described the meeting he and his colleagues had with Johann, he was almost foaming at the mouth with outrage and jealousy. 'No wonder his factory is massively outselling us,' he lamented, 'they're using *our* name!'

'And *our* crest!' Farty cried. 'And right next door! Virtually on our doorstep!'

They were all united in their desire to destroy Johann's venture as soon as possible.

27

The dastardly plan for Werner to procure the bombs and hire two men to plant them in Johann's factory and detonate them that afternoon was Kunnikunde's brainchild. And, as a grand finale to the bomb blasts, she wanted to demonstrate her own awesome firepower. To facilitate it, she had the large picture window in the boardroom removed.

'I will unleash a barrage of fire bolts on what's left of that lousy factory after the bombs explode. It will be razed to the ground. After that, no one will ever mess with me again!' Kunnikunde threw her head back and shrieked, 'I'm tough! I'm tough!'

When she finally calmed down Werner found that she was glaring at him.

'Why are you still here, Werner?' she hissed.

'Just leaving, my countess,' the little man squeaked as he ran off, puffed up with self-importance as the man chosen by Kunnikunde to carry out her plan of chaos and destruction. He was beside himself with pride and excitement.

'I have arranged a minibus to take us to and from the circus,' she told the three remaining men. 'On our return this afternoon we shall meet in my company boardroom. And I'm issuing each of you a taser gun in case something should go wrong at the circus.'

'That really should not be necessary, my dearest aunt,' Rollover gently objected.

'Better to be safe than sorry,' Kunnikunde retorted, summarily dismissing his opinion.

Mr Broombridge, by contrast, was delighted to be getting a taser. 'With one of those, I can have my revenge on that monstrous Heger woman!'

'I would steer well clear of her if I were you,' Farty Ritter von Krumm smirked. 'You have no more room for bandages!'

28

A buzz of excitement and anticipation was building rapidly as people streamed into the giant circus tent. The entertainment had started even before the main event began; clowns were moving among the crowd performing their wacky antics, and the circus band played to a parade of magnificent horses. The stage was set for a spectacular show ... and not just in the ring.

The actors in another thrilling drama under the big top had begun taking their places. First to arrive was Kunnikunde and her advisory board. The evil countess managed to slip in unnoticed due to a large floppy hat she was wearing that covered most of her face. Next to appear were Lady Heger-Steel and husband Jim Steel, who entered to loud applause. Gusto's thugs also slipped in unobtrusively, without their boss anywhere to be seen, although Umberto soon ruined their low profile by loudly announcing that Prince Ulla Dulla Bulla had arrived.

The figure that Umberto pointed out was certainly dressed like the prince in white robes and veiled hood, but the clothing looked about five sizes too big for him.

Not far away, Andy Belle was getting anxious. 'Should I give Commander Wurstling the signal?' he asked the pencil.

'No—this is not the time!' the pencil responded curtly. 'Gusto plans to capture Kunnikunde, and we should let him try ... even help him a little by identifying his target. The hat she is wearing is almost covering her face completely, and Gusto won't know it's her.'

The pencil gave Andy Belle a brief command.

Andy Belle smiled. 'I'm on my way.'

A minute later Andy Belle was whispering into the ear of the white-robed figure everyone assumed was Prince Ulla Dulla Bulla, who, for just a second, reacted sharply.

'Now, Andy,' the pencil said, 'start walking slowly through the crowd. The commander is following your progress with his binoculars.'

Commander Wurstling had positioned himself next to the animal entrance with Sergeant Fritzel standing beside him.

All was going to plan until Werner Little Werner launched a plan of his own, with the help of two shady-looking characters. They crept up to the animal cages unseen and opened five of them. An instant later they jumped onto motorcycles and sped off.

The commander, who was watching Andy Belle intently through his binoculars, had a small dilemma. All this intense concentration was making him hungry. He had put a sausage roll in his back pocket for just such an eventuality, but he didn't dare take his eyes off Andy Belle or allow himself to be distracted. 'Sergeant Fritzel,' he said. 'Would you please retrieve the sausage roll from my back pocket and hand it to me, thank you.'

There was no response from Sergeant Fritzel who seemed to have disappeared. After several silent seconds went by, Commander Wurstling suddenly reacted angrily.

'Sergeant Fritzel! Please! Tell me I'm hearing things; it sounds like you are chomping on my sausage roll!'

The commander temporarily forgot his binoculars duty and turned around, only to find himself staring into the face of a huge male chimpanzee with very large fearsome teeth that had just made short work of his sausage roll.

Wisely, Sergeant Fritzel had left the chimpanzee to his chief's sausage roll and taken refuge behind a big barrel nearby.

'Sergeant Fritzel!' Commander Wurstling boomed. 'This greedy monkey is a criminal ... arrest it immediately!' When he saw Sergeant Fritzel emerge from his hiding place he revised his order. 'OK ... arrest that big bear behind you first, then this monkey!'

When Sergeant Fritzel turned round he made a loud gurgling sound as a bear reared up on its hind legs and growled ferociously. The sergeant's legs seemed to start running before his body finally followed. He ran towards the main ring in the middle of the big top, pursued by the bear. Meanwhile, the commander had been hitting the chimpanzee with his police truncheon, which was making the creature very angry. When it bared its fearsome teeth at the police chief, the chief ran off too, hot on the heels of Sergeant Fritzel.

29

The huge steel mesh lions' cage took up most of the central ring. Standing at its open door, Ringmaster Elbow was explaining to the crowd the dangers of lion taming. For added drama and effect he said that the door of the cage through which he was about to enter could only be opened from the outside; so, once the lion tamer was inside, he couldn't get out until someone let him out.

Just as he was about to step through the door, he was knocked to the ground by two terrified men in a frantic dash for safety. Commander Wurstling and Sergeant Fritzel ran straight over the ringmaster into the cage and slammed the door behind them.

'Arrest that greedy monkey!' Commander Wurstling shouted. He ate my sausage roll! To steal from the police is a serious crime!' But the chimpanzee, along with the bear, had already been arrested, in a sense, by their handlers and led away.

The crowd thought it was all part of the act and applauded wildly, delighted to see two of their own participating in a circus act—especially their police chief and his sergeant.

Meanwhile, Ringmaster Elbow was back on his feet desperately trying to open the cage door, but the two policemen had slammed it after them so hard that it had jammed shut.

As a spur-of-the-moment strategy to escape the bear and the chimpanzee, taking refuge in the big cage seemed like a good idea. With almost immediate hindsight, however, it was revealed to be a particularly bad idea.

Several lions, programmed for the day's lion taming event, were about to enter the big cage from a tunnel on the other side. The automatic tunnel gate opened briefly, letting the first lion through then closed behind it, blocking the others.

'Andy—quick!' the pencil commanded, 'telehop into the cage and take care of the lion! Now!'

Seconds later, Andy Belle was standing in front of a big male lion close enough to reach out and touch it. The lion was agitated, its tail swishing and a deep growl rumbling in its throat.

'OOOOHHH,' Andy Belle trembled.

'Calm down,' the pencil said firmly. 'Channel your inner love for animals and slowly, slowly try to touch him.'

The lion roared and Andy Belle almost dropped dead on the spot with fright. But he trusted the pencil implicitly and found the courage to slowly stretch out his right hand and place it ever so gently on the lion's huge muzzle. To the amazement of the spectators, and the stupendous relief of Andy Belle, the lion calmed down, scrutinised him from head to toe and then gave him a big lick with a tongue so huge that it wet his whole face in one go.

The crowd went ballistic; never in the history of the circus had there been such tumultuous cheering and applause.

The two policemen at the far side of the cage were wholly focused on getting the jammed door open and had their backs to the action with Andy Belle and the lion and missed it all.

Kunnikunde, though, missed nothing. The evil countess was so excited by the prospect of human slaughter and mayhem she imagined she was at the Colosseum in ancient Rome. To get a clear view she removed her large, floppy hat. Her eyes were fixated on Andy Belle and the lion. She did see something extraordinary, but it wasn't the violence and mayhem she'd hoped for.

Following the pencil's instructions, Andy Belle led the lion to a podium and had it perform its tricks as if he were a lion tamer. It was then the pencil's spell on Andy ended abruptly and he instantly turned from a girl back into a boy, in full view of everyone at the circus. Once again, the crowd erupted into uproarious applause, showing their appreciation for what they thought was an amazing magic trick.

Kunnikunde nearly fell off her seat. Her look of astonishment quickly turned to a glare of pure hatred when she recognised the transformed boy in the lions' cage as Andy. 'How stupid of me!' she hissed at herself. 'To kill the spirit that lives in that boy, I will need Lucifer himself!'

'Oops!' the pencil said. 'That was not good—very unfortunate timing.'

'Why?' Andy asked.

'Because we exposed ourselves to evil,' the pencil said.

Andy was about to respond when Commander Wurstling turned around and saw him standing in front of a big lion. His instant reaction was to assume Andy was in terrible danger and try to save him.

'Andy!' he yelled, rushing forward. 'Stand back! I'll handle this oversized pussycat!'

'This man needs brain-enlarging pills,' the pencil muttered to himself. 'Andy! Grab hold of the commander's hand—I have to give him the animal-love gift!

By then, the commander had reached Andy and the lion, which didn't look happy and snarled ferociously at the police chief. Andy grabbed his hand and saw him engulfed by a pale blue flash for just a split second—too quick for anybody else to notice.

The lion instantly stopped snarling and acted like the "oversized pussycat" the commander had called him. The big cat set about licking the police chief's face while he determinedly tried to lecture it on Teutonian Police authority.

Circus staff finally prized open the cage door, and the panic-stricken ringmaster rushed in to thunderous applause from the crowd. This completely gob-smacked him and stopped him in his tracks. He wasn't sure whether he should bow or wave. While he thought about it, Andy convinced Commander Wurstling and Sergeant Fritzel to leave the cage with him.

Gusto Calamari was also trying to get someone to leave with him. As he snuck up behind Kunnikunde his feet became tangled in the oversized white robes he was wearing, and he almost tripped and crashed into her. His Prince Ulla Dulla Bulla disguise was becoming a hindrance, but he managed to steady himself just in time. 'Come with me, lady—we need to talk,' he said to Kunnikunde, as she once again felt the cold steel of a pistol on her neck.

'Not now, I'm busy,' she replied calmly. Quick as a flash she withdrew a taser gun from her bag with her magic arm, jabbed it between Gusto's legs and pulled the trigger. The gangster boss cried out and started quivering all over, dropping his pistol.

At this point, the pencil intervened. 'Roger! The person in the white robes behind Kunnikunde is not Prince Ulla, it's Gusto Calamari. Please knock him out, as well as the three men around him.'

'Roger!' Roger said.

'Andy!' the pencil commanded. 'Identify Gusto Calamari to your small-brained police chief and help him arrest him and his three men.'

Already, Roger's drone darts were finding their targets as Gusto and his men collapsed to the ground one after the other.

None of them heard the announcement booming through the loudspeakers: 'LADIES AND GENTLEMEN ... WE ARE STOPPING THE CIRCUS! WE APOLOGISE TO YOU ALL, BUT WE HAVE NO CHOICE. OUR ANIMALS ARE THE STARS OF THE SHOW AND MANY OF THEM HAVE ESCAPED. ALL OUR STAFF ARE BUSY RECAPTURING THEM. PLEASE LEAVE THE BIG TOP IN AN ORDERLY FASHION. THANK YOU!'

While disappointed, the crowd felt they had already gotten their money's worth; their jaws were still sore from the constant laughing.

Roger, Hermann and Fritz helped Sergeant Fritzel take care of Gusto and his men, under the supervision of Police Chief Wurstling, while Kunnikunde and her board members left with the rest of the crowd.

30

As Mr Broombridge shuffled out with everybody else, he saw an opportunity to make his most fervent dream come true. He couldn't believe his good luck! Rocking side-to-side right in front of him was the broad beam of Lady Heger-Steel. With a grin almost as broad, he took out his taser gun, jabbed it firmly into Lady Heger-Steel's abundant bottom and pulled the trigger.

Despite the shock of over a thousand volts of electricity being delivered directly into her delicate derriere, some deep instinct within Lady Heger-Steel told her that she was the victim of the same pervert who had assaulted her backside on previous occasions. Without hesitation and with a speed belying her impressive bulk, she spun round and landed a slap on Mr Broombridge's cheek that sounded like a small cannon being fired. It prompted some of the departing crowd to stop in their tracks, thinking that perhaps the circus was continuing after all.

With the force of this stupendous blow, poor Mr Broombridge became airborne. He cannoned into Rollover von Cracklingen who fell backwards knocking Kunnikunde over who, in turn, clutched frantically onto Farty von Krumm, dragging him down with her.

Observing the fiasco, Roger remarked, 'One could say that the advisory board of the Ritter von Krumm Pencil Factory was truly floored—mentally and physically.' He chuckled to himself at his little wordplay.

Andy, Jurgen and Hansi were also nearby watching the fun. When Kunnikunde got to her feet she saw three Andys standing there looking at her. It was all too much, and with a hysterical scream, she turned and rushed out of the tent.

A short time later, only two people remained inside the big top. Cornelia and her cameraman were looking at each other shaking their heads in wonder and astonishment at what they had seen and captured on film over the course of the day.

'This is, without question,' Cornelia remarked, 'the weirdest town I have ever visited.'

With perhaps the weirdest police chief, she might have added if she'd known what was going on in Commander Wurstling's brain—his 'small brain' according to the pencil. The commander was less interested in having captured one of the world's most notorious gangsters in Gusto Calamari than he was in arresting the big chimpanzee who had eaten his sausage roll. He was determined to interrogate the "thieving monkey" and stormed up to the cage to which it had been returned after being recaptured. Before its keeper could stop him, the police chief entered the cage. There was a loud metallic clang and click as the door locked itself behind him.

The keeper was panic-stricken—he knew no one should ever enter the cage of a large, aggressive chimpanzee, especially when it was feeding on a big bunch of bananas.

'Monkey!' Commander Wurstling boomed. 'Stand up and listen!' The police chief put on his most authoritarian voice. 'You have committed a serious crime!'

The chimpanzee stared at him for a second then calmly got up with a banana in hand and gently stuffed it into the commander's mouth.

'Yuuuuckkkkk!' shouted the police chief, taking it out of his mouth and looking at it in disgust. The magic animal-love gift he now possessed, without knowing it, had taken over. He grabbed the chimpanzee by the arm and walked it across to the cage door, which the keeper was frantically trying to unlock but was fumbling with the keys in his panic.

Commander Wurstling waved the banana at the keeper. 'Bananas just won't do for this magnificent monkey!' he shouted. 'They are simply not good enough. No wonder he couldn't resist my sausage roll! I demand you feed him a sausage roll every day for breakfast, lunch and dinner!'

By this stage, the keeper was a blubbering mess, but he finally managed to get the cage door unlocked. After getting a big hug from the chimpanzee, Commander Wurstling left the cage and wandered off, happy with the world once again.

31

'Andy!' the pencil ordered. 'We need to go to your father's factory urgently! Tell the others to meet you there. This will be the longest distance you've ever telehopped—so concentrate hard. Go! Go!'

Andy left his twins, Hansi and Jurgen, near the circus tent with instructions about where to meet up at the factory. 'See you there!' he said. He then disappeared before their eyes and reappeared moments later at the door to his father Johann's new pencil factory. He was delighted to see Sassy there waiting for him as well as the two Dobermans. All three greeted him with great enthusiasm and Andy was trying to pat them all at once.

'No time for happy reunions now, Andy!' the pencil scolded. 'Touch me to the dogs so I can see through their eyes and help find the hidden explosives Werner has planted.'

Andy complied, and the three dogs immediately rushed into Johann's factory. Andy had no hope of keeping up with the dogs, but he was surprised to find that he could see through the dogs' eyes too. Then the penny dropped: *Of course, I can, you idiot!* he rebuked himself. *The pencil has to use my eyes.*

By the time Andy caught up with the dogs they had located and retrieved the cleverly placed duffel bags containing the explosives.

'Open the bags, Andy' the pencil instructed, 'and through you, I will first neutralise and then recalibrate the bombs.'

Before Andy could say a word, the magic pencil took over his body. Andy found his hands busily fiddling with various wires, metal clips and what he correctly guessed were electronic detonators. As he worked, he was startled by several blindingly bright flashes. He watched his hands in amazement, having no idea what they were doing. After several minutes they suddenly stopped fiddling.

'Done!' the pencil said. 'Now touch me to the dogs again, Andy.'

No sooner had Andy done so than the dogs raced off. One of the Dobermans had the large duffel bag in its jaws and headed for the executive car park, with the other Doberman hot on its heels.

They quickly located Kunnikunde's big golden limousine and dragged the duffel bag containing the larger bomb under the car.

Sassy, in the meantime, ran off with the smaller bag in her mouth to Kunnikunde's factory and placed it under the pencil-making machine.

Andy and the pencil could see all this happening through the dogs' eyes.

'Good!' the pencil said. 'All done, Andy. Now we wait.'

While Andy and the pencil waited, various people began arriving. First on the scene were Johann and Anna, who went straight into the factory because Johann was keen to check the premises for any sign of sabotage. As they disappeared inside, Roger drove up in his magnificent silver machine with the journalist Cornelia on board.

Andy went over and opened the passenger door for Cornelia, who was strapped so securely in the seat she could only just wiggle her fingers and toes.

'Uh oh!' Andy exclaimed. 'You pushed the blue button, didn't you?'

Cornelia was too angry to speak.

'Yes,' Roger grumped. 'I told her not to, but she did anyway. So, I decided to leave her tied up until we got here. I didn't want to be interviewed by a nosey journalist, anyway!'

He pushed another button and released Cornelia from the straps. She virtually leapt from the car and stomped off straight into Johann's factory.

Roger just scowled and shrugged. As he was about to lock his magnificent machine, Hansi and Jurgen arrived and asked if they could sit in it.

'Yes,' Roger said, 'but don't push any buttons!'

32

After carefully checking his factory and satisfying himself that nothing was amiss, Johann went upstairs to the office suites and stepped out onto a small balcony that faced Kunnikunde's office building next door. He noticed right away that the big picture window in her boardroom had been removed. 'Why would she do that?' he asked himself aloud. 'What is that evil woman up to now?'

A minute later Johann was no longer alone on the small balcony; it was becoming decidedly crowded. Andy had joined his dad, along with his twins, Jurgen and Hansi, and the cameraman, whose finely tuned antennae were telling him that some sort of filmable action was about to take place.

Inside the boardroom with the missing window, Kunnikunde had just been presented with financial year results and she was not happy.

'The stupid morals and ethics my former husband insisted on when he was running this factory have got to go!' she yelled. 'Highest quality and reasonable prices might be good for customers, but they are a disaster for us because they reduce our profits! We have to reverse our approach; that means the lowest quality and exorbitant prices! Use cheap wood in my pencils!

And half the ink in our marker pens! Double the prices, again! No more marketing spending! What we need is control! Control! And more control!'

Kunnikunde's yelling had increased several octaves to a screeching, 'I need money! Money! Money! My money! You idiots are sending me into bankruptcy! I'm broke! I'm broke! You fools have no idea!'

Her hysterical tirade continued for several minutes until her voice started to fail and she finally stopped screeching. She got up from her chair and jabbed a finger at each of her board directors in turn. 'I will show you idiots how it's done,' she hissed. 'Werner! Give me the remote control with the explosives button!'

Werner hesitated. From somewhere buried deep inside him, he found a measure of human decency. 'But, my countess,' he pointed out, 'Johann and his family and others are on that balcony over there. They'll all be blown to smithereens if you trigger those bombs!'

Kunnikunde almost spat her response at him: 'This is war! In war there are casualties, and I'm at war with that despicable family!'

She wrestled the remote control from Werner's hands and invited the others to join her at the windowless opening she had created. Putting on her most charming smile, she waved at Johann, who waved back. She then theatrically raised the remote control with her left hand to about shoulder level and slowly moved her index finger to the red button on the remote.

'Die, Johann ... die!' she hissed and firmly pressed the red button.

A mighty flash blinded everyone for a few seconds.

Once Kunnikunde had regained her composure and saw that Johann's factory building had not been blown up, she exploded herself—in rage. 'Do I have to do everything myself?' she shrieked, her face twisting with hate and fury. She immediately took her position at the open window and prepared to throw her deadly fire bolts at Johann and the others on the balcony. She screeched and threw her head back while thrusting her hands forward and kicking her feet wildly. But this time there were no lightning cracks from shooting fire bolts, only a loud sizzling sound. The only thing coming from her hands and feet was a lot of smoke, which quickly filled the boardroom. Soon the noisy coughing of the board directors drowned out the sizzling sound Kunnikunde was making.

'What's happening to Kunnikunde?' Johann asked. 'She looks like a human smoke machine.'

'She has fizzled out!' the pencil laughed.

Her firepower had fizzled out but not her fury, which she was directing at Werner Little Werner. 'Werner! Where are you?' she screamed. 'You're a total failure! I'm going to throw you out the window! Show yourself!'

Far from showing himself, Werner had made himself scarce. He ran out to the executive car park, taking the remote bomb control with him and hid in the big golden limousine.

Kunnikunde turned her attention to Johann and the others and shook her fist at them. 'I shall kill you all!' she screeched.

Driven out of the boardroom by the smoke, Kunnikunde's advisory board members decided to call it a day. They headed for the executive car park where Werner was hiding in the limousine. To their shock and dismay, the car park appeared to be empty.

'Someone has stolen our cars!' Rollover von Cracklingen yelled.

The car park was almost directly below Johann's factory balcony next door. Rollover stabbed his finger furiously up at Johann. 'And we all know who is behind it. ... Don't we, Uncle?' he shouted.

Johann just calmly shook his head.

'Rollover!' Farty von Krumm yelled. 'Look at this!'

The board directors stood around in stunned silence staring down at tiny, exact replica models of the cars they had parked there earlier that day. At that point, Kunnikunde arrived on the scene, still in a rage. It didn't help her mood any when she saw what had happened to the cars. She snatched up the replica of her golden limo and threw it into her big handbag.

As she turned to go, she stopped and looked up at the group on the balcony, giving them her best evil stare. That was the moment the twin Andys turned back into Jurgen and Hansi. The real Andy gave Kunnikunde a friendly wave.

She didn't return it. 'I underestimated the power of this boy,' she muttered to herself. 'But never again!'

'Countess!' a voice called out with alarm.

Kunnikunde turned to see Mr Broombridge striding towards her. 'I have some bad news! I've just inspected the factory and all the pencil-making machines have disappeared. ... In their place are tiny, exact replica models of them!'

'AAAAARGH!' Kunnikunde howled. 'My machines! My money-making machines! My money! I'm broke! I'm broke! But I will get my revenge—you'll see!'

With that, a mini tornado began whirling around Kunnikunde. Seconds later she had disappeared, leaving Mr Broombridge choking on the cloud of dust she had left in her wake.

Those watching from the balcony began to move back indoors.

'Do you think we've won?' Andy asked the pencil.

'No, unfortunately not! Gusto Calamari is in gaol and will be there for a long time. Dr Folterknecht has been officially declared insane and is out of action. Ohama Bin Schaden has managed to spectacularly escape the big city prison, but he definitely won't dare ever show his face here again.'

'So that leaves us with my Aunt Kunnikunde,' Andy said.

'Unfortunately, yes,' the pencil replied. 'Countess Ritter von Krumm ... the incarnation of jealousy and paranoia ... the embodiment of evil ... a true living devil. She believes you have some incredible magic powers or are the medium for a powerful spirit of some kind.'

'How?' Andy asked, scowling.

'Your sudden appearance in the lions' cage, your handling of wild animals and last but not least, your transformation from a girl into a boy right before her eyes.'

'Yeah, that's true,' Andy shrugged. 'But what can we do to stop my evil aunt doing bad things?'

'We have to break her relationship with the devil—that's the only way,' the pencil replied. 'I hope she is falling into the trap I set for her through Werner. If she does, it should buy us one year free of her and her evil deeds.'

Andy didn't look happy with the pencil's answer: 'And what happens after one year—we have to start over and fight her again?'

'It's your eleventh birthday tomorrow, Andy,' the pencil responded, deflecting the question. 'But you won't be turning eleven,' he added cryptically—tomorrow you will be twelve years old! That's all I can predict.'

Andy was totally mystified. He simply frowned and shook his head as he started walking home. But after a few minutes, his mood brightened considerably as he anticipated the big party that night and his birthday the next day.

And what a party it turned out to be. About sixty people attended, all eager to celebrate the capture of Gusto Calamari and his thugs, the banishment of Ohama Bin Schaden and the apparent defeat of Countess Kunnikunde. The festivities went on until the early hours of the morning and all seemed well in the village of Stone.

33

You never know when the devil might come calling. For most people, that's true; but Kunnikunde was expecting him. The Prince of Darkness arrived at the countess's home in Snobtown dressed in red trousers, light tan shoes, a black shirt and a multi-coloured jacket. Above a pale and drawn face, his hair was pitch black.

When Kunnikunde opened the door, she didn't bother to hide her disappointment, assuming that once again Lucifer had sent her a minor devil instead of coming himself. Nonetheless, she waved him in. The instant she sat down with her visitor in the living room Kunnikunde launched into a semi-hysterical tirade about the recent events at Stone. She hissed, she screamed, she moaned, she wailed, and she cried. When she finally finished her rant, she angrily rebuked her visitor for not taking notes.

'You minor devils are all the same!' she fumed. 'Unhelpful! Incompetent! I need Lucifer himself to know what is going on!'

'You're right,' her guest admitted calmly. 'Minor devils can be incompetent—but very few are as incompetent as you. And Kunnikunde, your bag is moving. Why is your bag moving?'

Kunnikunde looked at her bag in astonishment.

'Actually,' her guest observed, 'it's not just moving, it's expanding.'

Kunnikunde continued to stare at her bag in a daze, lost for words.

'Throw it out the window!' her guest demanded.

When Kunnikunde failed to respond, the man with the pitch-black hair and pale face turned into a scary, vile-looking monster that snarled at her so ferociously that she snapped out of her daze, leapt to her feet, grabbed the bag with both hands and hurled it through an open window like an Olympic hammer thrower.

A moment later Kunnikunde saw the monster turn back into her guest and she nervously sat down again.

'Did you tell me everything?' the man asked.

'You *are* Lucifer, aren't you?' Kunnikunde whispered. 'The devil himself?'

'Yes.'

Kunnikunde was momentarily overawed but quickly reverted to her arrogant, aggressive self. 'I have acquired an amazing laser gun that may be of alien origin! It is an incredible weapon, far more deadly and destructive than my fire bolts! With all due respect, Lucifer, this gun turns me from a mere fire witch into a great and powerful devil!'

She paused and went to the window where she focused a stare of pure malice on the house next door.

'This incredible gun of mine can also make things disappear,' she hissed. 'I want to try it out first on my neighbour Princess High Duty's house. She has money! Disgusting! It should be my money! Then I will get rid of my lousy brother-in-law and his entire family!'

'No, Kunnikunde,' the devil said. 'Let me examine this gun first.'

Kunnikunde opened her mouth to reply when a loud banging on the door cut her off. She opened it to a very distraught Werner Little Werner, who stumbled inside looking bruised and exhausted. He was so agitated he barely noticed Kunnikunde's guest.

'I had a nightmare, a terrible nightmare!' Werner wailed. 'I dreamt I was in your limousine while it was being thrown around like a toy. Then everything went black. The next thing I knew, the car was parked in your garden bed!'

Kunnikunde looked out the window and saw her golden limo in amongst the roses and azaleas. She suddenly realised what it was inside her handbag making it expand—the miniature replica car returning to its normal size. *Lucky I threw the bag out the window,* she told herself, *otherwise, we'd now have a huge car here in the living room with us!*

Werner collapsed into a lounge chair and Lucifer sat staring at him with an amused smile on his face.

'You're a total failure, Werner!' Kunnikunde screeched, looming over him. 'Now get out of—'

The devil interrupted her. 'Wait, Kunnikunde,' he whispered, grabbing her arm and taking her aside. 'The Werners of this world are precious to us. They blindly follow orders. They are the people who become dictators. They are the ones who sell their souls. They can turn happy lives into sad ones.'

He moved a short distance to a big timber desk. 'I want you to give Werner the two bundles of one-thousand-dollar notes hidden in the drawer of this desk.'

'What?' Kunnikunde cried. 'No way! That's my money! Mine! All mine!' She stood defiantly with her arms folded, staring aggressively at the devil. But when he repeated his vile monster transformation, she quickly grabbed the two bundles of money and handed them over to a gob-smacked Werner.

'Now, go back to Stone before I change my mind!' Kunnikunde screeched.

Werner didn't get a chance to thank her; the devil simply touched his hand and the little man disappeared.

'Why didn't you give me some warning you were going to do that?' Kunnikunde shouted. 'I could have grabbed the money back just before you touched him. Now I'll have to get it back tomorrow when I'm in Stone!'

'I don't want you to take the money back from him,' the devil said sharply. 'At least until we have caught that boy!'

'OK! OK!' Kunnikunde hissed, picking up the laser gun. 'And anyway, there are plenty of hostile countries who would pay billions for this gun. If I make them bid competitively for it at auction it'll be worth even more!'

She lifted the gun to eye level and aimed it at the house next door. 'I'll show you how it works!'

Before the devil could stop her, Kunnikunde pulled the trigger.

A split second after she fired the laser gun an awesome electrical storm engulfed Kunnikunde's house. Anyone passing by on the street would have seen the house hit by continuous lightning strikes in rapid succession for about thirty seconds. And they would have been astonished that such a violent, spectacular lightning event didn't make a sound.

Inside the house, the reaction was way beyond mere astonishment. Kunnikunde was hysterical with shock and bewilderment. The devil howled like a pack of hounds from hell, shouting obscenities in a furious rage.

34

'What happened? What happened?' Kunnikunde screamed as she stumbled over the old hubcaps and tools from which the pencil had constructed the fake gun, now scattered across the living room floor.

'You!... you,' the devil shouted, pointing furiously at Kunnikunde, 'you fool! You were tricked again! Why can't you listen? This is a catastrophe! That was a Good Thought bomb, designed to strip my minor devils of their powers for at least one year! Now they can't do their evil work; they will be useless to me! Even I will have a headache for a few weeks!'

Kunnikunde didn't care about the devil's problems. 'Why me? Why always me?' she wailed. 'What have I done to deserve this? A poor old widow. It's not fair!' She turned to the devil, filled with hate and rage. 'I want you to destroy my former husband's brother and his family! All of them, now!

'Cannot do! Will not do!' the devil retorted. 'You have also lost all your powers for at least a year, and you will never be able to teleport yourself again! I really should take you back to my place and make you burn all your silly money anew every day, for eternity!'

'Noooooooo!' Kunnikunde squealed. 'Not my precious money! Mine! Mine! Burning everyone else's would be fine—but not mine!'

'OK, I won't do it yet,' the devil said with an evil sneer. 'But take it as a warning! I will be back next year and will go with you to this terrible place Stone and take out this dastardly spirit myself. How dare it attack Lucifer himself—me! ... the Satanic Majesty, the Prince of Darkness, the King of the Underworld, the Evil One!'

'Yes! Yes!' Kunnikunde goaded. 'Outrageous! Unforgivable! Destroy the boy with the spirit now as well as his family! And while you're at it, get back the money you made me give to Werner!'

The devil glared at Kunnikunde with a mixture of pity and disdain. 'That train has already left the station.' With that, he disappeared in a puff of smoke.

'Lucifer!' Kunnikunde screeched, throwing her hands in the air. 'Lucifer! Come back! Come back!' She collapsed in an armchair, yowling like a wounded cat.

Pink and Rose came running down the stairs and into the living room.

'Mum! What's wrong? What happened!' they cried together.

'Everyone is after my money,' Kunnikunde wailed. 'Even the devil himself! I'm broke! I'm broke! You have no idea! Stealing all that money was hard work and now that little worm Werner has got it! Is that fair? Is that fair?'

Her wails turned to sobs and her two daughters tried in vain to comfort her.

35

With his car now a miniature replica, Mr Broombridge was forced to take the train to get around. He was finding it quite comfortable and convenient and decided it was a sensible alternative to driving himself. What wasn't so sensible though was carrying his miniaturised car in his suit pocket.

Soon after he settled into his seat, he heard a loud ripping sound as his pocket started to come apart at the seams. He looked down and saw that it was starting to bulge. A second later the pocket tore open completely, and his tiny replica car fell onto the floor. Within several more seconds, it was the size of a shoebox and growing rapidly. Half a minute later, it was as big as a lawnmower.

His fellow passengers began to freak out and quickly vacated their seats, huddling together near the door, watching the expanding car with alarm and disbelief. Mr Broombridge joined them.

Someone eventually pressed the emergency stop button and the train slowly came to a halt. By this time, the car had grown to about half size and was beginning to crush seats as it expanded. By the time the passengers fled, and the police arrived, the car had regained its full size, taking out five rows of seats on both sides of the aisle.

Mr Broombridge could find no way to explain to the police officers how his car came to be parked inside a train carriage.

Farty von Krumm's sports car appeared deep in his wine cellar and had to be dismantled piece by piece to be removed. Rollover von Cracklingen's car returned to full size in a tree in his garden, completely destroying his kids' treehouse. Fortunately, the kids weren't in the tree at the time.

Andy had a fabulous birthday. While he received lots of presents, what he valued even more was that there would be peace in Stone once again and life would return to normal, at least for a while anyway.

He was feeling very happy, and everything seemed right with the world, except for one thing; the pencil was unusually quiet and that worried him. The answer he got when he asked why dismayed him.

'Andy,' the magic pencil said, 'I am a good spirit sent here to protect your family from evil, which I managed to do, this time. I feel quite confident taking on minor devils and earthly criminals, but I could never be a match for the devil himself. I don't have the powers yet to take on Lucifer. And I fear that's what I will have to do next time. My superiors tell me we have attracted the devil's attention through your Aunt Kunnikunde's connection with him. I'm a young spirit with limited powers and still learning, so they want me to return for further training.'

'That's OK!' Andy said with false bravado, forcing himself to smile, even though deep down he knew what the pencil was saying. 'It will be just for one night, like last time.'

'No!' the pencil replied firmly. 'It will be for at least nine months.'

Andy went pale. 'No!' he gasped. 'That is far too long! You are my friend. I can't do without you for such a long time.'

Andy took a few deep breaths to calm himself. 'You know,' he said, 'even though you are my special friend, I don't even know your name.'

'Michaela,' the pencil said.

'Michaela,' Andy repeated.

'Yes,' the pencil replied. 'And I'm sure when I return with greater powers and more advanced training, we will have another grand journey together.'

But that's another story.

Illustrations by Caroline Webb

www.ingramcontent.com/pod-product-compliance
Lightning Source LLC
LaVergne TN
LVHW011712060526
838200LV00051B/2872

Copyright © 2011 by Tom Frye
ALL RIGHTS RESERVED

Villian Logo Copyright © Mosley Street Melodrama
Hero Logo Courtesy of Monte Wheeler
Heroine Logo Courtesy of Monte Wheeler
Vamp Logo Courtesy of Monte Wheeler

CAUTION: Professionals and amateurs are hereby warned that *THE MOSLEY STREET MELODRAMAS VOLUME IV* is subject to a licensing fee. It is fully protected under the copyright laws of the United States of America, the British Commonwealth, including Canada, and all other countries of the Copyright Union. All rights, including professional, amateur, motion picture, recitation, lecturing, public reading, radio broadcasting, television and the rights of translation into foreign languages are strictly reserved. In its present form the play is dedicated to the reading public only.

The amateur and professional live stage performance rights to *THE MOSLEY STREET MELODRAMAS VOLUME IV* are controlled exclusively by Samuel French, Inc., and licensing arrangements and performance licenses must be secured well in advance of presentation. PLEASE NOTE that amateur licensing fees are set upon application in accordance with your producing circumstances. When applying for a licensing quotation and a performance license please give us the number of performances intended, dates of production, your seating capacity and admission fee. Licensing fees are payable one week before the opening performance of the play to Samuel French, Inc., at 45 W. 25th Street, New York, NY 10010.

Licensing fee of the required amount must be paid whether the play is presented for charity or gain and whether or not admission is charged.

Professional/Stock licensing fees quoted upon application to Samuel French, Inc.

For all other rights than those stipulated above, apply to: Samuel French, Inc., at 45 W. 25th Street, New York, NY 10010.

Particular emphasis is laid on the question of amateur or professional readings, permission and terms for which must be secured in writing from Samuel French, Inc.

Copying from this book in whole or in part is strictly forbidden by law, and the right of performance is not transferable.

Whenever the play is produced the following notice must appear on all programs, printing and advertising for the play: "Produced by special arrangement with Samuel French, Inc."

Due authorship credit must be given on all programs, printing and advertising for the play.

ISBN 978-0-573-69954-2   Printed in U.S.A.   #29994

The Mosley Street Melodramas
Volume IV

by Tom Frye

A Samuel French Acting Edition

SAMUELFRENCH.COM

No one shall commit or authorize any act or omission by which the copyright of, or the right to copyright, this play may be impaired.

No one shall make any changes in this play for the purpose of production.

Publication of this play does not imply availability for performance. Both amateurs and professionals considering a production are strongly advised in their own interests to apply to Samuel French, Inc., for written permission before starting rehearsals, advertising, or booking a theatre.

No part of this book may be reproduced, stored in a retrieval system, or transmitted in any form, by any means, now known or yet to be invented, including mechanical, electronic, photocopying, recording, videotaping, or otherwise, without the prior written permission of the publisher.

MUSIC USE NOTE

Licensees are solely responsible for obtaining formal written permission from copyright owners to use copyrighted music in the performance of this play and are strongly cautioned to do so. If no such permission is obtained by the licensee, then the licensee must use only original music that the licensee owns and controls. Licensees are solely responsible and liable for all music clearances and shall indemnify the copyright owners of the play and their licensing agent, Samuel French, Inc., against any costs, expenses, losses and liabilities arising from the use of music by licensees.

IMPORTANT BILLING AND CREDIT REQUIREMENTS

All producers of *THE MOSLEY STREET MELODRAMAS VOLUME IV must* give credit to the Author of the Play in all programs distributed in connection with performances of the Play, and in all instances in which the title of the Play appears for the purposes of advertising, publicizing or otherwise exploiting the Play and/or a production. The name of the Author *must* appear on a separate line on which no other name appears, immediately following the title and *must* appear in size of type not less than fifty percent of the size of the title type.

FROM THE AUTHOR

All four of these melodramas were premiered at Mosley Street Melodramas in Wichita, Kansas under the love and guidance of owner/producers Patty Reeder and Scott Noah. The scripts were given the chance to grow and do what was intended by their author, to entertain.

Each play may use various sets, drops, scenery pieces or space available to that theatre. The names of Kansas towns, local celebrities and politicians make the script more enjoyable to the audience. Feel free to change those names to your particular area of the country.

A warm and loving thank you for many of the character names that have been drawn from my family and friends.

I dedicate this volume to my grandparents Cecile Mae Hoggatt Adams, Walter Harry Adams, Orpha Lela Frye Turkington, and Roy Pickard.

CONTENTS

Fast Food Frenzy 7

Little School House on the Prairie 43

Where's the Gold? 67

Old McDonald Had a Farm 103

FAST FOOD FRENZY
OR
WOULD YOU LIKE FRYES WITH THAT?

For

My Beloved Parents

Margaret Helen and Kenneth Minor Frye

FAST FOOD FRENZY was first presented at Mosley Street Melodramas, Wichita, Kansas on February 5, 2004 under the direction of Tom Frye. It ran for 24 performances. The production featured lights, sound and stage management by Marty Gilbert, costumes by Patty Reeder, properties by Pat Szlauderbach, musical direction by Steve Rue, choreography by Kyle Vespestad, and set design by Scott Noah and Nick Saverine. The cast was as follows:

MAGGIE "MA" FRYE	Bambi Stofer
K.M. FRYE	Tim Robu
LENDY FRYE	Kim Des Jardin
ETTA WOODS	Patty Reeder
SOUR KRAUT	Scott Noah
SAM L. MADISON	Cody Chambers
TRIXIE	Scott Noah

CHARACTERS

MAGGIE "MA" FRYE - Matronly and full of spunk.
K.M. FRYE - Simple but loves Maggie.
LENDY FRYE - Our Heroine. She is sweet and goofy.
ETTA WOODS - Crazy neighbor. Big butt and wild hair.
SOUR KRAUT - Our villain and a big business thug.
SAM L. MADISON – Our hero. New principal. Not too bright.
TRIXIE – A Rat Terrier with an attitude.
PIANO PLAYER

THE SETTING

Wichita, Kansas.

Scene I: Frye Homestead
Scene II: Office of Sour Kraut
Scene III: Somewhere Outside
Scene IV: Lendy's Restaurant

Scene I

(The Frye homestead in Rose Hill, Kansas in the living room of the Fryes. In the center is a table and two chairs. Music opens the scene, "Home Sweet Home."

*(**MA** enters with a pie, holding it with two oven mitts. She is wearing bib overalls, a flannel shirt, and a L.A. Dodgers baseball cap. She is humming and smiling. Sitting in one of the stuffed chairs is a small, white and brown, stuffed dog named **TRIXIE**.)*

*(**MA** enters stage left and crosses to table and places pie in the middle of the table)*

MA. And that's the last one. My oh my, I've baked twenty seven pies this morning. *(She speaks with great love.)* But this one is for Pa.

*(She looks at **TRIXIE**.)*

Now Trixie, you know you're not suppose to be sitting on the table.

*(She pats **TRIXIE**'s head.)*

Okay you can stay, but stay away from this pie. Pa should be back any minute now. Bless his little heart, he's been out all morning training those polo ponies for Mr. Kraut. How Pa loves them animals, and how I hate ol' man Kr—

(She quickly puts her hand over her mouth and begins to sob and then sits at the table.)

Now Maggie Frye that is not the Christian thing to say or think.

(She looks towards the Heavens.)

MA. I didn't mean that. But it's so difficult to like a man who eats chips and dip from his belly button. And he is always trying to come up with a new recipe that will make him famous. Imagine when he tried to sell his belly button lint and salsa dip. *(beat)* Why, he barely broke even. At least he pays my husband a meager wage. Enough to keep us out of the poor house.

(She rises and picks up dog.)

Oh Trixie, with all our sorrow - and your doggie breath - it's just unbearable at times. At least my darling daughter, Lendy, is due home from Manhattan, Kansas where she was attending college at Silo Tech. Hopefully she can get a job and help Pa and me.

(There is a knock at the door.)

Now I wonder who that can be this early.

(She puts dog on the table and starts to go.)

Now stay.

(Goes off stage right and says)

Oh it's you, Etta. Good morning. Come in and have a cup of coffee.

*(She enters with **ETTA WOODS**.)*

ETTA. Oh landsake, a good cup of coffee sounds wonderful.

MA. Well, have a seat and I'll go get us a cup. *(Starts to exit stage left)*

ETTA. Oh Maggie, you wouldn't mind rustlin' up a doughnut with that would you?

MA. Why certainly, Etta. *(Starts to go off stage left)*

ETTA. And maybe a couple of eggs, some toast and a few flapjacks.

MA. Eh? Well... *(Starts again to leave)*

ETTA. A side order of grits, sausage and a T-bone steak, eh, medium rare.

MA. Is that all?

ETTA. Maybe a few biscuits and gravy.

(MA pulls a pencil from her hair and a waitress' order pad out of her apron pocket and starts writing.)

And some Sweet'N Low for the coffee, I'm watching my weight.

MA. No prob, I'll just go out and butcher a hog and be right back.

(She exits shaking her head.)

ETTA. Well, good ol' Trixie. Are you looking at that pie like I am?

(She is eyeing the pie. Looks around to see if anyone is watching her.)

Well, I'll just have a little pie.

(She picks up the pie and starts to take a big bite out of the side of it.)

(Over microphone we hear the voice of the TRIXIE. The actor who plays the villain may do this role, or another actor with a great speaking voice.)

TRIXIE. Put down that pie.

(ETTA freezes and looks around, then tries to take another bite.)

You could save energy on the chewing and apply that directly to your butt.

ETTA. *(Puts down the pie)* Who said that?

(She rises and looks around the room and under the table.)

Boy hunger is making me crazy.

TRIXIE. Naw, you were already crazy.

ETTA. *(Rises and takes a fighting poise)* That does it, come out here and I'll break yer face.

TRIXIE. With what? Yer looks?

ETTA. *(She speaks to herself.)* Now there ain't no one here but me...and this stupid dog, Trixie.

TRIXIE. Who's stupid? You don't see me following you around the park with a plastic bag picking up yer poop.

(ETTA freezes, looks back at the dog, and then looks back at the audience.)

ETTA. Naw, it can't be. Dogs can't talk. *(She suddenly realizes it must be something else.)* I know, I forgot to take my pills this morning.

TRIXIE. Pills for what? Ugliness?

(ETTA quickly turns and looks at dog.)

OOOhhh, it ain't working.

(She then turns back to audience with an angry look, so her backside is towards the dog.)

It ain't working from this side either.

(ETTA turns and picks up TRIXIE.)

ETTA. That does it dog. You want a piece of this?

TRIXIE. Hell there's enough for the entire audience.

ETTA. Wait a minute. What's goin' on? I'm talkin' to a dog.

(Beat)

TRIXIE. So am I.

ETTA. Now listen here you, you...

(She suddenly realizes the dog talks and sets him in a chair.)

You can talk.

TRIXIE. Bingo Einstein. Finally. You must be one of the whiz kids from _____. *(Insert local school name)*

ETTA. But, but, but.

TRIXIE. No you only got one butt, but it is worth saying three times.

ETTA. Oh my goodness, I'm in pain. I got to sit down.

*(She starts to sit on **TRIXIE**.)*

TRIXIE. AHHH! Not on me. *(**ETTA** jumps and moves to the other chair.)* My life just flashed before my cute little Rat Terrier eyes.

ETTA. Trixie?

TRIXIE. Yeeeeesssss?

ETTA. I don't understand. Dogs ain't suppose to talk. But you're talking.

TRIXIE. Yeah, well. Men ain't suppose to leave the toilet seat up either. I rest my case.

ETTA. But why are you talking to me? You never have before. Do you talk to Maggie?

TRIXIE. Well, I've never had to before. But there's lots of trouble in this house, and I need someone to help me save Ma and Pa Frye. So listen to my plan.

(Long pause)

Wait, here comes Ma...Dummy up.

*(**ETTA** makes a blank look on her face.)*

Oops, too late.

*(**MA** enters stage left. She carries out two coffee cups and places them on the table.)*

MA. Well, everything is cooking on the stove. Here's your coffee.

*(She sees **TRIXIE** on the chair.)*

Now Trixie, you need to get down so I can rest these old bones.

(She picks up the dog and places him on floor.)

There you go. Now, Etta, what brings you over here today? It couldn't be just the 18-course meal you ordered is it?

ETTA. *(Still flabbergasted, she blurts out and yells at* **MA.***)* NO. NO REASON. CAN'T A FRIEND JUST DROP OVER AND HAVE A CUP OF COFFEE? WHY DOES THERE HAVE TO BE A PROBLEM? THERE'S NO PROBLEM. NOPE. NO PROBLEM HERE. I'M FINE. ARE YOU FINE? I KNOW I'M NORMAL. NO ONE TALKS TO DOGS HERE. NO SIR. JUST ME AND YOU AND OLD SILENT DOG, TRIXIE.

MA. *(Looking at* **ETTA** *with concern)* OK. As long as everything is normal. Well, why don't you just have a drink of your coffee. I'll go check on your breakfast.

*(***ETTA** *gulps down the whole cup as* **MA** *exits stage left.)*

But be careful it's really hot.

(Beat. The dog speaks after **MA** *leaves.)*

TRIXIE. How's your mouth, Etta?

*(***ETTA** *jumps up and runs around the room screaming.)*

ETTA. AHHHHH. Hot! Hot! Oh that's hot. Water. Water.

*(***ETTA** *grabs water off a front table, throws it at her mouth, and collapses in a chair.)*

TRIXIE. That was subtle. Listen hippo hips, you can't fall apart. I need someone to help me save this family from that creep Sour Kraut.

ETTA. *(Speaking with a scorched tongue)* Awwite. Ut an I oo. At an owns aw a ores in own. I ust a imple arm ooman.

TRIXIE. Excuse me, I don't speak grunt. What the hell did you say? Nevermind. I'm sure it was stupid.

*(***MA** *reenters with a can of whipped cream, plate, and fork and sets them on the table.)*

MA. There, now after breakfast you can have a piece of pie for dessert if you want.

*(***MA** *exits again.* **ETTA**, *still fanning her burning tongue, looks at the whipped cream, grabs it, and fills her mouth with the cooling whipped cream. She smiles as it soothes the pain.)*

TRIXIE. And they say I'm disgusting because I drink out of the toilet.

ETTA. *(Trying to speak with whipped cream all over her tongue)* Ah ge er oh...

TRIXIE. Ok, toots. This is quiet time. Shhhh. Just listen. I've got a plan and you can help.

(Suddenly there is a knock at the door. From offstage, we hear MA.)

MA. Oh Etta, would you get the door?

(ETTA looks scary with all the whipped cream on her face. She looks at the dog and pantomimes him to go to the door.)

TRIXIE. Oh yeah, and it wouldn't be weirder for me to answer the door. Answer it, Cool Whip kisser.

(ETTA reluctantly goes to door stage right and lets in our hero, SAM.)

(SAM enters, poses centerstage, and faces audience, but speaks directly to ETTA.)

SAM. Howdy ma'am. I'm Sam L. Madison *(He quickly poses for the audience.)* at yer service. I'm new to Wichita, *(He pronounces it "Wa-Chee-ta".)* so I'm going around and introducing myself to everybody. I'm the new school principal. Are there any children living in this humble home?

(He gets no answer and turns and sees ETTA, screams and jumps back.)

Ahhhh. Help! Help! This woman has gone mad. She's rabid, get a gun.

(ETTA points to the whipping cream and shows him the can. He looks puzzled, and she pantomimes what happened with the coffee. Of course, he's an idiot and doesn't understand.)

SAM. Oh, I see, must be a family custom to shoot whipped cream directly in your mouth.

(ETTA does a take to the audience.)

SAM. Well, I want to be welcome here, so I'm glad to oblige, ma'am.

(He shoots mouth full of whipped cream and sits in other chair. ETTA collapses in the opposite chair in disbelief.)

MA. *(Offstage she starts her line and enters stage left and sees the two of them sitting with whipped cream all over their mouths.)* Etta dear, who was that at the do...

(She freezes and stares. SAM waves at her really big and smiles. MA walks over to piano and takes whiskey bottle from within the spittoon and takes a big swig. She crosses back and says.)

Is this a new Jehovah's Witness thing? Jes what in the world is going on here? Etta, who is this man?

ETTA. *(She is finally able to speak.)* Maggie, this here is the new principal of the school. His name is Sam L. Madison. Mr. Madison, this is the lady of the house, Maggie Frye.

(MAGGIE offers her hand, and he kisses it with all this whipped cream all over his mouth.)

MA. Thanks. How come you two got whipped cream all over your mouths?

ETTA. Well, I burned my mouth with the coffee and I had to cool it. And Mr. Madison... *(They both look at him in disbelief.)* ...well, he's an idiot. *(He smiles.)*

MA. *(She takes out her hanky and cleans his mouth.)* Here, let's just clean this up.

SAM. Thank you, ma'am. Pleased to meet you. I jest came by to see if there were any youngin's livin' here that would be comin' to my new school.

MA. Well sorry, son. I only have one child, and she's jest finished college in Manhattan Kansas. *(Underscored through this scene, "The Wabash Cannonball")*

ETTA. That's right she grad-ye-ated from K.S.U. or as we call it "Cow Pattie U."

MA. That's Silo Tech.

ETTA. Well, when I was walking there once, it was Cow Pattie U. *(She laughs.)*

SAM. So Mrs. Frye, she's a wildcat then, just like me.

ETTA. I'll say! That gal kin whip her weight in cowpokes.

SAM. No, I meant a wildcat. Silo Tech's mascot is the Wildcats.

ETTA. Yeah, that too.

MA. Yes. And she's due home at any time. I've prepared her favorite food as a welcome home dish. She loves Mexican food. So I made her Fiesta Frejoles Soup. But the problem is I can't serve it in a bowl.

SAM. Why not?

MA. If'n I serve a KSU Wildcat fiesta in a bowl, she'll jest lose it.

ETTA. Maybe you should serve her Jayhawk pie. Okay, eh, well, I need to go. Nice to meet you, Sam. Maggie, I need to go home. Thanks for the first degree burns.

MA. But what about your breakfast?

ETTA. Oh yeah. Jest put it in a doggie bag and I'll take it with me.

MA. Alright. Excuse me, Mr. Madison, I'll be right back. *(She picks up* **TRIXIE**.*)* Come on, Trixie, I'll git you something to eat. *(They exit stage left.)*

ETTA. So tell me, Sam. You hitched?

SAM. No, ma'am.

ETTA. Well then, *(She's now moving in on him.)* what say you and me git better acquainted? Eh?

SAM. Well...er...I don't know, miss?

ETTA. Woods. You know, like Woods with lots of trees... *(Underscored music plays a slow love ballad, something like* "Killing Me Softly"*)* and cool breezes...and babbling

---

*Please see Music Use Note on Page 3.

brooks…and couples neckin'…and heavy breathin' and clothes fly everywhere and whipped cream.

(By this time, she has grabbed the whipped cream and backed him against the stage right portal.)

Whatever Etta wants, Etta gets. And little man, little Etta wants you. *(She has him pinned against a wall.)*

MA. *(Entering stage left)* Etta. What are you doing?

ETTA. Nothin' Maggie, jes showin' Sam the country two thrust.

MA. You mean two step?

ETTA. You dance yer way, and I'll dance mine.

MA. Well, here's yer breakfast.

(She goes to get bag offstage left. It's a huge bag and she brings it center stage with great effort.)

ETTA. Thanks, Maggie. And, Sammy Poo, I'll see you later.

(She smiles and shoots whipped cream under his nose giving him a mustache.)

Men with mustaches really turn me on.

*(**MAGGIE** runs over and grabs whipped cream and throws **ETTA** towards the bag.)*

MA. Now Etta, behave yerself. This poor boy is liable to run away. He'll think the women in this town are as loose as those in _____. *(Insert a local town to make fun of)*

ETTA. Ok. But jes remember, Sam, I saw you first, and there's a whole lotta woman here. The good thing about me, is that I'm warm in the winter and shady in the summer. Toodle-oo.

(She drags bag offstage stage right.)

MA. You'll have to forgive Etta, Mr. Madison. She's…well, the clinical term is…nuts. Anyway, may I offer you a cup of scalding coffee?

SAM. No, thank you. I think you're running low on whipped cream. It was nice meeting you. But I must go.

MA. Oh please, Mr. Madison, stay! I jest heard Pa coming in the back door. I want you to meet him.

(She calls off stage left.)

Oh, Pa! Come in here I want you to meet someone. Oh Mr. Madison sit down.

*(**PA** enters wearing **MA**'s dress and bonnet. **MA** sees him.)*

Oh Pa.

*(She looks at their clothes as does **SAM**.)*

Pa, you dressed in the dark again this morning. This here is the new principal, Sam Madison.

*(**PA** crosses to him. **SAM** rises. They shake hands.)*

PA. Howdy there son. Any friend of Ma's is a friend of mine.

MA. Pa, we ain't friends, we jest met.

PA. *(Quickly turning on **SAM** and grabbing him)* Then git out, you scoundrel! How dare you come in here and take advantage of my wife.

MA. No, Pa. He's not a stranger either. We jest met.

PA. *(Releasing **SAM**)* Oh sorry there, fella. It's jest this little woman here is hot property.

MA. Oh, Pa. *(She is embarrassed.)*

SAM. Yes sir, she seems real nice.

PA. *(Angrily grabbing **SAM** again)* Are you givin' my woman the eye, boy?

MA. Oh Pa, he was jes being pleasant.

PA. *(Releasing him again)* Sorry, son. It's jes this little woman gits me hot jest walkin by her. Why, when I think of her my bunions start to twitch. I remember once when we was out in the barn...

MA. Pa! *(Cutting him off, she hits him with the hanky.)*

PA. Come here, you little tart.

(He grabs her, and they start to make out passionately. Choreographed, they run around the room groping and kissing. **SAM** *just can't quite get out of the way as they lay on him and make out. He is mortified.)*

(They finally end up in a clump stage left as **LENDY** *enters from stage right with her suitcase. She has bright red hair fixed like the Wendy's restaurant logo, freckles, and dress. She enters and sees them.)*

LENDY. Mom, Dad, I'm home.

(They break and end up in a line centerstage; **MA**, **PA**, *and* **SAM**. **LENDY** *goes to each. She kisses* **MA** *on the cheek.)*

Oh Ma.

(She kisses **PA** *on the forehead.)*

Oh Pa.

(She kisses **SAM** *on the lips.)*

Oh my.

(She realizes she doesn't know this person, but liked the kiss.)

MA. Oh Lendy, this is the new principal, Mr. Sam L. Madison.

SAM. I'm so happy to meet you, Miss Frye.

LENDY. Oh please, Mr. Madison, call me Lendy.

(She runs offstage right as the other three take centerstage pose.)

MA. Who's peeking out from under her hairdo?

PA. Calling a name that's lighter than air.

SAM. Who's bending down and gave me a big kiss?

ALL. Everyone knows it's Lendy. *(She pokes head out of stage right curtain.)*

PA. Who's tripping down the streets of Manhattan?

MA. Looking around to find a big bird.

SAM. Who's reaching out to kill a Jayhawk.

(**LENDY** *grabs* **SAM** *and drags him stage right.*)

MA & PA. Everyone knows it's Lendy.

PA. Oh, Lendy, we're so glad you're home.

LENDY. *(Looking at* **SAM.***)* Oh me too.

MA. But Lendy, I'm afraid there's bad news.

LENDY. You mean something worse than that description of me?

MA. I'm afraid so. Oh this is so hard for me to say.

PA. Oh Ma, just spit it out.

(**MA** *starts hacking and coughing like she's hurling up a fur ball.*)

LENDY. No Ma, he just means tell me.

MA. Ok, but that was gonna be a good one. It felt like it had some cream corn with it.

LENDY. *(Cutting her off)* Ma. Just what is the problem?

MA. Well, as you know, that mean nasty polecat Sour Kraut still owns this place, and he's raising the rent again to drive us out. We need money and bad.

(They all look at **SAM.***)*

SAM. *(Smiling)* Are you kidding? Don't look at me, I'm broke, I'm in education.

PA. It don't look good, honey. If we don't come up with the money in one week, he's going to send us packin'.

SAM. Boy, that sounds terrible. You poor folks are in a world of hurt. It just isn't fair. This Sour Kraut sounds like he needs a good thrashin'.

(They all look to **SAM** *as a savior.)*

Well, be sure and write when he throws you out. *(Starts to go.)*

LENDY. Wait, Sam. You have to help us.

SAM. Me? What can I do?

LENDY. Well, I know if the four of us put our brains together, we're bound to have at least one full one.

(They all gather in a circle with the tops of their heads together and grumble.)

(After they are in position in a circle, **PA** *raises his head and looks and says:)*

PA. Say, does this bonnet make my butt look big?

Scene II

(**KRAUT** *enters from front theatre doors as spotlight hits him. Music blares a recognizable movie theme, like the theme from "Rocky"*. He is dressed in a boxer's robe with "COCKY" in letters on the back, sunglasses, and has a big cigarette holder with a cigarette. He is in a dark pinstriped suit, yellow shirt, and red tie. He has boxing gloves on.*)

(*He stands at door, poses, and waves to crowd. He turns and bends like he's in the boxing ring corner, showing his "COCKY" on the back. Slowly, he meanders through the crowd, shaking hands and schmoozing. Once he begins walking the music switches to a 1950s gangster Sinatra-style tune.*)

KRAUT. Drinks all around for this table.

(*He moves to the next table.*)

Bill it to this table.

(*He moves to the next table.*)

Hey fella, nice lady, too bad she's going home with me.

(*He coaxes another lady to rise and waltz with him.*)

Hey doll, what's your phone number? If you don't give it to me, I'll just copy it off the bathroom wall.

(*He finally arrives on the stage, and he prances around the stage shaking hands with the front row.*)

Wow, this is how it must feel like to be Paris Hilton, only fully clothed and with brains.

(**KRAUT** *backs to stage right and a hand comes out and takes his robe. He then turns and sticks his left hand offstage, and someone takes off his boxing glove. Then he sticks his right hand off and someone takes off his right glove and replaces it with a drink.* **KRAUT** *swaggers centerstage and addresses audience.*)

---

*Please see Music Use Note on page 3.

KRAUT. Good evening and welcome to your worst nightmare. *(He laughs and then looks at a lady in the audience.)* No lady, I'm not talking about your honeymoon night. May I introduce myself to you. My name is Sour Kraut. *(He bows. He loves all the booing and smiles.)* You think that bothers me. You don't understand. What I love more than anything in the world is booze. *(He laughs and then toasts the audience with his drink.)* Like most of you here tonight, I have very little tolerance for distasteful entertainment. Therefore this man right here agrees to keep his clothes on all night. *(He laughs.)* Enough mingling with the minions. I have work to do. I believe there are people to destroy, animals to cage, damsels to undress.

(He reaches in his pocket and pulls out a remote control and aims it at the curtain, steps back and hits forward button.)

Forward.

(Curtain starts to slowly open.)

Rewind.

(Curtain starts to go down.)

Forward.

(Curtain starts back up again.)

Pause.

(Curtain pauses midway up. He turns and smiles at the audience.)

I love high tech. Forward.

(Curtain goes up.)

He starts to turn and go upstage and he catches sight of the **PIANO PLAYER**. *He looks at him and then the audience and then the remote control. He grins. He aims it at* **PIANO PLAYER** *and hits button.)*

Play.

*(***PIANO PLAYER** *starts playing* Take Me Out to the Ball Game. *After a few seconds,* **KRAUT** *again aims at* **PIANO PLAYER** *and hits button.)*

Stop.

(He laughs and re-aims.)

Play.

*(**PIANO PLAYER** starts where he/she left off. **KRAUT** waits and then aims again. He hits button again.)*

Mute.

*(**PIANO PLAYER** mimes playing.)*

Play.

(He resumes where he/she left off. The villain is having a ball with this.)

Stop.

*(**PIANO PLAYER** stops.)*

Play.

(He/she plays.)

Fast Forward.

(He/she plays double time.)

Stop.

*(**PIANO PLAYER** stops.)*

Reverse.

*(**PIANO PLAYER** plays unrecognizable chords. Villain is laughing. He aims again and says.)*

Pause.

*(This time the **PIANO PLAYER** plays in mime. **KRAUT** looks at him in disgust and then looks at the button. He says to audience.)*

Sorry, I hit the mute button. Pause.

*(He re-aims and hits pause, **PIANO PLAYER** freezes again. **KRAUT** walks upstage and then decides to give the **PIANO PLAYER** a break. He aims and hits button.)*

Stop.

*(**PIANO PLAYER** is now resting and panting at piano. **KRAUT** smirks and says.)*

KRAUT. Oops, I forgot. Be kind. Rewind.

(Aims and pushes button. **PIANO PLAYER** *is frantically playing gibberish until he collapses. Sometimes he slows down and then speeds up like a video tape does.*

*(***KRAUT*** laughs. He skips to behind desk, sits, and picks up stack of papers.)*

KRAUT. Hmmm. Foreclosure. Foreclosure. Foreclosure. Send to Haysville. Foreclosure. Foreclosure. Send to Prison. Foreclosure. *(Goes back to send to prison. Looks at paper.)* No, prison is too good for him. Send him to Haysville. *(He laughs and goes on.)* Foreclosure, and finally we come to the last decision, the Frye family. *(He menacingly laughs.)* Do I raise their rent again or do I have a heart? *(Takes paper to audience)* I'm going to show you I do have a heart. I'm going to let you the audience decide what to do with these lowlifes. All those who think I should raise their rent and shove them into poverty raise your hands. *(He quickly raises his.)* Okay, I count one. Now all those who think I should let them stay, lower their rent and be sweet to them, raise your hands.

(He turns his back to audience and pretends like he's looking around the stage. Still with back to audience.)

Well, well. It looks like it's one to nothing. What an apathetic group. *(Laughs)* So I raise the rent. *(He turns around. If there are any hands still up he says:)* Yes, you may, *(Points to the restrooms)* they're right over there.

(He crosses behind desk.)

Well, I've sent for these losers. They should be here any time. And you get to watch me throw them out.

(There is a knock at the door.)

I bet that's the Frye family now. Well, I can't wait to fry them. *(He laughs.)* Come in.

*(***MA*** *and* **PA** *enter and* **KRAUT** *crosses between them.)*

KRAUT. Good morning Maggie, K. M. I see you've come to pay your rent and the small increase.

PA. You know that ain't true, Mr. Crap.

KRAUT. Eh. That's Kraut.

MA. No, he was right the first time.

KRAUT. Now, now, business is business.

PA. Yeah, and you're givin' us the business. You know we ain't got that much money.

KRAUT. You don't? Tsk Tsk. Well, that puts me in an awkward situation. Let's see, I know, I have a file for what to do when you don't have your rent check. *(Goes to desk and rifles through files)* Ah, here it is. *(Opens file)* And it says... *(Yells:)* Throw the bums out!

(As he laughs, MA cries on PA's shoulder. Hearing all the noise, LENDY enters stage left.)

LENDY. Ma. Pa. What's all the yelling and crying? Is something wrong?

(Immediately KRAUT eyes LENDY and starts drooling and licking his lips.)

KRAUT. Sweet mother of disaster, who is this vision of loveliness?

PA. Have you forgotten our daughter, Lendy? She's been away at college.

KRAUT. And what did you get your degree in? Photography? 'Cause there's been a lot of developing going on here! WOW!

LENDY. Mr. Crotch.

KRAUT. Eh, please call me Sour.

LENDY. Why is my mother crying, Sourcrotch?

(KRAUT sighs at this.)

PA. Because this fiend is throwing us out of our home.

KRAUT. Oh my goodness, no. You misunderstood, Mr. Frye.

(Aside to audience) I must think of something fast. I had no idea there was this beauty within my grasp. But what can I do? I must have this wench as my secretary, slash mistress, slash wife. Think Kraut think. I got it. Back to the show.

(He speaks to the **FRYES**) Why, my dear Frye family, I failed to mention the very fine print here at the bottom of this document.

(He picks up document and reads.)

Whereas the party of the first part. That's me, is renting to the party of the second part, that's you. And the second party fails to pay rent to the first party, then the first party has the obligation to the second party of lending a helping hand. Which means the first party must set up a business with the second party so they can make some money to pay the first party and they all make enough money to have a party.

MA. Where does it say that?

KRAUT. *(Pointing to bottom of document)* Right there.

MA. That looks like a period at the end of a sentence.

KRAUT. Do you read short hand, Mrs. Frye?

MA. No.

KRAUT. Well, that's short hand. Now all we have to do is come up with a business that we can all agree on. Now what talents do you all have?

PA. *(Putting his hand under his armpit)* Well, I can make some pretty funny sounds. Just listen.

KRAUT. No. That's not quite what I had in mind.

LENDY. Well, I have a college degree.

KRAUT. *(Looking at her and waiting)* And? What is your degree in?

LENDY. Animal husbandry.

PA. Great, we'll open up a wedding chapel in the barn.

KRAUT. How about you, Mrs. Frye? Do you have any thing that you're good at?

MA. Well, I'm a good cook.

KRAUT. Wonderful. That's perfect. We'll open a restaurant.

PA. Oh great. Ma you can prepare some of yer great meals and folks will come from all over to enjoy fine dining.

KRAUT. Naw. None of that crap. Get 'em in and get 'em out. We'll serve thousands in seconds. A fast food restaurant.

LENDY. Are you sure a fast food restaurant will make it here in Wichita, Kansas?

KRAUT. You're right. Not without a gimmick. We need a catchy name and logo.

LENDY. How about some golden arches, and we'll call it McCowpattie?

MA. No, Mexican food. Maybe, Taco Barfo?

PA. I got it. A fried chicken place. A 1950's motif. We'll call it "Strangles." Where you get to strangle your own chicken.

KRAUT. No. *(Starts to pace)* We need a friendly name. With a wholesome look. A girl. All American. Cute dress. Redhead. Freckles. Pigtails.

(They all freeze and look at LENDY.)

I know. We'll call it Long John Silvers Sour Krauts.

(They all look at him in disbelief.)

What?

MA. *(Bringing LENDY centerstage)* We'll call it "Lendy's".

(And the curtain falls.)

(Blackout)

Scene III

(The next scene takes place stage right portal. Curtain is down. **ETTA** *is holding* **TRIXIE**.*)*

ETTA. Okay, it's safe. No one is around. Now what's your plan?

TRIXIE. Alright. Ma and Pa need money fast.

ETTA. But they're making lots of money since they opened up Lendy's. The business is going gang busters. Their hottest item is cream pies. They can't make 'em fast enough.

TRIXIE. Don't you see, that's the problem. Old man Kraut is going to work them to death, marry Lendy, and keep all the money. We've got to get hold of some cash to bail them out.

ETTA. But how? *(Pauses, looks at dog, and laughs)* I am talking to a stuffed animal.

TRIXIE. It's not the only thing that's stuffed.

ETTA. Hey.

TRIXIE. It's simple. We just rob the place.

ETTA. What? We can't take money from the Fryes.

TRIXIE. Listen, Twinkie breath. They ain't going to see that money. We steal the money. You use the money to buy the Frye home and Kraut will think you're going to throw them out. Instead you give it to them as a gift. It's a brilliant plan and this from a dog.

ETTA. Boy, that will fix Kraut.

*(***TRIXIE*** screams in horror.)*

What? What's the matter?

TRIXIE. *(Very distressed)* Never say fix to a dog.

ETTA. Sorry. But wait, I don't know anything about robbing a restaurant. I've never held a gun on anyone...well, there was that one boyfriend back in Iola.

TRIXIE. Look, it'll be easy. I'll lay out the plan and I'll be with you all the way.

ETTA. Just one problem with that idea, Rin Tin Tin. Dogs are not allowed in places that serve food. Except in Europe. Also Asia, but in Asia, dogs are actually on the menu. *(She laughs.)*

TRIXIE. How would you like fleas?

ETTA. Been there done that.

TRIXIE. Wait. *(Chuckles)* They will let some dogs in.

ETTA. Naw, the only dogs that are allowed are the ones with blind people.

TRIXIE. Come on, Stevie Wonder, we got work to do.

(Blackout)

Scene IV

(The restaurant: we are at the counter and the menu is posted on the front of it. Behind the bar is **LENDY** *and* **PA** *wearing stupid, paper hats and goofy Lendy outfits. There are tables stage right and stage left and one chair at each. Also,* **MA** *and* **PA** *have switched clothes.)*

LENDY. Boy, Pop, I'm worn out. We've sold a ton of pies today. It's nice to have a break.

PA. You're telling me, honey. These old legs are ready for the bed.

LENDY. But Mr. Kraut won't let us close until midnight. It's only five o'clock now. The dinner rush should be starting any time.

(From stage left, **MA** *comes roller skating by with two pies. She puts the pies on the counter and exits quickly stage right.)*

*(***KRAUT*** enters.)*

KRAUT. *(Laughs and speaks to the audience)* Yeah, but how about table dancing.

*(***PA*** comes from behind the bar where he has grabbed a boa. He starts moving sexy towards* **KRAUT**. **KRAUT** *can't see him.* **PA** *grabs him from behind with his hands on his chest.* **KRAUT** *feels his hands a moment and smiles and then he looks at the size of his hands and then the hair on his arms.)*

Eh, Lendy.

(By this time **PA** *has put his face next to* **KRAUT***'s. Now he feels his face, his beard or mustache He really is puzzled now. They turn in towards each other as* **PA** *has his lips puckered.* **KRAUT** *screams and jumps away.)*

PA. Well, you ain't no beauty either. *(***PA*** goes behind bar and puts boa away.)*

KRAUT. *(Barking at* **PA** *and* **LENDY**) Bring me a another rum and coke.

PA. Lendy, the Coke tank is acting up. I'm going down to the basement to adjust it.

(A bell rings and he slowly lowers his body so it looks like his descending in an elevator. He smiles and waves to audience as he goes down.)

KRAUT. Lendy, where is your mother? She not loafing somewhere is she?

LENDY. No. My poor, sweet mother is in the back baking pies. She has been going non-stop for six days.

KRAUT. Yeah, well, so have my kidneys, and they ain't complaining.

LENDY. *(Crossing to him)* Mr. Kraut, you're mean. Just a big ol' meany, mean, mean.

KRAUT. Oooh, that hurt. Now come give me a big wet kiss, or get your tail back to the grill.

(She storms off behind the bar. He laughs. Once again, **MA** *flies through again stage right to stage left.)*

*(***SAM*** enters from stage right and goes to the bar.)*

LENDY. Yes sir, May I help you?

SAM. Lendy, it's me, Sam.

LENDY. Shhhhh. *(She points to* **SAM** *and whispers to him.)* The boss is right there. *(Loud again)* So sir, may I offer you our special?

SAM. Yes.

LENDY. And would you like fries with that?

SAM. Yes. Especially if you're the Frye. *(He grins and she blushes.)* I'll just sit at the table until it's ready

*(***MA*** flies past him stage left to stage right nearly knocking him down. He sits at opposite table he pulls out a children's book to read.)*

*(We hear bell ring. **PA** ascends like he's climbing the stairs. **LENDY** looks puzzled because it was an elevator and now it's stairs.)*

PA. The elevator was broken, I had to use the stairs.

*(**ETTA** enters from stage right. She has on sunglasses, a wig with her own hair hanging out, and a white cane. **TRIXIE** is sitting on the ridge of her butt and has sunglasses on also. She bumps around the room, hitting both **SAM** and **KRAUT** before she goes to the bar.)*

LENDY. Yes ma'am, may I help you?

PA. *(Whispers to **LENDY**)* Lendy, don't she look familiar?

LENDY. Pa we don't know any blind people. Especially with black and blonde hair.

ETTA. *(Speaking with a stupid voice)* Yes, I would like a number two.

PA. Well, you'll have to use the outhouse for that, ma'am.

(He points.)

LENDY. No Pa. Not that. I'm sorry ma'am, we don't have an extended menu yet. All we have is a number one.

*(**MA** comes flying by with two more pies stage right to stage left.)*

MA. Two more incoming.

ETTA. *(Suddenly pulls out a gun and swings it around the room)* All right, this is a robbery. Everybody just stay calm and no body gets shot.

KRAUT. *(Screaming and hiding under **SAM**'s table)* Help! Please don't shoot me. Shoot the help. I'm just a customer.

*(**SAM** is oblivious to all this commotion. **PA** and **LENDY** run around opposite ends of the bar and begin clinging to each other.)*

ETTA. Get over there.

*(She motions for **LENDY** and **PA** to get on the other side of the table where **KRAUT** is hiding.)*

SAM. *(Laughing)* Boy, that Curious George just kills me.

*(He is showing book to **KRAUT** who is still under the table.)*

Look at this. This just cracks me up.

ETTA. *(Handing **SAM** a note)* Here, read this and do exactly as it says.

SAM. *(Reading note and very puzzled)* What is a guk?

ETTA. What?

SAM. A guk? It says here that you have a guk. *(Showing her the note)*

ETTA. That's not guk, that's gun.

SAM. Oh no, that's definitely not gun, that's guk.

PA. Well, what is a guk?

SAM. That's what I'm trying to find out.

ETTA. *(Getting angry)* It's not guk. It's gun. See that's an "N" not a "K".

PA. Well, it sure looks like a "K" to me.

*(**SAM** nods in agreement.)*

ETTA. Well, it's not. It's an "N" and that word is gun.

LENDY. So what's a guk, then?

ETTA. You idiots there is no such thing as guk. It's gun, gun, gun.

SAM. Well, if that's an "N", your penmanship leaves a lot to be desired. Who was your first grade teacher?

*(During the above **KRAUT** is going crazy over the stupidity of these three and grabs the note.)*

KRAUT. It says "I have a gun". Gun. G-U-N spells gun. Not "guk," you morons. There is no such word as "guk."

PA. I don't know. Sometimes I get guk out of my ears.

ETTA. *(To **KRAUT**:)* Do you have a pen? *(He hands her one and she rewrites the note.)* There. G-U-N. Gun, I have a gun. Can you read that?

SAM. *(Looking at note)* Oh yes, that's much better. *(Asking for the pen)* May I? *(Marking the paper)* Excellent, A+ much improved. Your parents are going to be so happy. *(Reading again)* Give me all your money. I have a gun. *(He screams.)* Gun? It's a robbery, quick someone do something.

KRAUT. May I have my pen back?

SAM. Oh, I'm so sorry. Here you are. *(Hands him the pen)* And thank you very much.

ETTA. All right, you four. No one gets shot if no one tries anything funny.

KRAUT. Fat chance with this script.

ETTA. You, Pippi Long Stockings. Get the money and be quick about it.

SAM. *(Whispering to **LENDY**)* Psst, Lendy, give her a hamburger instead, she'll never know, she's blind.

KRAUT. *(Picking up the children's book and giving it to **SAM**)* Here, read.

*(**SAM** does as **LENDY** goes to get money off the other tables. She returns and hands it to **ETTA**.)*

LENDY. Would you like fries with that?

KRAUT. Someone just shoot me now.

*(**ETTA** aims at him.)*

Kidding. I'm just kidding. Geez.

ETTA. *(Backing away as **MA** comes flying through again with two more pies.)* Now no one follow me.

KRAUT. Someone do something, she has my money.

*(During this sequence, **MA** scares **ETTA** by running behind her. **ETTA** screams and throws the gun in the air and **KRAUT** catches it. She then throws the money in the air and **LENDY** catches it. **KRAUT** laughs and aims it at **ETTA**. **LENDY** yells as the gun is flying. **SAM** is still reading.)*

LENDY. Quick Pa, get the gun.

(PA grapples with KRAUT as he yells:)

KRAUT. Not from me you idiot. Grab the robber.

(PA grabs at ETTA and misses and gets MA from behind and is swinging her around while she still has two pies.)

LENDY. *(Yelling at KRAUT.)* I got your money, Mr. Krunch. Here–catch.

(LENDY throws it to KRAUT. He panics and then he throws the gun. ETTA catches it and he catches the money. KRAUT ducks under the pies and just narrowly dodges as MA is spun around on the last toss. The gun goes off and everyone freezes because no one knows if they've been shot. All are afraid to look. Each does so one at a time. At last KRAUT realizes it must be him, and he confesses during this death scene.)

KRAUT. Oh what a world, all my beautiful wickedness. I'm melting, er dying, I'm dying.

(He collapses as all but SAM timidly approach him. He suddenly springs up and everyone jumps back and screams.)

But not before I tell you boobs off. You think I was ever going to let you catch up on your rent? Even share the profits from this place? Hello? As soon as I made a little more money. I was going to marry you little Lendy and throw your parents to the winds. But that's all right, at least I'm dying rich and you all are right back where you started...in Wichita, Kansas... Nowheresville. So I can die happy.

(He has made his way down to stage right table and dies.)

SAM. *(Looking up from his book and closing it)* Oh George, you silly monkey.

(Everyone is looking at SAM and he sees them and is puzzled.)

What?

LENDY. Well, it looks like it's back to the poor house again.

ETTA. *(Removing her sunglasses and wig)* Gosh, I didn't mean to shoot anyone.

PA. Etta?

ETTA. Yes, it's me.

PA. I didn't know you were blind.

LENDY. *(To* **PA***:)* Okay Rainman, go over there with a beautiful mind. (**PA** *goes to* **SAM***.)*

MA. Etta, I don't understand. You were trying to rob us.

ETTA. I know, but I was trying to help. You see I was going to give the money to you and Pa so you could pay off ole man Sour Kraut. I guess I goofed.

TRIXIE. This just in.

(They all look puzzled, and **ETTA** *turns around to see* **TRIXIE***.* **MA** *takes her off her of* **ETTA***'s butt.)*

MA. Trixie?

ETTA. That's right she kin talk. This whole thing was her idea.

(If the actor portraying **KRAUT** *is also doing the voice* **TRIXIE***., when* **KRAUT** *dies on stage, a wireless mic can be preset at the table so he can keep his back to the audience and use it to do the voice of* **TRIXIE***, or he can die off stage and do the voice offstage as he has been doing.)*

TRIXIE. And it would have worked if I hadn't had to work with Bozo the big butt. But don't worry, I'll save the day again. I didn't want to do this, but you leave me no choice. I'll go on David Letterman and do stupid pet tricks and earn enough money to set you all up for life.

LENDY. *(Hugging the dog)* Oh Trixie, you saved the day.

PA. Now all we got to figure out is how to git rid of the dead body.

ETTA. Yea that still puzzles me, I only had blanks in that guk. Er gun.

(All look at **KRAUT** *who looks up or reenters from off-Stage and is as astonished as they are.)*

KRAUT. I'm alive, I'm alive. Oh goody. Now you Frye Family Freaks get out of my restaurant and leave the money and leave the girl.

(He pulls out a gun and holds it on **LENDY**. *They all react in horror.)*

LENDY. Oh Sam, help me, do something.

SAM. *(Rising and looking baffled)* Unhand that lady, you cad, or you'll have to answer to me. *(He takes a hero pose.)*

KRAUT. Right, I'm trembling Rain Man. 247. 247. 247.

(He laughs and **LENDY** *cries.* **SAM** *starts towards him and he fires three shots directly at him. All freeze in wonderment that he hasn't fallen. Suddenly we hear heroic music.* **SAM** *quickly runs stage left and snaps off his very geeky glasses and steps offstage. The actor playing* **SAM** *should be underdressed with a good break away costume. Under it is a complete Superman costume, including cape. This costume change should literally only take 3 to 5 seconds. He leaps back on stage and takes a Superhero pose. He grabs* **KRAUT** *and throws him out stage right.)*

LENDY. Oh Sam, I never knew you had it in you. Why did you wait so long to show your true self?

SAM. Well Lendy, all good stories must come to an end. I just figured these people had suffered enough and this story weren't never getting any good. So I had to save the day.

*(***LENDY*** leaps into his arms and says:)*

LENDY. Oh, you're super....man.

The End

LITTLE SCHOOL HOUSE ON THE PRAIRIE

OR

TEACHER GOES WILDER

For

My Grandparents

Cecile Mae & Walter Harry Adams

LITTLE SCHOOL ON THE PRAIRIE was presented at Mosley Street Melodramas in Wichita, Kansas on May 27, 1999. The production was directed and choreographed by Tom Frye. It ran for 24 performances. Lights and sound were by Marty Gilbert, stage management was by Amy Saker, musical direction was by Steve Rue, costumes by Karen Robu, properties by Amy Saker & Scott Noah, and set design by Scott Noah. The cast was as follows:

SHERIFF JOHN HOGGATT	Scott Noah
CECILE MAE HOGGATT	Cara Statham
MISS ANGINA PICKARD	Randy Ervin
WALTER HARRY ADAMS	Kevin McKelvy
J.D. PICKARD	Mike Roark
MAMY PICKARD	Ali Spurgeon
OLIVE PITTS/MASKED PIMENTO	Angela Geer

CHARACTERS

MRS. ANGINA PICKARD – Mother of the twins.

HARRY ADAMS – Hero and a mild-mannered school teacher.

CECILE MAE HOGGATT – Heroine and a mild-mannered telegraph operator.

SHERIFF – Cecile's pa.

MISS OLIVE PITTS/THE MASKED PIMENTO - Superintendant of schools/thief.

MAMY PICKARD – Evil girl sixteen year-old twin.

J.D. PICKARD – Evil boy sixteen year-old twin.

STAGE MANAGER

PIANO PLAYER

LATE AUDIENCE MEMBER

THE SETTING

Wacheta, Kansas 1886

SYNOPSIS OF SCENES

Scene 1: Along a Dusty Trail

Scene II: Riley School

AUTHOR'S NOTE

In this melodrama, things are a little twisted from the norm. The male school teacher is very shy and frightened and is more like the put-upon heroine. It's ideal if his body type looks very tall and masculine. The female telegraph operator is a lovely attractive woman, but is very much a tomboy. She is the tough and no-nonsense hero type. As a matter of fact, this is a very role reversal play. Have fun cheering the woman and "ooh and ahhing" the man.

Scene I

(CECILE comes riding through the house on a stick horse. She stops in the middle of the house to speak.)

CECILE. Whoa, Cowpie. Well, it looks like anuther beautiful day in Wacheta, Kansas.

(She begins to smell something around her, then looks behind her and sees a lady in the audience.)

Oh now, Cowpie, why didn't you do that before we left the stable. Sorry lady, you'll probably wanna scrape that off yer foot, or ya jest might want to save it fer yer garden. Just put it in yer purse. I love ridin' out on the prairie and communin' with nature and the animals. Looky here! *(She has a man in the audience stand up.)* A fine example of a snake. *(She goes to another man in the audience.)* Here's a skunk! *(She goes to a woman in the audience.)* And here's an old bat. Well, it's off to work at the telegraph office.

(She goes up on stage and notices telegraph wires have been cut.)

Well, snap my corset, if them telegraph wires ain't been cut again. This is no doubt the work of the Masked Pimento. That varmit keeps cuttin' the wires so as I can't get word to Governor _____ *(Use the name of your state Governor)* 'bout the new railroad that wants to purchase Widda Pickards land. I got to tell Pa 'bout this and right away *(She pulls out a cell phone from saddle.)* Pa, it's me Cecile Mae. I'm out here onstage. Heck no, they ain't laughin. This audience is dead. The only thing might liven 'em up is if I bring out the strippers. Now hurry up and git out here.

*(The **SHERIFF** rides out on another stick horse.)*

SHERIFF. Hold on, Cease, I'm on my way.

*(He rides through the house the same way **CECILE** rode. Passes the lady and stops and looks at her foot)*

Oh man. Lady, would you clean that up? Put it in yer purse or somethin'.

CECILE. I told her that already, Pa.

SHERIFF. Dern city folks. You know the outhouse is right over there. *(He points to the restrooms.)*

CECILE. No Pa, it twern't her. It was Cowpie.

SHERIFF. I know cow pie when I see it, and this ain't it.

CECILE. No, Pa. *(She points to her horse.)* CowPIE!

SHERIFF. Oh! Sorry, ma'am. *(He goes up onstage.)*

CECILE. Look Pa, that danged Masked Pimento has cut the tellygraph wires again.

SHERIFF. Dog gone his hide! If'n I find out who he is, I'll lock him up till Kansas elects a democratic governor.

CECILE. *(Pointing to the ground)* Look Pa, tracks. Let's foller 'em. Maybe they'll lead us to that ornery critter.

SHERIFF. Now Cease, this is man's business. You know a womern ain't suppose to chase bad men.

CECILE. *(She comes out of character.)* Now ya tell me.

SHERIFF. You head back to the tellygraph office and git some equipment to fix this line and I'll foller these tracks.

(He rides off stage right into audience.)

CECILE. Well, he might be my pa, but I ain't standin' fer the Masked Pimento to cut my wires. I am woman hear me roar. I'll find that bandit if it's the last thing I do. *(She is again out of character.)* Right after I get my nails done.

(She exits as the lights fade.)

Scene II

*(The setting is a one room school house with teacher's deck, chalkboard, and two benches for the students. Our teacher **WALTER HARRY ADAMS** is discussing enrollment to a parent, **ANGINA**. Ideally, our teacher has a shaven head. The parent is a woman, but usually funnier if it's a man in drag. The twins, **MAMY** and **J.D.**, are dressed as if they were about six years old, since they're only in elementary school.)*

HARRY. Now Mrs. Pickard, as you know it is the new policy of our school superintendent, Miss Olive Pitts, that we have on record all available information of new enrollees. What are your children's names?

ANGINA. Well, there's Mamy, my daughter, and J.D., my son.

HARRY. Alright. And what does the J.D. stand for?

ANGINA. Juvenile Delinquent.

HARRY. *(He laughs.)* Oh, that's very funny.

ANGINA. I'm not kidding.

HARRY. But why would you name him Juvenile Delinquent?

ANGINA. Wait till you meet him.

HARRY. Well, I'm sure he's not as bad as you say. Now what are their birth dates?

ANGINA. April 1, 1886.

HARRY. Oh I see, they're twins.

ANGINA. Nope.

HARRY. But if they were born on the same day and the same year, they must be twins.

ANGINA. Nope. There was another one, Billy Bob. They's triplets.

HARRY. And why aren't you enrolling him?

ANGINA. He's dead. J.D. shot him.

HARRY. Oh my! He was shot by his 6 year-old brother.

ANGINA. Naw! He was shot before he was born.

HARRY. He was shot by his triplet brother before they were born? I don't understand?

ANGINA. J.D. hates crowds.

HARRY. Life must have been awful for little Mamy then?

ANGINA. Naw, she's spent the last 3 years in the pen.

HARRY. Three years in a play pen?

ANGINA. Naw, the state pen. She's got out in time for the first day of school.

HARRY. Oh, goody! Well, I can hardly wait to meet your... children.

ANGINA. Why? They're rotten. Last week they burned down the pig sty.

HARRY. Oh for heaven's sake, what for?

ANGINA. They wanted crispy bacon.

HARRY. Well, I'm sure they're not as bad as you say.

ANGINA. Well, what they need is a good strong male teacher role model to straighten them out. You know where I can find one? *(She starts to ogle the teacher.)* Hey! Teach, you know I'm a widda. Been one for 15 years.

HARRY. But you said the children were only 6 years...

ANGINA. *(She interrupts him.)* Don't ask! Anyway, I'm always lookin' fer a Pa fer the kids.

HARRY. Mrs. Pickard, you're old enough to be my mother.

ANGINA. There may be snow on the roof, but there's still a fire in the fireplace. Whaddya ya say, Harry?

*(**MISS OLIVE PITTS** enters.)*

PITTS. Well, is this the kind of behavior I am to expect out of my teachers, Mr. Adams?

HARRY. Oh my! Miss Pitts. This isn't what you think it is. I was just enrolling the widda...er, widow Pickard's children for the school year.

PITTS. Oh yeah, the kindergarten James Gang.

ANGINA. Olive Pitts, you can't say that about my children! I can say that about my children, but you can't.

PITTS. Mr. Adams, when I hired you to teach in this district, I thought I made it quite clear that you were to teach, keep your mouth shut, and have no fun. And as for you, Angina Pickard, have you decided to turn your late husband's farm over to the school board?

ANGINA. Olive Pitts, you are meaner than the devil himself! If you think you can brow beat me like you've done to all the other people in this town, well, you're wrong.

PITTS. Look here. How do you spell your first name again? With a "V"?

(She screams with laughter. Then she speaks an aside to the audience:)

This women has been a thorn in my side long enough! I need that land if I'm going to have access to the new Kellogg Covered Wagon Fly over, then I'll be rich. Let's see if they begin construction this year 1877, they should be done by 2021, as projected.

*(She speaks to **ANGINA**:)*

You know we need that land to build a playground for the kiddies.

(She speaks another aside:)

As soon as she signs over that deed I'll quit the school board and keep the land for myself. I'll build some quality motels like those on south Broadway.

ANGINA. You'll never get that land as long as I'm alive!

PITTS. *(She smiles at the audience.)* Good riden– er, goodbye Angina. And as for you Mr. Adams, I'll be back and we'll have a little talk about your behavior here today.

HARRY. Yes, sir... er, ma'am.

*(**PITTS** glares at him and exits.)*

ANGINA. Oh look, here come the kids, Mr. Adams, or are you Harry? I mean may I call you Harry?

(He laughs with embarrassment.)

*(***J.D.*** enters very confidently.)*

J.D. Yo, Ma, what's cookin'?

ANGINA. Nothing dear, I'm just talkin' to yer teacher.

J.D. No, I mean what's cookin'? I'm hungry now.

(She slaps him.)

ANGINA. Shut up and talk to me. Where's your sister Mamy?

J.D. Aw, she'll be here. She stopped to kick a lamb.

(A lamb comes flying in. **J.D.** *picks it up and speaks to the lamb.)*

Hey stupid, what'd ya follow me for? Do I look like a Mary?

HARRY. *(Laughing loudly)* I get it, "Mary had a little lamb, he followed her to school." Very clever...

*(***J.D.*** approaches the teacher very menacingly and speaks a la Robert De Niro.)*

J.D. Are you laughin' at me? Are you laughin' at me. You better not be laughin' at me.

HARRY. Oh no! It's just that your little joke about Mary Had a Little...

(They're not responding at all.)

Never mind.

J.D. Boy, you're a geek.

*(***MAMY*** enters.)*

MAMY. Hey Ma, what's shakin'? *(Looks at* **J.D***)* Yer butt?

(The twins laugh very loudly.)

J.D. Hey sis, look at the goober we got fer a teacher.

HARRY. Children. Since this is the first day of school for me, I'll need your help. Now, what have your other teachers had you do on the first day of school?

(The twins reluctantly look at him, then they both walk to the back wall and take police "frisking" positions.)

ANGINA. Now look Harry, why don't I...

(She drapes across desk quite seductively.)

...take you away from all this?

HARRY. Please Mrs. Pickard...

MAMY. Hey Ma, where's our lunch?

J.D. Yeah, we're hungry, ya old bat!

ANGINA. Look here, Bonnie & Clyde, you cross me one more time and...

MAMY. And you're gonna do what? J.D.?

(He takes out pistol and takes six shots at his mother. **ANGINA** *falls into chair.)*

HARRY. Now children, I will not have toy guns here in school. *(He stomps his foot.)* You and your mother can play your games somewhere else. Mrs. Pickard, I must ask you to please leave. Mrs. Pickard? *(He checks her pulse.)* Oh my, I think she's dead.

(The twins do "high fives.")

MAMY. Great job, bro.

J.D. Yeah! Let's git her outta here. How about hiding her under the school steps?

MAMY. Great, then she can be our stepmother!

(They both laugh and carry body out.)

HARRY. Oh Goodness! My first day on the job and a parent tries to seduce me, my students are criminals, there's a shooting in my classroom, and the superintendent harasses me. *(He smiles.)* Oh well, welcome to USD 259!

(He picks up books and exits and immediately the twins reenter.)

MAMY. Hey, J.D.? That new teacher is gonna be a push over.

J.D. Yeah.

(They both start to roll their cigarettes.)

Once we rough him up a little he'll change our grades so next year we're in the fifth grade.

MAMY. Hey, I like bein' in the fourth grade. Six of the best years of my life have been in the fourth grade.

*(The **SHERIFF** enters the classroom with his gun unholstered.)*

SHERIFF. Hey, I heard shootin' coming from in here. What's goin on?

*(They immediately become sweet kids and polite for the **SHERIFF** and hide their cigarettes.)*

J.D. AND MAMY. Oh, good morning, Sheriff Hoggatt, and how are you today?

SHERIFF. Mornin', J.D. Mornin', Mamy. I thought I heard gun shots.

MAMY. Naw, that was J.D. He ate at Atomic Burrito for lunch.

SHERIFF. Oh man, I know how that is. Say, did you notice how lumpy that front step is when you come in the school?

J.D. No, sir. We were too busy studying for our chemistry test.

SHERIFF. I tell, you kids, you make me proud. Who would have thunk it, that after you got out of reform school you would become such model citizens?

*(The **CHILDREN** are behind him making faces.)*

Say where's yer Ma?

J.D. Oh, she's underfoot somewhere.

MAMY. Come on, brother dear, we still have to do all our chores before we go to prayer meeting. Goodbye, Sheriff Hoggatt.

J.D. Bye, Sheriff.

*(**CECILE** enters the classroom.)*

CECILE Hey Pa! I followed them tracks of the Masked Pimento and they lead back here to the school house.

SHERIFF. Now Cecile Mae, I told you this was man's business. I'll take care of that varmit, you tend to the tellygraph office.

*(**HARRY** enters.)*

HARRY. Oh, I seem to have forgotten my grade book.

*(**SHERIFF** and **HARRY**'s eyes meet and music begins playing some well known love song and they smile and float to each other, **CECILE** is looking puzzled. As they almost meet, **STAGE MANAGER** comes out with prompt book and yells "Hold it! Hold it!" and shows all three the book.)*

SHERIFF. Oh, it's those two. I'm so embarrassed.

*(**STAGE MANAGER** exits shaking his head and muttering, "stupid actors.")*

HARRY. No.

*(To the **PIANO PLAYER**:)* Don't worry about it, it's an honest mistake.

CECILE. Yeah.

*(To the **PIANO PLAYER**:)* You just got caught up in the moment. Can we start that again?

*(The same song, only this time **CECILE** and **HARRY**'s eyes meet and they float towards each other. They meet and ogle each other.)*

Howdy! My name's Cecile Mae Hoggatt. Pleased to meet cha.

(She shakes his hand quite vigorously.)

HARRY. Oh the pleasure is all mine. I'm the new school marm, eh, mame, eh, man. My name is Walter Harry Adams, but you can call me Harry, Miss Hoggatt.

CECILE. Oh no, the pleasures all mine, Harry Miss Hoggatt.

HARRY. No, no it's not...

SHERIFF. And I'm glad to meet you too, Harry Miss Hoggatt. I'm her pa, but you can just call me Sheriff Hoggatt.

HARRY. No, you don't understand Sheriff Hoggatt. Harry Miss Hoggatt is not my name.

CECILE. Well, of course it's not, who would have a silly name like Sheriff Hoggatt Harry Miss Hoggatt?

SHERIFF. Yeah, that's confusin'. Why don't you just go by Walter Harry Adams, that's easier.

HARRY. No, Walter Harry Adams, Sheriff Hoggatt, is fine but I prefer just Harry, Cecile Mae. Sheriff Hoggatt, Harry Miss Hoggatt is not my name.

SHERIFF. Let me get this straight, it's hunky dory to call you Walter Harry Adams Sheriff Hoggatt but you'd rather us call you Just Harry Cecile Mae Sheriff Hoggatt Harry Miss Hoggatt even tho it ain't yer name?

HARRY. Where are those kids…and their guns?

CECILE. Look, why don't I just call you Teach?

SHERIFF. Yeah, son. Yer makin' things too difficult with all yer names.

(He's looking shell shocked, he smiles and laughs.)

Well, I can see you two want to be alone, so I'll just slip out the back and track down that dern Masked Pimento. Good luck, Cece.

(CECILE and **HARRY** *both giggle and shy away from each other.)*

CECILE. Shucks, Walter Harry Cecile–

HARRY. *(He quickly cuts her off.)* Teach!!!!

CECILE. Well then, Teach, teach me.

(He's very embarrassed.)

HARRY. Oh my, Miss Cecile Mae, this is so sudden. I don't know what to say. I'm just a poor innocent school teacher out here in the wild wooly plains of Kansas with no one to protect me from the dangers of "wild.... women".

CECILE. Don't you worry! As long as I'm here, no woman will touch a hair on that pretty little head! Yer safe with me, Teach.

HARRY. Oh, if I could be sure of that! I feel so vulnerable and scared.

CECILE. I'll protect you, no matter what. It's the creed of the Old West. "If yer man's in trouble...he probably deserves it." *(She does a hero pose.)*

(He looks very confused.)

HARRY. Oh, thank you! I think. Tell me, what's all this talk about the Masked Pimento?

*(**PITTS** sticks her head around corner to observe scene without being seen by the couple onstage, but very obvious to the audience.)*

PITTS. Well, look who's here it's that Telycrap operator! Cecile Mae Hogface. What's she up to?

CECILE. Don't you worry yer pretty little head about that coyote. Me and my pa will take care of him. But ifin' you do ever get into trouble, we'll work out a signal that says, "Help me, I'm in distress." I got it. You get the chicken pox.

*(**HARRY** is really confused now.)*

Well, I got to get back on the trail. It's sure been nice meetin' ya.

HARRY. Oh. Will I ever see you again?

CECILE. Oh yeah. I'm in the next scene with ya.

*(She exits as he crosses to desk, while **OLIVE PITTS** enters.)*

PITTS. Well, Mr. Adams. I'm back. Now that those awful Pickards are gone, we can be alone.

HARRY. Yes, ma'am. I hope you don't think badly of me.

PITTS. *(Becoming seductive)* Oh, please, Mr. Adams, or may I call you Harry? Let's forget about that first meeting, I really find you quite a hunka hunka burning love.

HARRY. Eh...Miss Pitts...please. You're the Superintendent of schools...

PITTS. I know, and you're only a teacher. But if you play your flash cards right, I can take you away from all this.

HARRY. Miss Pitts, I must insist that you cease at once.

PITTS. What's wrong? Don't tell me there's another woman in your life.

HARRY. Well, to be truthful there is.

*(The **PIANO PLAYER** plays love music under this.)*

I'm in love with Cecile Mae Hoggatt.

PITTS. So that's how it is, huh? Well, we'll see about that, Hairless.

HARRY. That's Harry.

(She pulls out a small mirror from her cleavage and shows him.)

PITTS. Hello! Reality check. Alright Mr. Adams, wait until you're in trouble and you need me. Like if the Masked Pimento should drop in, then you'll need me.

HARRY. Oh no. I can always get the chicken pox.

PITTS. *(Confused)* I'll be back mister.

(She exits quickly and changes into a disguise.)

HARRY. What a terrible woman. But oh well, I can't worry about her. It's like my mamma always says, "Life is like a box of chocolates, you never know what kind of evil woman you're going to get."

*(**PITTS** enters wearing same dress but with cape, cowboy hat, mask outlined in green olives and a whip. She is now **PIMENTO**.)*

PIMENTO. Ah ha!

HARRY. Good afternoon, you must be the new principal.

PIMENTO. Principal! You idiot, I'm the Masked Pimento!

HARRY. Oh I see.

(He goes to desk and gets out the gradebook.)

Well, Mr. Pimento, why don't you sit in row...

PIMENTO. I'm not a student you bald baboon, I'm the bad guy.

HARRY. *(Very nonchalant)* Oh, I see!

(He suddenly realizes what she's said and screams and runs around the room.)

Oh my! Help! Help! Help! Someone help me.

PIMENTO. *(She is advancing on him.)* Oh you can't escape my clutches my pretty...eh handsome. You will be mine.

HARRY. Oh heavens, what shall I do, I'm just a poor helpless, defenseless, brainless...man. I know! I'll do the distress call.

(He grunts and strains.)

PIMENTO. What the heck are you doing?

HARRY. I'm trying to get chicken pox.

(He continues looking like he's passing a kidney.)

PIMENTO. You keep doing that and you're gonna make a mess on the stage.

(Aside to the audience:) Now to put my scheme into place, I'll make him call for Olive and then I'll save the day by beating myself up.

(She has a puzzled look on her face as to what she said.)

There's only one person who can save you teacher and that's Olive Pitts. If she showed up, I'd really be scared.

(She winks to the audience.)

HARRY. Well, obviously the chicken pox ain't workin'. Help! Help! Miss Pitts, save me.

PIMENTO. Oh drat. Here comes that beautiful Olive Pitts, my nemesis.

(She exits and changes quickly and runs back onstage.)

(CECILE enters and sees what is transpiring. She says to the audience.)

CECILE. What's this? My true love is in the arms of an olive.

(She speaks to HARRY.)

Harry, how could you?

HARRY. Oh Cecile, I signaled you but you didn't come, and that terrible Masked Pimento was forcing itself on me.

PITTS. That's right, Hoggatt. I saved his life.

CECILE. I've failed my true love.

HARRY. Oh no, Cecile. I know if that Masked Pimento was here, you would show it a thing or two.

(He runs and hugs her.)

CECILE. Yes, but he's gone and I just got the deed to Widow Pickards property from Topeka.

(CECILE pulls out the deed.)

(PITTS speaks an aside to the audience.)

PITTS. The deed! I must have that land! This looks like a job for the Masked Pimento.

(She speaks to CECILE and HARRY again.)

Eh, well, I've got a cake in the oven, so glad I could help save your life. Buh bye.

(She quickly exits.)

(SHERIFF enters.)

SHERIFF. Cecile, what are you doin' here? Ain't you got that tellygraph wire fixed yet?

CECILE. Yes, Pa. And I just got a wire from Haysville about this here deed to Widow Pickard's land that the Railroad wants to buy.

SHERIFF. Well, what's it say?

(PIMENTO enters with gun.)

PIMENTO. Well, look who's here, Sheriff Hoggnose and his daughter Sow Ill Mae. All right, give me that deed.

SHERIFF. Why, you dastardly villainess. You got the drop on me now but...

PIMENTO. Quiet!

(She speaks to CECILE.)

Now give me that property.

CECILE. Alright Masked Pimento, but it won't do you any good.

PIMENTO. Oh yeah, well that land will make me rich with the Kellogg Covered Wagon Fly over goin' through.

CECILE. Except for one minor detail. That land is willed over to the public schools and has to be approved and signed by the Superintendent of schools, Miss Olive Pitts before anyone can hold the deed.

PIMENTO. Eh...I knew that. Well, you haven't seen the last of me.

(She exits.)

HARRY. May I see that deed, Cecile dear?

CECILE. Of Course, Harry Hon.

*(**PITTS** enters with a cake.)*

PITTS. So, cake anyone? Just thought I'd drip, er drop by and see if anyone had anything for me to sign or anything? *(She is wearing a cheesy grin.)*

SHERIFF. Something smells here, and it ain't me.

CECILE. Why yes, Miss Pitts it just so happens that you have to approve and sign this document.

PITTS. *(Pulling out huge stamp and pen and then stamping and signing it.)* There we go, always glad to help out. Now I'll just take this to the deed office.

HARRY. Oh excuse me, Miss Pitts, but there's one other minor detail.

PITTS. Now what?

HARRY. It seems that the will is made out to the school system and must be signed by the county Sheriff before its official.

SHERIFF. Why that's me, and I ain't signing nothing to you Olive Pitts unless there's a gun pointed at my head.

(**PITTS** *exits and scrambles back as the* **MASKED PIMENTO** *with only a cowboy hat with knitting needles through it. With a gun that she points to the* **SHERIFF***'s head, all the while panting from the quick costume change.*)

PIMENTO. Alright, Sheriff, I want that deed signed and right now.

SHERIFF. *(Signing deed.)* Something's mighty strange goin on here.

PIMENTO. Yeah, well I got the deed so now I'm rich and you all will be out on your keisters.

HARRY. Mr. Pimento, what about the legal heirs to the deed?

(**PIMENTO** *stares in anger at him.*)

CECILE. Say that's right. J.D. and Mamy have to sign these papers too.

SHERIFF. Them wonderful children are out back. I saw them playing with something under the steps. I'll call them.

(He yells offstage.) Children, come here.

(There is no response.)

I got a Martin Scorsese film for you to see.

(They both run on very excited.)

J.D. Which one, *Taxi Driver, Departed, Gangs of New York*, or *The Nazi Nuns Waste Bambi*?

MAMY. Hey, look it's the masked Pretzel!

(They both laugh.)

PIMENTO. Look here, you little cretins. Here's a deed and you must sign it.

J.D. You talkin' to me? Are you talkin' to me?

MAMY. Yeah, it's talkin' to us.

(They look at hat and needles then they confer.)

Say J.D., maybe we ought to sign. But of course we ain't signin over to anyone 'cept our Superintendent of schools Miss Olive Pitts.

*(***PIMENTO*** does a take and runs off, makes quick change and returns.)*

PIMENTO. Okay, here I am for the signing.

J.D. Ya know sis, maybe we ought to sign this over to our hero the Masked Pepperoni?

PITTS. That's Pimento!

MAMY. Yeah, only to him.

PITTS. You sorry sack of...*(She exits and returns as* **MASKED PIMENTO***, panting.)*

HARRY. Oh Sheriff, do something, don't just stand there.

SHERIFF. *(Looking at his pants)* I just did.

CECILE. Don't worry I'll save the day, or my name isn't...

(She has a puzzled look and **HARRY** *then whispers in her ear.)*

Oh yeah. Cecile Mae Adams. Cecile Mae Adams? Oh Harry, does this mean?

HARRY. Yes, it does. You finally got somebody's name right.

CECILE. Masked Pimento, you've cheated your last defenseless stud! *(She giggles.)* You're dead meat now.

(They begin to fight and at that very moment there is a **LATE AUDIENCE MEMBER** *who arrives and sits very close to the front and speaks very loudly to another audience member.)*

LATE AUDIENCE MEMBER. Sorry, I had car trouble. Did I miss much of the storyline?

J.D. Hey! Hey! Hey! What's up with the late arrival?

MAMY. Yeah, I believe curtain time is 8:00.

J.D. That's just great, now just for you we have to back up and show you what you missed.

*(The cast takes their place from the top of the show. Everything is done in quick step motion and there is no dialogue, except for a few sounds once in a while. The **PIANO PLAYER** accompanies the cast through this fast-paced reenactment. All actors should basically do the same entrances and exits and blocking as before. This is a shortened version, so you don't need all the actions. The director may feel free to add anything not in this version.)*

*(**CECILE** enters on horse and reacts to the same audience members. She pulls out cell phone and we immediately hear **SHERIFF**'s cell phone ring as he enters from the same entrance as before. They recreate same blocking and gestures in double time. Okay, you got the idea. It's good to keep any important props used before in this version. Also don't forget anything with sound effects. Also the quick costume changes with **PITTS** and **PIMENTO**, that don't quite make it, can be very funny. Don't forget to repeat any screams or squeals from the first time. Once you're finished everyone should be in the same spot as the show has ended. This fast paced run should be about three minutes in length.)*

CECILE. *(Speaking to the late comer)* There, you happy? All caught up?

ANGINA. Yeah!

*(The **LATE AUDIENCE MEMBER** is embarrassed and is starting to exit.)*

I was already backstage and I had to put this stupid dress back on. Hey, fella, do you know how difficult it is to put on a bra without help?

*(**ANGINA** exits.)*

HARRY. Just exactly where were we?

SHERIFF. I was just about to escort the Masked Pimento to jail.

CECILE. First, take off that mask.

(She removes her mask. The **CAST** *all gasps.)*

Olive Pitts. You are the Masked Pimento?

HARRY. Miss Pitts, you haven't been very nice.

CECILE. Nice? I'll show you nice...

*(***CECILE*** grabs ***PITTS***, just as ***SHERIFF*** stops her.)*

SHERIFF. Now, now, Cecile. The law says she gits a fair trial. I'll just take her to our little jail where she'll be safe. Come on, Pitts.

*(He takes her offstage. We hear a gong sound and we hear ***PITTS*** yell. Suddenly the ***SHERIFF*** reappears by himself and he is carrying a frying pan. He smiles at everyone.)*

I'm afraid that might leave a mark.

(He laughs and runs offstage.)

CECILE. Well, Walter Harry Adams, what say you and me make a trip to the barn? *(She grins and takes his hand.)*

HARRY. Wouldn't it sell more tickets if I just kissed you right here in front of all these people?

(They kiss as the kids act like they're getting sick and run offstage. The lights fade out.)

THE END

WHERE'S THE GOLD
OR
I DON'T KNOW, ALASKA

For
Kenneth Eugene Frye
"Sonny"

THE KISS OF THE VILLAIN was first presented at Mosley Street Melodramas, in Wichita, Kansas on February 10, 2005. under the direction of Mike Roark. It ran for 21 performances. Lights, sound and stage management by Marty Gilbert, costumes designed by Patty Reeder, musical direction and keyboards by Steve Rue, properties by Pat Szlauderbach, and choreography by Kyle Vespestad. The cast was as follows:

KLONDIKE IKE	Marty Gilbert
JONESY	Steve Rue
FANNY FAIRBANKS	Patty Reeder
SAM DE MILO	Monte Wheeler
JUNEAU JACK WHEELER	Scott Noah
MARGARETTE SIMMONS	Tara Hoffman
YUKON YETTE	Monte Wheeler
SONNY DAY	Kyle Vespestad
KAREN YOUNG	Heather Bloomgren

THE KISS OF THE VILLAIN renamed *WHERE'S THE GOLD* was presented again at Mosley Street Melodramas in Wichita, Kansas on February 5, 2010. It was under the direction of Tom Frye and ran for 25 performances. Lights, sound and stage management by Marty Gilbert, costumes by Patty Reeder, Musical Director/Keyboards by Angela Steiner, Properties by Amy Saker, and Choreography by Steve Hitchcock.

KLONDIKE IKE	Monte Wheeler
FANNY FAIRBANKS	Barb Schoenhofer
SAM DE MILO	Monte Wheeler
JUNEAU JACK WHEELER	J. R. Hurst
MARGARETTE SIMMONS	Scott Noah
YUKON YETTE	Scott Noah
SONNY DAY	Steve Hitchcock
KAREN YOUNG	Christina Hink
MINERS	J R Hurst, Scott Noah, Steve Hitchcock & Christina Hink

CHARACTERS

KLONDIKE IKE - Prospector who spins the tale.
JONESY - A rinky tink piano man or woman. In costume.
FANNY FAIRBANKS - She's the vamp. Sings like a boid.
SAM DE MILO - Don't get up in arms, he's just a bartender.
JUNEAU JACK WHEELER - Our oily, oozing ogre of oafullness. A true villain.
MARGARETTE SIMMONS - Town sot. We still love her.
YUKON YETTE - Stagecoach driver. He rude, crude and tattooed.
SONNY DAY - A Canadian Mountie. What a stud.
KAREN YOUNG - Our pure young heroine. We hope.
FEISTY FRYE FOUR – Johnny, Earl, Garry & Tommie

THE SETTING

The coldest spot in Alaska. 1879

SYNOPSIS OF SCENES

Scene I & III: Blood and Guts Saloon

Scene II & IV: Hotel lobby

Scene I

*(The scene opens in a saloon. The piano is blaring and patrons are all in heavy coats and beards to look like Alaskan miners and to disguise them as they are actors who come out later in the play, women included. There is lots of drinking and yelling and the piano is banging very loudly. The actors are choreographed drinking, playing cards, yelling, gambling, etc. This should continue for about 15 seconds and then suddenly the music stops and everyone is in a ridiculous freeze. The lights fade to dim and out of the crowd steps **IKE**.)*

IKE. This is it folks, the Blood and Guts Saloon. It's not a pretty place. It's the home to the scum of the earth, the dregs of the coldest part of Alaska, where men would kill you for your last nickel, where children never go to school and where women refuse to shave their legs...or their chests. I mean it was tough. The patrons were every low life heathen imaginable...kinda like you folks. They came out from under every rock on earth, they came from Turkish prisons, Chinese opium dens, Australian slave gulags, Girl Scout camps, the big house, the little house, the outhouse, the little house on the prairie, the house of pancakes and... HAYSVILLE. *(We hear ominous music.)* Just look at 'em folks, they're just butt ugly.

*(Light resumes and the cast comes down to a chorus line in ugly poses for audience. The raucous piano is playing through this again, and after their poses, they freeze again, lights dim and **IKE** begins again.)*

Why would anyone want to live here? The weather was unbearable. Liquor was expensive. Women were cheap...well, maybe it wasn't that bad. Anyway, no one

IKE. *(cont.)* wanted to live in this hell hole. But one thing drove everyone here… *(He whispers.)* GOLD!

*(Spotlight hits each actor one by one as they change to another ugly position and say in their crudest voice, the word…."GOLD". With each 'gold,' the intensity and volume rises until the last, very **FEY MINER** (**MARGARETTE**) says…"SHOPPING!" The other patrons look at him and run him offstage. Yelling at him all the way. The lights dim again and the narrator continues.)*

I told you they were mean. These men eat muskrat… raw. They kill for sport. They shoot moose from helicopters. And when someone rubs them the wrong way…well they marry 'em.

*(The miners reenter in the dark. They have caught the **FEY MINER** and are holding him center in a menacing mob scene pose. The lights are up again and they're yelling out at him. After each suggestion, the crowds yells and growls.)*

JUNEAU JOHNNY. I say hang him.

ESKIMO EARL. No, That's too good for him.

GRIZZLEY GARRY. Strip him down naked and leave him in the snow.

JUNEAU JOHNNY. Naw. Cut off his fingers and feed 'em to the wolves.

ESKIMO EARL. Send him to Dillard's without a credit card.

*(The **FEY MINER** is appalled as the others all look surprised and freeze as the lights fade. **IKE** starts again.)*

IKE. I told you they were mean! Folks, here's where the story gets pretty gritty and not suitable for humans. So if you think it might be too much for you…

*(During **IKE**'s last line, they are all resuming their table positions for the floor show.)*

…then I suggest you leave now and remember our friendly policy. We want to make you happy, so Miss

Helen Hunt, our box office manager, will be glad to refund your money. So please, if you want a refund you'll have to go to Helen Hunt for it.

(Lights resume, piano resumes and noise resumes.)

Now let's begin our saga of greed, glory, gambling, and gold.

*(There's an echo on the word "gold". **FANNY** comes onstage, waving her arms and trying to quiet the crowd.)*

FANNY. Quiet down! Shut up, ya varmits. You heard me, shut yer traps.

*(During all the above lines, the miners yell and pay no attention to **FANNY**. She finally pulls out a gun from one of the miner's holsters and fires into the air. They immediately freeze in stupid positions.)*

(There is a beat and a bird falls from the air. They all stare at the bird.)

Let that be a lesson to y'all! Ya either shut up when I yell, or things are gonna get pretty foul around here. *(She kicks the bird offstage.)* Now since ya all paid yer two bits cover charge...

(She points to the audience.)

...except fer these suckers, and you all paid waaay too much, the floor show is about to begin.

(The miners begin to hoop and holler.)

Quiet down. Quiet down. Now this next little lady is gonna sing a song fer ya and ya better listen, because she's my favorite hummingbird and she's got a body to boot.

(More cat calls and yells.)

So here she is...your favorite gal in all of Alaska and mine too...ME.

*(More yells. **FANNY** crosses to piano and sits on top as two miners hoist her up. A spot hits her. She sings a bawdy saloon song. She can come off the piano at any*

time and work the audience. The miner doubling as **SAM** *needs to exit before number is over to change. Once he has completed his change, he enters and yells out.)*

SAM. *(Looking at his pocket watch)* Listen up ya scumbags, last call for alcohol!

EARL. Oh yeah? Well, last call this.

(He shoots **SAM** *and then exits stage right.)*

SAM. *(Dying, he says)* Oh my arm, my arm. I've been shot. Boy, this is a tough town.

(The miners drag him offstage.)

FANNY. *(To the miners who were dragging the body:)* Make sure you clock him out.

(Only person left is **FANNY**. *She goes up to the bar and pours herself a shot of whiskey.)*

(Our villain enters. He is wearing a black western outfit and cape. He poses and gets his boos and hisses and then crosses to her at the bar.)

JACK. Fanny!

(She slowly looks at her butt and then back at him and then to the audience.)

FANNY. Yeah, and a great one too.

JACK. Has the noon stage arrived from Nome?

FANNY. Naw, it's only 1:30 in the afternoon, you know the noon stage don't get here till 2 pm. The 9 am stage arrives at noon. The 6 o'clock stage arrives at 4 pm. And the midnight express don't leave at all. If you need to get to this hell hole on time, you gotta leave two hours later then when you arrive.

JACK. I'm expecting a little package on that stage and I'm chopping at the bit to git at it.

FANNY. This package's measurements wouldn't be 36-24-36 by any chance?

JACK. *(He grins.)* Now Fanny, you know I'm all business.

(He crosses very close to her.)

Women are nothing but trouble. If I want trouble, all I have to do is come to you.

FANNY. You know what I do to rattlesnakes like you, Jack? I bite their heads off and make new shoes outta their skin.

JACK. Is that a promise, Fanny?

FANNY. Yeah.

JACK. Oh yeah?

(They laugh.)

Can I get a drink in this dive?

FANNY. Sure, honey. Hey Sam, get out here and get Juneau Jack a whiskey.

*(**FANNY** grabs a bar rag and crosses downstage left to clean a table.)*

*(**SAM** only has one arm in a sleeve. The other is hidden and his shirt sleeve is all bloody as if his arm has been shot off at the shoulder. He enters as if nothing is wrong.)*

SAM. Sure, Miss Fanny.

*(He pours drink as **JACK** looks at his bloody sleeve.)*

JACK. Sam someone shot yer arm off! Are ya okay?

SAM. Ah, it's just a flesh wound.

(He smiles and exits.)

*(**JACK** speaks to the audience.)*

JACK. This is a tough town.

*(**MARGARETTE** staggers in from stage right, crosses to the bar and scares **JACK** as he's drinking. She is a fright with bad hair, bad teeth and a bad outfit.)*

MARGARETTE. Ah ha. I thought I'd catch you here you scoundrel. Drinking again? I told you that whiskey will rot yer guts out. Now gimme that bottle.

JACK. Margarette, you old coot, one little drink ain't never hurt no one.

MARGARETTE. *(Very somber and reflective)* That's all I ever had was one little drink.

SAM. *(Looking at her.)* What was it served in…a water tower?

(They all laugh at her.)

MARGARETTE. *(Crossing behind the bar to confront* **SAM***)* You shut up, you slot machine, before I put my evil spell on you and turn you into a frog.

FANNY. *(Over her shoulder at the down left table)* How ribbeting.

MARGARETTE. You shut up too, you bar fly.

JACK. Look here you old hag, my best friend is Fanny.

MARGARETTE. Yeah? *(Crossing towards* **FANNY** *and looking at her butt)* Well, she's got enough of it!

(The two women start to confront each other as **JACK** *crosses between them.)*

FANNY. Look here, ya Sarah Palin wannabe!

JACK. All right, that's enough. You get back to the house and wait for me.

MARGARETTE. I'm going, but mark my word, you cross me again…Fanny…and that's what you'll be singing through.

(She grabs bottle and speaks to the audience.)

If my boss is gonna drink, then I'm gonna drink.

(She self-reflects.) Yea, that's as good a reason as any.

(She grins and exits stage left with bottle.)

JACK. Sorry about that Fanny, but Margarette has never liked you ever since you threw her false teeth into the two holer.

SAM. *(Crossing to stage left table to clean it.)* Does that make her your indentured servant? Some people just can't take a little joke.

JACK. Yeah, well, she's still carrying a grudge.

SAM. Fanny, send her a box of gummy bears and shut the ol' bag up. Jack, why do you keep that ol' bat on the payroll?

JACK. Because she's the best housekeeper I've found. She works for booze only.

(They all laugh.)

(We hear the stage approaching. The driver, **YUKON,** *enters. He is a real tough character.)*

YUKON. Howdy, Fanny. Howdy, Jack. Sam.

SAM. Howdy, Yukon Yette. Any trouble gitten here from Oklahoma?

YUKON. You know there's one good thing that comes out of Oklahoma.

SAM. What's that, Yukon?

*(***SAM*** crosses back behind the bar.)*

YUKON. I-35.

(They all laugh.)

I been drivin that stage so long, I feel like my butt is made of jello? Want to see the jiggle?

(He crosses to the stage left proscenium and jiggles his butt.)

YUKON. Here's ya mail, Fanny.

(He hands her some mail.)

FANNY. *(Looking through the mail)* Hmm. Let's see. Cable bill. *(She throws each piece of mail behind the bar.)* Electric bill. Hey here's my Alaskan absentee voting ballot. Hey Sam, how do you spell Murkowski?

JACK. Say, Yukon, was there anything on the stage fer me?

(He grins and crosses to down right table and sits.)

Like a woman?

YUKON. Come to think of it there was. She's around back. Had to use the little girls room.

FANNY. Juneau Jack Wheeler, I smell a rat!

(She crosses to him.)

And I think he's in your pocket. What's the skinny on this gal?

JACK. Oh now, Fanny! What makes you think there's something rotten?

SAM. There's always something rotten when it concerns you, Jack.

(He crosses behind the bar and approaches the bartender.)

JACK. Well, you don't know Jack!

(They all do a take to the audience and then laugh and we hear rim shot.)

YUKON. No, but I know a bad script and bad puns and that was it. And I'm gettin off the stage before the stage leaves.

(He exits stage right.)

SAM. So spill the beans, Juneau. Who's this gal?

JACK. Well, let's just say she's a little investment. Her pa was an old acquaintance of mine.

FANNY. I'll bet. Where is he now?

JACK. Well, he found a gold mine and when I found out, I made him a deal. We split 50/50. I got the mine, and he got the shaft.

(He cackles and they all laugh again.)

FANNY. *(Aside to the audience:)* Oh no, he's bringing up old heartaches. But I mustn't let him know about our past.

(She speaks to him.)

I don't understand, what's the girl got to do with this?

*(**JACK** crosses stage left and around the bar to downstage center.)*

JACK. Well, once I got the map for the goldmine, I realized there would be claim jumpers after it, so I transferred the map to something else and destroyed the original.

SAM. *(Crossing stage right around the bar to downstage center.)* Where is the new map then? And why is the girl involved?

JACK. Look here, you barkeep! This is between me and Fanny, so why don't you go git a job hangin wallpaper.

(SAM exits angrily stage right.)

At the time of the demise of the old prospector, she was only 6 years old. I wanted to hide the map in a safe place. So I hid it on the gal. That was 20 years ago.

FANNY. You idiot, she's grown up. She's not going to still have the map.

JACK. *(Laughing)* Oh yes, she will! *(This is underscored with ominous music:)* I branded it on her back.

(FANNY is appalled.)

FANNY. You fiend! What did the poor child do when you did that?

JACK. Hmmmm...I'm not sure...I...believe...she...said... "ahahahahahahahh"! *(He laughs again.)* Pardon me a moment Fanny, but I'm gonna go check on my property out...(*He points to his own back and laughs.)* back.

(He exits stage left.)

FANNY. Someday that man is gonna step into the wrong two holer and talk about your royal flush.

*(Our hero, **SONNY**, enters from stage right and crosses down center and poses. He is a Royal Canadian Mountie, and boy is he cute. He sees **FANNY** and removes his hat and approaches her.)*

SONNY. Excuse me ma'am, I'm looking for a place to get a drink.

FANNY. Well, step right up, Handsome. This is the only place to get a drink.

(She slowly slinks up to him.)

FANNY. What's yer moniker? Long, tall, and gorgeous?

SONNY. They call me Sonny. *(He is embarrassed.)*

FANNY. Well, Sonny, I'll git ya something smooth. *(She calls for* **SAM**.*)* Sam, we got another customer. Git on out here!

*(**SAM** enters from stage right. This time he has no arms and two bloody sleeves.)*

SAM. Sure, Miss Fanny.

FANNY. Sonny, this is my bartender. Sam de Milo.

SAM. What'll ya have partner?

*(**SONNY** looks at **SAM**'s lack of arms.)*

SONNY. Eh? Gee, Mister, what happened to you?

SAM. Don't EVER try to slice ham with one arm! Now name yer poison.

SONNY. Gee I don't know. Let me think.

FANNY. Oh Sam, go ahead and give him the house specialty, the Grizzly Grunt Gristle Grog.

SONNY. That sounds yummy. What's in it?

FANNY. You don't wanna know. Just mix it up, Sam.

SAM. Okay.

*(**SAM** looks at the two bottles on the bar and the glass. He looks puzzled because he has no arms. He finally shrugs. He picks up the first bottle in his mouth, tips it back, and then puts it down, and spits the contents into the shot glass. Then he does the same with the second bottle. He looks around for a swizzle stick and doesn't see one. He shrugs and then sticks his tongue in the shot glass and stirs it. **FANNY** acts as if nothing is wrong. **SAM** then pushes it towards **SONNY** with his nose.)*

FANNY. *(To the audience:)* I hired him away from _____ *(Insert the name of a local bar)*, that's how they mix all their drinks.

(**SONNY** *looks disgusted at the drink.*)

SONNY. Got milk?

FANNY. Milk? Hey Sam, we got any milk back there?

SAM. Well, we had some. We ain't served any in quite awhile. I'll go get ya some.

(*He exits stage left.*)

FANNY. So what's a Royal Canadian Mountie doin' in Alaska?

SONNY. Well ma'am, I'm here looking for a man named Juneau Jack Wheeler, also known as Nome Ned, Fairbanks Frank, and Wichita Wanda.

FANNY. Oh yeah? What fer?

SONNY. Well, he's wanted in every province in Canada and six other countries. He's done everything from robbery to white slavery to embezzlement to rigging elections in Ohio and Florida.

FANNY. Wow, all that work. He must be Bushed.

(*They both refuse to look at audience. After the boos, she says:*)

Are they still there?

SONNY. Oh yeah!

(**SAM** *reenters with free standing milk. He is holding it in his mouth with the straw that is out of it. This prop needs to look like hardened milk with a piece of wood out of it made to resemble a straw.* **SAM** *puts it down on the bar.*)

SAM. Well here ya go, one milk.

SONNY. (*Crossing to the milk and looking at it*) It's not even in a glass.

SAM. Nope, didn't need one.

(**SONNY** *picks up milk by the straw and pounds it on the bar.*)

SONNY. It seems a little curdled.

FANNY. Yep, that's how we drink our milk here in Alaska.

SONNY. Boy, what a tough town.

SAM. Miss Fanny, I'm goin' to the back to make them doughnuts you wanted?

(**SONNY** *looks at him very puzzled.* **SAM** *glares back.*)

SONNY. Make doughnuts without any arms. How does he do that?

SAM. *(Smiling)* Don't ask.

(He exits stage left.)

SONNY. Well, ma'am. I appreciate all yer hospitality. But I need to find the hotel. I've got to get a room fer the night. Good night, ma'am.

(He nods, puts on his hat and exits stage right.)

JACK. *(He enters from stage left and he is not happy.)* Well, if that don't beat all.

FANNY. What's the matter Jack? Where's the gal?

JACK. She ain't even gone in the outhouse yet.

FANNY. Why not?

JACK. She said, she'd have to wait til some girlfriends showed up, that women only go to the bathroom in groups.

FANNY. Oh yea, I forgot. Well, I'll go see what I can do.

(She starts to leave.)

Oh Jack, before I forget, ya had a visitor jest in here lookin fer ya.

JACK. Great. I bet they we're delivering my "George Foreman Grill."

FANNY. Nope. This was a Royal Canadian Mountie.

JACK. *(He quickly hides behind the bar.)* What? Did you tell him I was here?

FANNY. Naw, but he's lookin fer ya and he ain't selling Girl Scout Mountie Mints.

JACK. Man those are great, especially when you put them

in the freezer and eat them with a cold glass of mil... did he say what he wanted?

FANNY. He didn't have to. Your reputation speaks for itself.

(She starts off again.)

Well Jack, I'm headed to where yer life is headin'.

JACK. Where's that?

(She laughs.)

FANNY. In the crapper.

(She exits stage left.)

*(***JACK** *crosses downstage center to address the audience. The curtain drops in behind him for the scene change.)*

JACK. So the Mounties are lookin for me are they? *(He laughs.)* Fat chance they'll ever catch Juneau Jack Wheeler *(Ominous music builds after each name.)* or... Nome Ned, or...Fairbanks Frank, or...Wichita Wanda.... *(He glares at audience.)* Hey it was before the surgery alright? Now all I need to do is git the gal alone. Read the map. *(He uses fingers like he's reading Braille.)* It'll be a tough job, but somebody's got to do it. *(He laughs again.)* Then I'll be richer than Charlie Sheen, Robert Blake, and Nick Nolte...before the lawyer fees!

(He exits, laughing.)

Scene II

(Played in front of an olio curtain)

(KAREN *enters from stage right portal and crosses downstage center. She is carrying a bright pink suitcase with the words "WOMANLY LUGGAGE" written on it.)*

KAREN. Wow! What a grand hotel. I'd better check into my room right away and get freshened up.

(She exits stage left.)

(SONNY *enters from stage right portal and crosses downstage center. He is carrying a black suitcase that has boldly written on it. "MANLY LUGGAGE".)*

SONNY. Wow! What a Grand Hotel. I'd better check into my room right away and get manlyed up.

(He exits stage left.)

(KAREN *enters from stage left crosses downstage center. She carries on her suitcase and sits it down center stage and forgets it as she leaves.)*

KAREN. That hotel manager was swell. *(She holds up a room key.)* I can't wait to see my room, room 112.

(She exits stage right.)

(SONNY *enters stage left and crosses down center. He sets suitcase down next to hers. He doesn't notice her suitcase.)*

SONNY. That hotel manager was swell. *(He holds up a room key.)* I can't wait to see my room, room 212. *(He realizes there are two suitcases and he doesn't know which is his.)* Oh goodness which is mine? *(He picks up hers and reads.)* Oh this is mine, it says "Manly Luggage."

(He crosses stage left with wrong suitcase.)

(KAREN *enters stage right and crosses down center.)*

KAREN. Oh silly me. I've forgotten my luggage. *(She sees the black luggage.)* Oh, here it is. *(She points to it and reads it.)* Yes, this is mine: "Womanly Luggage."

(She picks it up and crosses stage right and opens the suitcase.)

Gee, I hope I remembered to pack my toothbrush.

(She pulls out boy's boxer briefs.)

Goodness, these are not mine.

SONNY. Gee, I hope I remembered to pack my toothbrush.

(He begins to open suitcase and pulls out a woman's negligee.)

Goodness, I wish these were mine.

KAREN and SONNY. Oh my goodness, I must have gotten the wrong luggage.

(They quickly start to repack. After they are packed they turn and cross to opposite sides of the stage, passing each other. They don't notice each other until they get to the opposite side. They suddenly they turn and look out at the audience. They both say. Wow! They drop their suitcases.)

SONNY. I'm so excited.

KAREN. I just can't hide it.

SONNY. I'm about to lose my mind.

KAREN. And I think I like you.

SONNY. Like you.

KAREN. And I know, I know, Know

SONNY. I need you.

KAREN. Need you.

SONNY. I'm so delighted.

KAREN. I just can't fight it.

SONNY. I'm about to lose control

KAREN. And I think I want to.

SONNY. Want to.

(They end facing each other in romantic pose. He removes his hat.)

SONNY. Oh…I…Don't think I've introduced myself, ma'am. I'm Sonny. Sonny Day of the Royal Canadian Mounties, at your service.

KAREN. How do you do Mr. Day. I'm Karen F. Young of Greensburg, Kansas.

SONNY. Not the home of the world's largest hand-dug…

KAREN. Yes, it is.

SONNY. Well, well, well.

(They wait for the groans.)

Karen F. Young. What's the F stand for?

KAREN. Forever.

*(**PIANO PLAYER** plays something sappy as she coos.)*

SONNY. Gee, Miss Young. May I carry you suitcase to your room for you?

KAREN. Well yes, but there seems to be some mistake. I think I have someone else's luggage.

SONNY. Really? Me too.

(They each go and get the luggage they have been carrying and bring them back center.)

But mine says "Manly Luggage."

(It doesn't.)

KAREN. And mine says, "Womanly Luggage." *(It doesn't.)*

BOTH. I don't understand.

PIANO PLAYER. *(Walking over and handing each their own luggage.)* We don't hire 'em for their brains, folks. *(He/She goes back to the piano.)*

SONNY. Now where is your room, Miss Karen?

KAREN. I'm in room 112.

SONNY. Really, I'm in 212. I guess that makes me right on top of you.

(She squeals. They both are shocked and embarrassed.)

Eh…I mean…well…we should go now.

(He takes her bags and they exit stage left.)

(MARGARETTE enters from stage right. She obviously has been hitting the bottle.)

MARGARETTE. I don't know where I went wrong. I tried to be a good mother, but something happened.

(She notices the audience and then picks out a lady to talk to. During this speech she is drinking and crying.)

Hey, you look like a mother. Come to think of it there's a lot of muthas out here. We don't got it easy do we? Having a baby is awful, 56 hours of absolutely screaming hell. The pain, the pushing, the sweating, and that was just to get the doctor to accept my HMO.

Why me? I'm just a poor southern beauty who tried her best. *(She sits on a man's lap.)* I am a beauty right? Damn straight. Are you married? You are? Wanna neck anyway? Never mind…I'm not that drunk. *(She gets back on stage and starts to exit)* I am making a vow as of this moment. And all of you will take it with me. Raise your right hand. *(She raises her left.)* Now repeat after me. I…State your name. *(And they'll probably say, "State your name.")* Do hereby promise to never drink again. *(She looks at audience, brings her right hand from behind her back and her fingers were crossed.)* SUCKERS! *(She laughs, drinks and exits stage left.)*

Scene III

*(We find **FANNY** at a table drinking stage left, She is talking to **SAM**.)*

FANNY. That Juneau Jack has got a grip on me and I ain't happy about it. He made me hire that sweet little gal off the stage and it's breakin my heart, but I mustn't let on to Jack. Tonight's her first night too. We're having a big blast here and there's gonna be lots of drinking and dancing and I'm afraid for the girl. I've got to keep Jack away from her. Sam, go carry them beer kegs in from the back room. Do you need a hand. Here comes the little filly now.

*(**KAREN** enters from stage right.)*

KAREN. Excuse me, Miss Tushe.

FANNY. That's Fanny.

KAREN. Eh, yes, ma'am. What do I do until I start my songs?

FANNY. Just sit over there at that table and make eyes at the customers, and remember: no touchy feely!

KAREN. Yes ma'am.

*(She crosses and sits at stage right table and proceeds to do stupid things with her eyes. During this **YUKON** enters from stage right and sees her. He watches her a minute.)*

YUKON. She's a right pretty gal, ain't she, Fanny? A little cockeyed, but pretty.

*(**FANNY** rises quickly and glares at **YUKON**.)*

FANNY. Are ya saying I ain't?

YUKON. Oh no Fanny, it's just...eh...well...the way she's makin eyes at me.

*(**KAREN**'s still doing stupid eye ogles.)*

FANNY. Eh...I need a drink. Sam's busy Yukon, make me a drink.

*(She crosses to bar to drink and brood, as **YUKON** goes behind bar, he sees **MARGARETTE** passed out behind the bar.)*

YUKON. Hey Margarette, are you drunk again, get out from the behind the bar.

(YUKON stoops down and changes to MARGARETTE.)

(SONNY enters from stage right and crosses to KAREN.)

SONNY. Good evening, Miss Karen.

(She really tries to ogle him. He looks at her very concerned.)

Gee ya got the pink eye?

(She stops.)

(She rises.)

KAREN. Oh gee Sonny, I'm just not cut out for this saloon girl stuff. I'm supposed to sing in a little while and I'm scared to death.

SONNY. Now, now Miss Karen, you just need a stiff…glass of milk.

(MARGARETTE comes out from behind the bar and she is ripping drunk.)

MARGARETTE. Hey, where's Yukon Yuckie.

FANNY. That's YETTE.

MARGARETTE. Ok, where's Yette Yukie? Say, have you seen the degenerate Juneau Jack?

FANNY. Yeah…I know Jack.

MARGARETTE. Well listen to me, when he gits here you tell him I need to see him. I'll be under the bar.

(She crosses behind bar, away from FANNY.)

SONNY. So Miss Karen, what brings you to this awful place?

KAREN. Well, my father died and his old partner sent for me. He said I could come to work for him up here in Alaska.

SONNY. Well, that was nice of him. What's his name?

KAREN. Juneau Jack Wheeler.

SONNY. *(Gasping)* What? Why that crook is wanted in every town south of the North Pole.

KAREN. Oh my, do you think he means to do something evil to my little body?

(YUKON arises from behind bar.)

YUKON. You just ain't whistling Dixie, ma'am.

KAREN. Excuse me?

(He crosses to their table.)

YUKON. Remember me little lady, I drove ya here on the stage.

KAREN. Yes, of course, Yukon Yuckie was it?

YUKON. YETTE. What an abominable curse.

KAREN. Mr. Yette, this is Sonny Day of the Royal Canadian Monkeys.

SONNY. At your service, sir.

*(**YUKON** takes his chair and sits.)*

YUKON. Good. Get me a beer.

*(**SONNY** is puzzled and goes for the beer at the bar.)*

Now I'm gonna give ya some advice, ma'am. You watch out fer that Juneau Jack Wheeler. He's up to no good and you could git hurt.

KAREN. Thank you sir, Mr. Day already told me he was wanted by every police station around.

YUKON. Jest remember, he's a bad one! Well, I got to git back to the hotel. Got an early trip tomorrow. The stage is due out at 4 am, so I got to be up by 5. Fanny do ya mind if I slip out through the cellar in case Jack is around?

FANNY. Yeah, that's fine, but be careful.

YUKON. Careful? Hey, I know how to go down stairs.

*(**YUKON** goes behind bar and falls downstairs. We hear his long scream as he falls many, many feet. Suddenly, there's a large crash and **FANNY** yells:)*

FANNY. Hey, them steps is broken!

SONNY. *(Yelling down to **YUKON**)* Mr. Yette, do you still want your beer?

YUKON. Yeah, just drop it down.

*(He drops the bottle of beer. We hear sound effects of something whistling though the air for a VERY long time. **SONNY** even checks his watch. Finally, it gets there.)*

YUKON. Hey you bozo, I don't drink lite beer, it's for sissies. I'm throwing this back up.

(He simply hands the bottle from behind the bar to him, We clearly see his arm and hand. **SONNY** *is embarrassed about the bit.)*

SONNY. *(Crossing back to the table)* Miss Karen, you look flush, is anything wrong?

KAREN. Oh, Mr. Day. I'm frightened. I want to go back home to Greensburg.

YUKON. *(Still behind the bar)* WHY?

FANNY. *(Crossing downstage center)* All right, everyone, quiet down. The dance will begin in 5 minutes.

*(***FANNY*** exits stage left.)*

SONNY. Miss Karen, you must stay here and help me catch that evil...

(He slowly looks around the room to see if he's around. Then he says to her:)

Juneau Jack.

KAREN. Yeah, I know Jack.

SONNY. No, I mean...never mind. Listen, he's got something evil up his sleeve. I can smell it.

KAREN. You smelled his sleeve?

SONNY. What I want you to do is be the bait in my plan to capture him.

KAREN. Bait, you mean risk my life, put my body in the clutches of that despicable villain, let him do unspeakable things to me just so you can apprehend him and get a big promotion.

SONNY. Yeah!

KAREN. Okay, Sonny. Anything for you.

SONNY. I'll wait behind the bar and watch his every move. You just go along with his plans.

(He pulls out a gun to give her.)

Oh yes, Miss Karen. If things go terribly awry, if it looks like he might take advantage of you, if your chastity should ever be in jeopardy, then I need you to do one last thing.

KAREN. Shoot the cad?

SONNY. No, the reward is to bring him in alive.

KAREN. Shoot myself?

SONNY. Oh heavens no, Miss Karen.

KAREN. What then?

SONNY. Would you clean my gun?

(He goes behind the bar and leaves the gun on the table.)

(JACK enters from stage right and asides to the audience.)

JACK. This is my chance. I'll ask her to dance and then I'll read *(He wiggles his fingers.)* the map. *(He crosses to her table.)* Well, my little ward, how about a little dance. Shall we?

(She reluctantly rises as the music starts and they dance a tango. With each pause in the music, she is turned so her back is to the audience. He desperately feels all up and down her back trying to read the map. This goes on for several turns. Finally–frustrated–he sits her back down.)

Thank you, my dear. But why don't you go find a dress that is maybe a little more suited for the dance. Like something...backless.

KAREN. Oh goodness sakes alive! I don't own anything like that.

JACK. Well, I do...er...I...mean...maybe Fanny has something. Don't move, I'll be right back.

Oh my dear Fanny!

(He exits stage left.)

*(**KAREN** reluctantly crosses downstage center and begins to sing quietly a sad song that eventually gets rowdy. By the end of the number, she has stepped out of her dress and is in a tiny show girl costume and is really selling the number.)*

*(**SONNY** slowly pops his head up from the bar. He's in disbelief and then happiness at what he sees. At the conclusion of **KAREN**'s song, he runs out to her, grabs her original dress, and helps her put it back on over the showgirl costume.)*

SONNY. Eh, Miss Karen, what was that?

KAREN. Oh Sonny, I'm sorry you had to see that. I was just practicing for American Idol.

SONNY. Here comes Jack and Fanny, play dumb.

(She already looks this way.)

Too late.

(He quickly hides behind the bar again.)

(JACK enters.)

JACK. Fanny, I want you take Miss Young upstairs and find her a dress a little more revealing in the back.

FANNY. Jack, I don't think–

JACK. That's right, you don't think. I do! Now do as I say or you'll be sorry.

FANNY. Quick, run, honey!

(She grabs her and roundhouses her accidentally into the proscenium.)

Oops, sorry.

JACK. Come here, gal.

SONNY. Stop! Unhand that lady.

(JACK pulls out his gun. This is the big shoot out.)

(JACK uses KAREN as a shield while he runs around the stage. SONNY, who has given up his gun to KAREN, who has left it on the table, is dodging and running around the room. FANNY is doing the same.)

FANNY. Don't worry, Sonny! I'll go get help. I'll go get Sam; he's great with a pistol!

(He looks at her in disbelief as she runs off stage left.)

(At first, JACK shoots one bullet at a time and people duck, then after a while it sounds like a gunfight with ten people shooting. Finally a very drunk MARGARETTE, who by the way, is the only one not ducking, but still drinking at the bar, slowly walks down to the table picks up the gun and tosses it to SONNY.)

MARGARETT. Here, ya moron.

(She turns and is looking at **JACK**.*)*

You always were a crappy shot.

(Just at that moment, **JACK** *shoots* **MARGARETTE**. *She starts to stagger. The shooting stops, and* **SONNY** *hasn't even shot one bullet.)*

*(***MARGARETTE** *has a slow lingering death around the stage. She falls into the piano player. We think she's dead. She jumps up and falls on the table. We think she's dead. She jumps up and falls on the bar, takes another drink. We think she's dead. Finally she falls in the arms of* **SONNY**.*)*

(During this death scene, **JACK** *has taken* **KAREN** *hostage and slithered out.)*

SONNY. Hang on, ma'am.

(He looks at **FANNY**.*)*

Miss Fanny, run and git the doctor.

FANNY. *(Pulling out a cell phone and dialing it)* No, I'll call 911 and get EMS. They'll get here faster than a doctor. Hello? Hello? Yes, is this EMS? What? Wait a minute, I can barely hear you. *(Moving around the stage)* Can you hear me now?

MARGARETTE. Forget it. I'm done for. I'm headin' for the last round up. Just about to meet my maker...I'm gonna bite the big one.

FANNY. *(Now she is above the stage hanging over the balcony.)* Is this better? Listen someone has been shot. Shot! No not pot. Hang on, I'm moving outside for better reception. Hang in there Margarette.

SONNY. You've got to hang on ma'am, she'll be calling for help.

MARGARETTE. I got one last confession to make..

FANNY. *(She crosses the stage from stage right to stage left.)* Listen you nitwit, this is serious, a woman has been shot several times. Yes she was shot in this bar. Hello? Hello?

Damn, lost them again. Hang in there, kid. Boy, I hope my battery holds out.

MARGARETTE. Listen, you've got to listen to me Sammy, er Scummy, eh Snoopy, Slimey. I mean Sony.

SONNY. No ma'am, not SONY, my name is Sonny.

MARGARETTE. No, it's Sony...you're not coming in too clear.

(FANNY enters from stage left with a land line telephone.)

FANNY. Hey, I can hear you great now. Address, hang on. I gotta go look.

(She exits stage left like she's looking for the address.)

SONNY. Is there anything I can do?

MARGARETTE. Yes there is...There's a locket around my neck. Do you see it?

(He pulls it out and looks puzzled.)

Ever see anything like this before?

(He stops and pulls a necklace out of his shirt.)

SONNY. Why they're exactly the same.

(FANNY reenters from stage left and is back on the phone.)

FANNY. The address is _____ *(Use the address of the theatre).* Say, when you come here do you pass by a McDonalds?

MARGARETTE. Yep. And there's one more necklace just like it.

SONNY. I don't understand.

MARGARETTE. Ya see. Years ago, I had me a set of twins. Shortly after their birth, we all got split up in a big traffic jam on _____ *(Local intersection).* I never saw my babies again. But before we got split up, I had three necklaces made, one for me and one for each of the twins. I knew you was one of my babies as soon as I saw you through my glass of whiskey.

(SONNY realizes what she's said and grasps her in his manly hug.)

SONNY. Oh Ma. At last I've found you. You've got to hang on.

FANNY. No not a Big Mac, I want a Quarter pounder, I said no cheese you idiot.

MARGARETTE. It's a good thing I'm dying, 'cause she's killin' me here. Ease up there King Kong.

*(**SAM** runs in quickly from stage right.)*

SAM. What's gonna on, I heard all the shootin'?

*(He sees the two of **SONNY** and **MARGARETTE**.)*

Oh cracky. What's happened to old Margarette?

MARGARETTE. I've been shot you idiot, twelve times.

*(She looks at **SAM** and gasps. He looks bewildered and flings his sleeves as to say, "I can't get it.")*

Whiskey. Whiskey.

SONNY. I'll git it.

*(**SONNY** drops her on the floor with a thud. He goes to get her a drink and brings it back. He gives it to **SAM** to hold in his mouth and then he picks her up again. **SAM** has drunk it by the time **SONNY** has **MARGARETTE** back in his arms..)*

MARGARETTE. Don't let me die here on the saloon floor. I've already spent too much of my life here.

SAM. Boy, you can say that again.

MARGARETTE. Put me where I'll be happiest.

SONNY. In your own warm bed?

SAM. In the arms of a loved one?

MARGARETTE. No! Put me on the bar, you moron.

*(They carry her to the bar and lay her out. **SAM** has no arms so **MARGARETTE** throws her legs over his shoulders and **SONNY** carries her by her arms.)*

Son, you've got to promise me you'll never give up on finding yer twin.

SONNY. I promise…*(He breaks down.)* Ma.

MARGARETTE. *(Fading fast)* Good bye, Sam. Good bye, Son.

FANNY. I got this, toots. *(She whistles loudly to **SAM** offstage.)*

Hey Sam get out here, the old lady is two seconds away

from a pine box. Get back here while she's still warm. Sorry, I think he's gone bowling.

MARGARETTE. Sonny, I have one last wish.

SONNY. What is it, Ma?

(**MARGARETTE** *quickly sits up and tries to strangle* **FANNY**, *as* **SONNY** *restrains her.*)

MARGARETTE. Help me kill this bi...*(Collapses)* Goodbye my Sonny...and tell Cher I forgive her for divorcing you, but I did love *Gypsies, Tramps and Thieves.*

Oh, my, the light is fading...

(At this time the stage lights start fading out. She quickly sits up and yells at the stage manager.)

Not the stage lights you nitwit, I was speaking spiritually.

(The lights come back up, she croaks. **SONNY** *steps down stage center.* **SAM** *reenters and says.)*

SAM. Hey, we got to clean this place up, we've rented this out for a bar mitzvah in here in thirty minutes.

(**SAM** *rolls the bar and* **MARGARETTE** *offstage. Then the olio curtain falls.*)

(**SONNY** *looks to the heavens and extends his arms upwards.*)

SONNY. I promise you, Ma.

(**MARGARETTE** *is on a mic backstage and clears her throat.*)

I promise you, Ma.

(Again, she clears her throat. Finally he realizes and looks down and points arms downwards.)

SONNY. I promise you, Ma. I will find my long lost twin.

KAREN. Hey what about me, you Canadian Cluck?

SONNY. Oh yeah, you too. I promise to find the girl of my dreams and as God as my witness I'll never go hungry again...

(Piano plays themes from movies.* Then suddenly we hear the heroine's voice on mic.)

---

*Please see Music Use Note on page 3.

SONNY. Eh, I mean, "play it again, Sam?", eh "We're gonna need a bigger boat?"

(He looks very puzzled. He is exiting and shaking his head.)

I know it's not, "Toto, I don't think we're not in Kansas anymore?"

Scene IV

(**JACK** *and* **KAREN** *are onstage.*)

JACK. Now, you take off that dress and let me see your back or I'll cut it off.

KAREN. Never, you cad, I'll die first.

JACK. Oaky, doaky.

(He crosses offstage a moment and drags on a saw blade and attaches it to the bar.)

KAREN. I thought you went to get a pair of scissors.

JACK. Yeah, well you thought wrong toots. Come here.

(She screams. He catches her and drags her to sawmill, ties her hands, and puts her on it. He then turns on the lever and the saw starts turning. Note: the actor playing **SAM** *is behind the mill turning the blade.)*

Now we'll just cut that ole dress off and then the map… ha ha…or should I say maps…will be mine!

KAREN. Help! Won't somebody help me?

*(***SONNY** *enters from stage right and poses.)*

SONNY. Yes, Miss Karen. Sonny is here to save the day.

(He enters to thunderous hero music.)

JACK. Not if I can stop you.

(They begin to struggle around the stage. First **SONNY** *getting loose enough to stop the blade. Then a struggle, then the villain starts the blade again. This happens two or three times.)*

(Each time **KAREN** *is yelling when the blade is running. Finally the villain pulls out a gun and backs* **SONNY** *away. He restarts the blade and cackles.)*

Sorry about that, Mountie Boy. Now you can watch as I make a few cutting remarks. *(More laughing)*

KAREN. Help me Sonny…Oh please…

(He starts to cross and suddenly **YUKON** *jumps from behind* **JACK** *and grabs the gun and a shot goes off and hits the* **PIANO PLAYER**. *They all freeze and slowly cross over to him.)*

(Then they start arguing about what they going to do now without a piano player. "I didn't know the gun was loaded," etc. Then they resume the show.)

*(***YUKON*** holds gun on ***JACK***. ***SONNY*** and ***YUKON*** are conversing about ***YUKON*** saving the day. Ad libbing and then suddenly, ***KAREN*** yells:)*

KAREN. Hey, I'm becoming sliced liverwurst back here.

*(***SONNY*** runs back and stops blade and helps her off and brings her downstage.)*

Oh, Sonny. You saved my life. My hero.

(They embrace.)

(Suddenly, **SONNY** *notices a necklace around* **JACK**'s *neck.)*

SONNY. Juneau Jack, this necklace is just like mine. *(He suddenly realizes:)* You're my twin brother.

JACK. What? We're brothers?

SONNY. Yes, and our mother was Margarette!

JACK. Are you nuts? That's impossible.

SONNY. But you have the necklace.

JACK. I stole that off of *(Points to* **KAREN***)* her when I bumped off her old man, er, I mean when she was just a child. She's your twin sister.

*(***SONNY & KAREN*** are still holding each other tightly and kiss just when he finishes his last line and they realize they are siblings.)*

SONNY & KAREN. Ew!

(They back away from each other.)

*(***YUKON*** sees ***FANNY*** and ***SAM*** entering from stage right.)*

YUKON. Fanny what are you doing here?

FANNY. Well, I came to straighten out a few things. I just couldn't live with my secret any more. Karen, you are my long lost daughter.

ALL. What?

SAM. You mean that Sonny and Karen are your twins?

FANNY. No.

KAREN. But what about the necklaces?

FANNY. When you were a baby. Your Pa got that necklace from his ole pal, who fell down a mine shaft. It belonged to his son who up and ran away when he was four years old.

SONNY. Then she's not my twin sister and Juneau Jack is not my twin brother?

SAM. Wait a minute, that's the necklace I lost years ago, before I ran away and joined Ringling Brothers, Barnum and Bailey's Canadian Circus. We had a wonderful act, we were known as the Canadian Bacons. We were so popular that people would come from miles around to see us. There were so many people that had trouble finding a place to pork...er park. But I broke up the act because he was becoming too much of a ham. He just didn't have the chops for it. Anyway, It's me. I'm yer twin brother.

(SONNY offers his hand and SAM has to use his foot to shake.)

SAM & SONNY. Brother.

YUKON. Boy this is great, I'm going to tell the Wichita Eagle.

(He exits stage left.)

FANNY. And that's not all...*(She crosses to JACK.)* You're Karen's father.

JACK. What?

FANNY. That's right. When you were young, you were a wonderful husband. But then one day you ate some bad pork and you just went to pot. You started to crack up. I put Karen in an orphanage, and I followed you around the country and tried to help you, but it was next to impossible, much like this script.

(He looks at **SONNY** *for pointing help.)*

SAM. So, Fanny and Jack are Karen's parents. Sonny and I are brothers. So who was the old prospector?

FANNY. His name was Clint Eastwood. He didn't really die in that fall, but if you can picture this, I don't think he ever amounted to anything of scope…

SONNY. Gee what a happy ending. Jack, now that you know the truth do you think you can ever stop your evil ways?

JACK. *(He starts to cry.)* Gee I think so. I just love happy endings.

KAREN. And I still have this map on my back. What does it mean?

SONNY. It means on our honeymoon night, I'm gonna strike it rich.

*(***MARGARETTE** *stumbles in stage left.)*

MARGARETTE. Hold it. Just hold on one stinkin' minute.

ALL. Margarette?

(She is mocking them.)

MARGARETTE. Yes. Margarette.

SONNY. Ma, look I found my brother.

(They hug.)

MARGARETTE. Oh son. *(Playing a joke, she then looks at* **SAM**.*)* High five. *(They all scream with laughter.)* No more pocket pool for you, boy. At last I've got my boys back.

SAM. But Ma, you was shot twelve times.

MARGARETTE. It was just a flesh wound.

KAREN. Boy, this is a tough town.

MARGARETTE. I've got my family back together and now we can all be happy.

PIANO PLAYER. Me too?

*(***MARGARETTE** *shoots her. As he slowly dies at piano, and everyone on stage says.)*

Boy this is one tough town.

The End

OLD MCDONALD HAD A FARM
OR
E, I, E, I, OH! JOHN DEERE

For
My Grandparents
Orpha Turkington
&
Roy Pickard

OLD McDONALD HAD A FARM was first presented at Mosley Street Melodramas in Wichita, Kansas on April 4, 2002 under the direction of Tom Frye. It ran for 24 performances. Lights, sound & stage management was by Marty Gilbert, costumes were by Nancy Reeves & Patty Reeder, musical direction was by Flint Hawes, properties were by Pat Szlauderbach, and choreography was by Kyle Vespestad. The cast was as follows:

NARRATOR	Marty Gilbert
CHICK LIE-SOME	Scott Noah
STOCKHOLDERS	Matthew Wright & Marty Gilbert
HOLOTTA TROUBLE	Adrian DeGrafenreed
CLOD HOPPER	Matthew Wright
MISSY DEERE	Jamie Dorfman
JOHN DEERE	Kip Scott
MARY MAE MUDGE	Angela Geer
UNCLE OLE	Matthew Wright

CHARACTERS

NARRATOR - May or may not be done offstage with microphone.
CHICK LIE-SOME - Our villain. Head of Lie-Some Foods.
STOCKHOLDERS - No lines. May be doubled with Clod, Narrator or Ole.
HOLOTTA - Our Vamp. Very sexy.
CLOD HOPPER - A country bumpkin. Very goofy.
MISSY DEERE - Our young heroine farm wife.
JOHN DEERE - Our gallant, handsome farmer hero.
MARY MAE MUDGE - Neighbor with an attitude and brashness.
UNCLE OLE - Good ole uncle. Older character.
PIANO PLAYER

THE SETTING

Independence, Kansas 1932

SYNOPSIS OF SCENES

Scene I & VII: Office of Chick Lie-Some

Scene II & IV: Train depot

Scene III & V: Living room of farm house

Scene VI: Deep in the woods

Scene I

(Curtain rises on office scene. We see a huge backed chair for **CHICK LIE-SOME** *and two tiny chairs for the two stockholders, an easel with several posters.* **CHICK** *is President, CEO, CFO, COD, DOA and BFD of Lie-Some Foods, corporate slime-ball who wants to create the perfect chicken with chemicals. As the curtain opens we hear the narrator. Lights are at half and come full at the end of the narrator's speech.)*

(During speech we hear a patriotic song played softly.)

NARRATOR. Many years ago in a far off country called the good ole U. S. of A., there was prosperity, decency and a code of ethics with the farming community. Now in the 21st century we are at the brink of destroying that rural charm by bending to the tactics of Big Business *("Big Business" echoes ominously. Two* **STOCKHOLDERS** *enter and stand in front of tiny chairs.)* So without further ado, let's visit the office of Lie-Some Foods, the world's biggest supplier of chicken to America's supermarkets. We find their boss Chick Lie-Some holding another meeting with his stockholders. Chick of course is the company's President, CEO, CFO, COD, DOA and BFD.

*(***CHICK** *enters and stands center.)*

CHICK. Gentlemen be seated...

(They sit.)

...and we'll begin our annual stockholders meeting. Now, we'll begin by reciting our company pledge:

(Puts on chicken head and says with dignity, pride and a tear in his eye.)

CHICK. "When it comes to America's farmers, America's consumers, and America's farm policy, we stand behind our name and what we do best

(He uses pointer to point to name on tablet.)

Lie...Some.

(The **STOCKHOLDERS** *applaud.)*

Thank you. Are there any questions?

*(***STOCKHOLDER #1** *raises his hand and* **CHICK** *takes out pistol and shoots him, and he staggers offstage.)*

CHICK. Good. Now let's get on with the financial report.

(He changes poster on easel to show a graph of the company's growth and it's line is increasing off the edge of the paper.)

You see here when my daddy, Rooster Lie-Some, started the company back in ought four, we were merely chicken scratches on the New York Stock Exchange. Today under my dictatorsh— er, directorship...

(The lights are fading out and **CHICK** *is picked up in a spotlight as he slowly gets maniacal.)*

...we see how every farm in Kansas is slowly but wonderfully evaporating until every last one is owned by little ole me, Chick Lie-Some, the king of FOUL farms everywhere!

(He laughs hysterically, stops suddenly and asks....)

Any questions?

(The second **STOCKHOLDER** *raises his hand and* **CHICK** *shoots him, and he staggers off stage.)*

And now finally we come to the REAL reason for today's meeting...my brilliant and fool proof plan to take over the very last pathetic family owned farm in Kansas.

(He laughs again.)

Now the rest of you silent stockholders raise your hands in the air.

(He indicates to the audience to raise their hands. When their hands are up, the spot goes out and the house lights come on.)

See, many hands make light work. Now I want to introduce my dear friend and public relations representative from KSU, our own state college

(He blows a kazoo.)

Kazoo University

(It's pronounced "kazoo".)

Miss Holotta Trouble.

(She enters in purple dress and her music is the Wabash Cannonball.*)*

Holotta…

(He motions for her to come center.)

HOLOTTA. You can just call me Ho.

(We hear vamp music again and she grinds and bumps.)

CHICK. Hoe! That's a very appropriate nickname…a farm tool.

HOLOTTA. *(Taking a long look at him)* Whatever.

CHICK. Now the reason for Miss Troubles visit today is to inform you stockhol…

(He looks and sees empty chairs.)

…is to inform you chairs about a scheme, er plot, I mean an idea to relieve the farmers of their terrible burden, their farms. Meaning their livelihood.

(They both laugh.)

I'll now turn the meeting over to Ho.

(He sits in large chair.)

HOLOTTA. Thank you, Cluck.

CHICK. Eh, that's Chick.

HOLOTTA. Whatever! Now the university has a new program where we are developing a new chicken from a petri dish. This of course will make millions for the Lie-Some Company and in turn Mr. Lie-Some...

(He rises and acts out football moves as **HOLOTTA** *speaks.)*

...will contribute fourteen bazillion dollars to the university for research, football scholarships, new buildings, football scholarships, football tutors, football scholarships and football players lawyer fees.

*(***CHICK*** resumes his sitting.)*

We have support from the university, the state lobbyists, beef packers, pork packers, backpackers, Green Bay Packers, woodpeckers, and politicians. The more animals we can clone or grow in the basement, the less the farmers have to worry about all those pesky dollars they could be making.

*(***CHICK*** crosses to center and then stage right.)*

CHICK. Yes, and I personally, with the help of Holotta Trouble, will travel to Cowpie, Kansas and visit with one of the last family farms left in the entire state and let them see the wonderful chickens we hope to develop through science and technology at good ole KSU *(He blows kazoo.)* Holotta, let's show the folks some of those great ideas.

*(***HOLOTTA*** plays Vanna White and goes to easel to change posters.)*

CHICK. First the Oct-o chicken,

*(***HOLOTTA*** exposes a picture of an 8 legged chicken.)*

for those families with at least eight children.

Second: Swine chicken

*(***HOLOTTA*** reveals a picture of a pig with two chicken legs.)*

this will be perfect for those breakfasts of ham and eggs.

Third, and my favorite, Lewinskychicken, *(She reveals a picture of a chicken wearing a beret and smoking a cigar.)* delicious, but it leaves a bitter aftertaste and a stain on your overalls.

And last we have chicken croquet *(She shows a chicken with a croquet mallet.)* not only good tasting, but this is a sporting bird.

*(**CHICK** crosses center stage as **HOLOTTA** puts easel away.)*

Now as soon as Holotta and I can get a train to Cowpie, Kansas, we'll meet with this family. So let's go Holotta and do our barnyard betrayal. You lead and I'll follow. *(She exits stage left and we see him smile after her.)* Oh come on, Holotta say it.

HOLOTTA. *(We hear her voice off stage.)* Don't make me say that.

CHICK. Oh please you know it makes me very happy.

HOLOTTA. *(She is still offstage yelling.)* Do I really have to?

CHICK. Oh please do it for daddy. Please, please, please…

HOLOTTA. *(She is still offstage.)* All right…here Chick, Chick, Chick, here Chick, Chick, Chick.

(He beams and chicken walks off stage left as she continues to call. Blackout and curtain falls to music of "Turkey in the straw.")

Scene II

(Scene change music until first light is "Chattanooga Choo Choo." Lights are low but increase throughout scene. We might hear a rooster crowing. On stage we see a bench center stage and a ticket booth stage right. Sign on ticket booth says "CLOSED". **HOLOTTA** *and* **CHICK** *are seated on bench.* **HOLOTTA** *has a bag and in it is a copy of* War and Peace, *a nail file, and a compact. On stage right are four small packages to be mailed.)*

CHICK. *(Crosses to booth and sees closed sign)* Well this is a load of chickenshi.....

HOLOTTA. Now, now, Chick.

(He rises and crosses right of bench.)

CHICK. How do people stayed cooped up in this hick town? I've got to be where the action is, lights, laughter, where the people are chick.

HOLOTTA. That's chic.

CHICK. Not with me, it ain't. Yea, there's no place like Kechi for action. *(He sits.)*

HOLOTTA. Well, Chick, I tell you I could never do this trip to Cowpie without having you with me. You know we could make beautiful music together.

CHICK. Well Holotta, it's no wonder you're the wind beneath my feathers.

HOLOTTA. Well, I'll just get out my lunch while we're waiting. *(She pulls out a huge prop hamburger from her bag.)*

CHICK. Oh yeah, that's the genetically enhanced beef patty you've been working on.

HOLOTTA. Yes, I call it my Holotta Burger.

(They laugh and the ticket agent, **CLOD**, *appears from stage left.)*

Chick, here comes the ticket agent. Go get our tickets.

(She puts burger away as he crosses to booth. The ticket agent crosses to ticket booth while singing. He takes packages, stamps it, and throws it off stage right.)

(CHICK *crosses to* **CLOD.)**

CHICK. Mr. Ticket Agent?

CLOD. Hold on, young fella. You got to ring the bell.

(He indicates front desk bell on counter.)

CHICK. Ring the bell? But you're right here.

CLOD. Now, let's not break the rules here. You may be a city slicker, but we here in the country play by the rules.

CHICK. *(Angry)* Very well, you idiot.

(He pounds the bell several times.)

CLOD. Yes, who is it?

CHICK. It's me you puddin' head. Who the…

CLOD. Sorry sir, I'm gonna have to put you on hold.

CHICK. Hold? This isn't a telephone, you moron.

*(**CLOD** hands **CHICK** the bell.)*

CLOD. Here HOLD this.

*(**CHICK** looks perplexed.)*

Now if you don't mind, I fergot that box.

(He points to second box and stamps it and throws off stage right.)

*(**CHICK** puts down bell and rings it feverishly.)*

CHICK. Yes I want…

CLOD. Eh, eh. Yer still on hold fella. I fergot that box. *(He points to third box and returns to booth.)*

CHICK. Yes, I want…

CLOD. Not so fast fella, I got to stamp it. *(He stamps it and throws it off stage.)*

CHICK. Look, I'm in a hurry…

CLOD. Hold it now, don't git yer drawers in a knot. *(He goes for the last package and reads it.)* OOOO!!! Waterford Crystal, very fragile.

(He slowly walks to booth, and very delicately stamps the package. He then quickly throws it off stage as we heard a huge crash.)

CHICK. Look I'm a very busy man…

CLOD. Busy? What do you think I'm doin', Buster?

CHICK. Not much, Grandpa.

CLOD. Hey, yer still on hold.

*(**CHICK** realizes he still is holding the bell.)*

I can't hear you.

*(**CHICK** replaces bell and angrily rings it several times. **CLOD** reaches below counter and exposes a sign that reads, "Gone To Lunch, Back in One Hour".)*

CHICK. *(He yells at **CLOD**.)* Now look here, Bud.

CLOD. Eh, that's Clod. Clod Hopper. *(He does a little delayed hop.)*

CHICK. Now look here Clem.

HOLOTTA. Clod.

CLOD. What?

CHICK. What?

HOLOTTA. Chick.

CLOD. No Clod.

CHICK. No…Chick.

CLOD. Who you callin a hick?

HOLOTTA. Clod.

CHICK. *(Yelling)* Clam up, everyone. Now listen.

CLOD. It's still Clod.

CHICK. Clod, I need…

CLOD. Eh, just a minute

(**CLOD** *eyes the last sack.* **CHICK** *sees it and doesn't want another slow pace, so he runs to it. Stamps it many times so hard he smashes it and angrily throws it offstage. He then looks at* **CLOD**.*)*

Eh...that was my lunch.

CHICK. *(Breaking down and crying)* I just need two tickets to...

CLOD. Tickets, eh? Well, you'll have to take a number.

(He points to numbers on ticket counter. **CHICK** *looks around and sees there is no one but* **HOLOTTA** *and himself at the depot.)*

CHICK. What?

CLOD. That's right, take a number. I just can't have people jest runnin' up here willy nilly and creatin' a mob scene for tickets. Now you take a number and have a seat over there with everybody else.

CHICK. Are you crazy?

CLOD. Do you want a ticket?

*(**CHICK** takes the next number, 42. He sits next to **HOLOTTA**.)*

All right now, number one.

*(**CHICK** reacts as **CLOD** looks around for number one. **HOLOTTA** pulls out* War and Peace *and starts to read.)*

Number one. Guess he ain't here. Number two. Number two.

*(**CHICK** buries his face in his hands.)*

Number two if you ain't comin up I'm movin' on to the next number. Ok, next number. Number three?

*(**HOLOTTA** grabs **CHICK**'s number and goes to ticket booth and puts her bust in **CLOD**'s face. He pauses and looks at her bust.)*

Eh, 42?

HOLOTTA. That's right baby, 42's. That's our number. Now can we have two tickets to Cowpie, Kansas on the next train?

CLOD. You bet they can.

*(He grabs two tickets. She goes over to **CHICK** and gives him one. He angrily grabs bag and starts to cross to exit, which is a security gate. He sets off the alarm.)*

*(**CLOD** indicates he should take off his shoes, then socks, pants, coat, hat, shirt, leaving him in his boxers and tee shirt on stage. He motions him through. **CHICK** storms out. **HOLOTTA** enters and all the sirens go off. **CLOD** smiles and motions her through.)*

CLOD. Yer clear, honey.

*(We hear train whistle as the train is pulling away and **CHICK** runs back in.)*

CHICK. You idiot you made us late and we missed the train.

CLOD. Well, you couldn't git on that train anyway. We got a dress code here in Newton.

(Blackout.)

Scene III

(Farm house interior. Enter **MISSY** *from stage left. She crosses downstage right and removes list from pocket and reads.)*

MISSY. Now let's see what needs to be done. It seems a farmer's work is never finished. Make a quilt, can 300 quart of beans, 200 quarts of yams, 80 quarts of strawberry preserves, 50 quarts of spinach, clean the house, milk the cows, churn the butter, slop the hogs, feed the chickens, do the wash, bake the bread, plow the south forty and make John's favorite apple pie. Check. Good, now what to do after breakfast. *(The clock strikes four.)* Oh goodness, it's 4 am already. I must have overslept. I hope John is up. *(She crosses and yells upstairs.)* Oh John, John dear are you up?

JOHN. *(Yells from off stage)* Yes my little chickadee, I'll be right down.

MISSY. *(She speaks to the audience.)* My husband, John Deere. He's my king and I'm his queen. We run this farm for my Uncle Ole. We just call him Ole. Anyway it's a hard knock life. But we love it. But it's been very difficult for us, *(Sad music is played under this speech.)* You see, we're a dying breed. America's family-owned farm. We work very hard, but we can't compete with the big business farms and those who remain will often become like indentured servants. My uncle is very old and poor John Deere is working his fingers to the bone. I try to be strong, I try to be brave, but it's difficult with money being so tight, the fear of crop failure, the farm aid bill being so favorable to the big guys, and to top it off I have to wear these crappy homemade dresses, but enough about the good life. I think I hear John. *(We hear the toilet flushing off stage.)* I know I hear the john.

*(***JOHN*** enters from stage right with hero music.)*

JOHN. Good morning, my little heifer.

(He picks her up in his arms.)

MISSY. Good morning, John dear. Are you taking the vegetables to market today?

JOHN. Yes, my little filly, *(Putting her down and crossing stage right)* but as you know we only make a small amount of money at the market. I just can't compete with the big city grocery stores. Although my vegetables are home grown, farm fresh, and free from toxic chemicals used by the big businesses, America seems to have forgotten the farmer.

*(**MISSY** crosses to **JOHN**.)*

MISSY. John, that's not true, just the other day on the news they said the working conditions for the farmer had drastically improved. The average farmer use to work eighteen hours a day and now it's only seventeen hours a day.

JOHN. No wonder I feel so much better. Well, my little piglet I'm off.

(He runs off stage left.)

MISSY. *(Crossing to center stage.)* Aw, nothing runs like a Deere. Well I must get busy I'm expecting my neighbor Mary Mae Mudge any minute. She's coming over to teach me how to prepare chicken a la compost. That's her specialty. Last year she won first place at the Kansas State Fair for most creative way to gag a judge.

(There is a knock at the door.)

Oh my, she's here already. Come on in Mary Mae.
*(Entering stage right a la Minnie Pearl is **MARY**. She is a fright. Bad hair, bad body, bad teeth and bad clothes.)*

MARY. Howdy neighbor! *(She slaps her on the back making her spin around.)* How you? Ye doggies, it's a pretty day for four a.m. Well, at least I think it's pretty, it's so damn dark I can't tell. *(She laughs uproariously.)* So you already for a lesson on cookin fer yer man? Honey, just remember to always stand by yer man, my man has been gone nearly three years and I still miss him.

(**MISSY** *indicates with a nod that he's in heaven.* **MARY** *shakes her head and points to hell.*)

MARY. *(cont.)* But just remember darlin'…Men, you can't live without 'em and you can't shoot 'em. Lord knows I tried both.

MISSY. What about the cookin' lesson?

MARY. Right, let's git started on that chicken dish.

MISSY. Oh yes, Mary Mae. I've been looking forward to this all week. You're the best cook in the entire county. I don't know how you do it. For the past twenty years you've run that three hundred acre farm, raised fifteen children, made their clothes, cook all the time and still managed to look the way you do.

MARY. *(Obviously flattered.)* Oh stop, honey. It's the farm life. You keep workin' hard every day and maybe someday you'll look like Mary Mae.

MISSY. Well we can only hope, Mary Mae. Let's go into the kitchen and start cookin.

MARY. Great. I took the liberty of wringing a few chicken necks as I was comin up the walk.

(She demonstrates her technique of twirling a chicken's neck. As she does we hear turning creaking sound effects.)

You know my recipe for chicken a la compost is very tricky to make, so I don't want you to get too cocky. *(She laughs again at her bad pun and* **MISSY** *is deadpan.)* Particularly in this foul weather, get it foul weather. Boy, that one laid an egg honey. Egg! Get the yolk? Oh man, can I shell it out.

(**MISSY** *is still stone-faced.*)

You don't get off the farm much, do ya honey? Are you from Yoder?

MISSY. *(Honestly)* I went to Kechi once.

MARY. Enough said. Okay, lead the way.

(We hear a knock at the door.)

MARY. You expectin' company Missy?

MISSY. Why for heaven's sake, who could that be at this time of day?

(She stands and does nothing.)

MARY. *(Looking at* **MISSY** *with a puzzled face.)* I got a great idea. Why don't you answer the door?

*(***MARY*** sits at the table.)*

MISSY. You're right again Mary Mae, I have so much to learn as a farm wife. *(She goes to stage right.)* Come in.

*(***HOLOTTA*** enters and then ***CHICK***.)*

CHICK. Good morning, charming lady. May I introduce myself to you, I'm Chick Lie-Some, Lie-Some Foods, the world's largest producer of foul. And this is Miss Holotta Trouble *(*Wabash Cannonball *music is played during her entrance.)* She is from KSU university. And you must be the lovely Mrs. John Deere.

MISSY. Yes I am, sir…

CHICK. And this must be your husband?

HOLOTTA. *(Looking at* **MARY***)* Talk about a tough life on the farm.

MARY. *(Rising and crossing to center)* Hey! Look here, you sorry sack of…

MISSY. Now Mary Mae, these are our guests, remember our warm rural manners. This is my neighbor, Mary Mae Mudge. What can I do for you Mr. Lie-Some, Miss Trouble?

CHICK. Well, I'd like to talk to the man of the house.

MISSY. I'm sorry sir, my husband has gone into town. Maybe I can help you.

*(***CHICK*** is moving in on her and taking her offstage.)*

CHICK. Yes, well I'm sure you can, little lady. You see I'm a very rich man and I want your husband to come to work for me at Lie-Some Foods and maybe I can find a spot for you in my office filing and running around my desk. Surely you don't want to stay cooped up here on this chicken farm brooding all day.

MISSY. But Mr. Lie-Some…

(MARY is moving towards them.)

CHICK. *(Smooth and sexy as he closes in to her)* Chick. Chick, please call me just plain Chick.

MISSY. Okay, Just Plain Chick. You see my husband is an American farmer. A proud profession and he doesn't want to see this chicken farm sold and go to work in the wicked city.

(CHICK begins to smell MARY who is right behind him.)

CHICK. Holotta, see if you can get Miss Sludge to show you the pigsty. She obviously knows where it is. I want to visit with Mrs. John Deere alone.

MARY. Excuse me Mr. Lie-Some. Crap, isn't it?

CHICK. Chick.

MARY. Right. Well listen, Chick Crap…I know yer type, you slither in here with all your high dollar suits and fancy words, why yer jes like most of them politicians in Toe-Peeky.

(She pushes him towards HOLOTTA.)

Well, I got news fer you bud, this here's our land and no high falootin' city slicker is gonna talk us into any company owned farms jes so you can make a whole lotta money and we git squat.

(CHICK ducks down and crosses behind HOLOTTA as MARY sees her bust up close.)

How do ya git those things in there like that?

CHICK. Now, Miss Fudge, my intentions are strictly honest. Lie-Some Foods would never run afoul of this chicken farm.

MARY. Well you better not, cause iffin' you try anything slick, then I'll have to wring yer neck jes like I do them other two-legged foul.

(**CHICK** *grimaces.*)

MARY. Come on girly, let's go to the pigsty where the smell is a whole lot better then in here.

(**HOLOTTA** *exits stage right while her music plays.* **MARY** *notices her bumps and grinds.*)

Oh yeah, well, watch this honey.

(*She exits bumping and grinding. Her music is* "Can't Touch This."*)

CHICK. Alone at last. Now, Miss.

MISSY. That's Missy.

CHICK. Missy?

MISSY. Yes, that's my first name Missy. Missy Deere. My maiden name was Ferguson.

CHICK. Missy Ferguson.

(*He looks at audience and then ogles over* **MISSY.**)

Well, looks like you're loaded with farm equipment.

MISSY. My husband will be home soon, but I know how he feels and he would never sell out to you. You see, we believe the government is already too much involved in controlling the farming industry. The farm bills just reward the big company owned farms and people like us are just getting pushed out.

CHICK. I assure you, that won't happen. If you would just look at this incredibly lucrative contract I have drawn up for him. (*He pulls out a contract.*) You see, he could work for the university and help create the perfect chicken. That's because the perfect Chick has already been made. (*He laughs at his own joke and she makes no response.*) You really don't get out, much do you? Anyway I have a picture of what I want as the perfect chicken. (*He pulls out a picture of a Jayhawk and* **MISSY** *gasps.*)

---

*Please See Music Use Note on Page 3.

MISSY. My husband would never create a monster like that. I'm sorry Just Plain Chick but you'll have to go. And before you leave, grab a Holotta Trouble and never darken our home again.

CHICK. Very well, little Missy, but you haven't seen the last of this Chick. There's more than one way to cluck a chicken.

(He exits stage left)

MISSY. *(Crossing downstage right)* Oh my goodness. What an awful man. He would make a great lobbyist.

*(**MARY** enters from stage right with rolled up picture.)*

MARY. Hey, was that Crack that just left?

CHICK. *(Offstage)* That's Chick.

MARY. *(Disgusted)* No, I was right the first time, pull up yer drawers. Well honey, what did that carpetbagger want, as if I didn't know.

MISSY. Oh Mary Mae, he wants John Deere to go to work in the research lab and create this.

(She holds up picture of Jawhawk.)

MARY. Oh sweetie, that ain't nothin'! Miss Trouble wants me to go work there too. She wants me to create a weird strain of wheat that looks like this.

*(She holds up picture of a WSU Shocker. **MISSY** gasps and passes out in the chair. **MARY** looks at the WU Shock and reacts with a big.)*

WOOOOOO *(She thinks a moment.)* I'm shocked. Woo....shock. Hmmm. Hey good name, maybe.

(Blackout.)

Scene IV

(**JOHN** *enters from stage left and crosses to center stage. He poses stage left in area light and then crosses center stage to other area light.*)

JOHN. Uncle Ole, are ya comin?

(*Slowly* **OLE** *is entering from stage left.*)

OLE. Yea John, I'm slow but I'm here. (*"Old McDonald" music is played during his entrance.*) Can we sit a spell? These old bones are achin'.

(*Stage right area light comes up revealing a piano bench.*)

JOHN. Sure, here's a piano bench out here on the road.

(**OLE** *and* **JOHN** *cross stage right, and* **OLE** *sits on bench.*)

(**HOLOTTA** *enters with* **CHICK** *stage right.*)

HOLOTTA. So any luck with the little wife, Chick?

CHICK. Naw! She's tough, but if I can talk to her hayseed husband... just maybe.

HOLOTTA. (*Noticing* **JOHN** *and* **OLE**) Hold the phone.

CHICK. I can't. It hasn't been invented yet.

HOLOTTA. I see something that makes my cannonball tingle.

CHICK. What?

HOLOTTA. Just look over there. Stand back and watch me do my stuff!

(*She vamps over and chugs in front of* **JOHN** *and* **OLE**.)

Hello there, gorgeous. How about you showing me the hayloft?

OLE. (*Rising*) You got it, baby.

HOLOTTA. Not you, you old fool. It's Mr. Beefcake that I want.

OLE. Oh, you mean my nephew, John Deere.

(He crosses in front of them to the left of **HOLOTTA**.*)*

Sorry, he's married, but not me, I'm hotter'n a two dollar pistol.

(He dances for her.)

HOLOTTA. I'd say more like a Derringer. Howdy, Farmer John.

JOHN. Howdy, ma'am. My name is John Deere and this here is my great Uncle, Ole McDonald. What brings you to these parts?

HOLOTTA. These parts. *(She wiggles her body.)* So you're John Deere? Well, walk this way.

(She wiggles over to **CHICK**.*)*

OLE. If'n he walks that way in this part of the country, he's gonna get arrested.

*(***JOHN** *goes to center stage.)*

HOLOTTA. *(Aside to* **CHICK***)* Chick, it's the farm boy himself, John Deere, let's work our magic before he gets home to the little woman. You show him the contract and I'll show the rest.

CHICK. *(Crossing to center stage to* **JOHN**.*)* So you're John Deere. Well, well, well...

OLE. It's over there.

CHICK. What?

OLE. The well.

CHICK. Yes, well maybe you can show Miss Trouble the well and *(He motions pushing him into the well.)* get her something to wet her whistle.

HOLOTTA. Yes, and my whistle is really dry right now.

*(***OLE** *gasps.)*

OLE. Ba, ba, ba.

HOLOTTA. Come on honey, let's take a dip.

(She exits to her music and he follows making train sounds.)

CHICK. John, John, John.

JOHN. It's over there.

CHICK. What?

JOHN. The john. It's over there.

CHICK. *(Looking at audience)* By any chance do you and your uncle share a brain? Never mind. Well, John…have I got a deal for you. Let me introduce myself. I'm Chick Lie-Some from the famous Lie-Some Chicken Farms.

JOHN. Golly, Mr. Chicken, I've heard of you. You're very rich and famous.

CHICK. Yes, John, and how would you like to be rich and famous too?

JOHN. Me? But how, I'm just a farmer from Cowpie, Kansas. Our farm don't make much money.

CHICK. Yes, I know John. It's very sad, the farm situation here in America. But I know how to make it all better. How would you like to sell me your farm and go to work at your alma mater as a research scientist developing a better chicken?

JOHN. Me? I don't know, Mr. Chicken. The farms means everything to my wife and uncle Ole and besides, America needs good farms.

CHICK. Of course they do, John, but if big industry takes over then they can produce vegetables, meats, and grains at a much lower price, and isn't that good for everyone?

JOHN. I don't know, I'm confused, maybe I should talk to my wife.

CHICK. Oh no, no. Let's not trouble your dear wife with silly details. Oh look here, Miss Trouble is right here.

*(**HOLOTTA** has entered stage left.)*

Did everything FALL into place, Holotta?

(They both scream with laughter and **JOHN** *joins in only to be polite even though he has no idea why he's laughing.)*

HOLOTTA. Yes indeedy. We went to the well, and Uncle Ole really got DOWN.

(They all laugh again.)

CHICK. Well, maybe he went to the well one too many times.

(Again there is more laughter.)

JOHN. Where's my Uncle Ole?

HOLOTTA. Well let's just say he's WELL preserved.

(Laughter continues from them.)

CHICK. He'll be fine, John. He's just bit the farm. Now if you'd sign this contract selling me your farm.

(He pulls out a contract for **JOHN** *to sign.)*

JOHN. But Mr. Chicken, I told you I needed to talk to my wife first.

*(***CHICK*** backs* **JOHN** *stage right as he is talking)*

CHICK. Are you one of those meelymouth men who has to check with his wife on everything? One of those spineless excuses for manhood who whimpers at every word of his wife? A nothing jellyfish who quivers when she walks into the room? Is that the kind of man you are?

*(***JOHN*** looks at* **CHICK** *blankly.)*

JOHN. Yeah.

*(***JOHN*** quickly runs off stage.)*

CHICK. All right, Holotta, you got your work cut out for you. Get that man.

*(***HOLOTTA*** smiles and as the train sound effects of a train departing with the building of steam and whistles blare, she is chugging off. Scene change music is the* Wabash Cannonball.*)*

Scene V

JOHN. Missy, Missy, where are you? Oh I know where she might be. I'll bet she's in the kitchen. I know cause I smell hot buns.

(There is a knock at the door.)

Come in.

(HOLOTTA enters and crosses very close to JOHN.)

HOLOTTA. Hello, BIG John. I hope you don't mind but I needed to talk to you before I leave for the university.

(Her lips get very close to his.)

Can we...talk?

JOHN. *(Very nervous)* Yes, ma'am. What is it you need? Er, I mean, what is it you want? No. I mean, what would you like to talk about?

HOLOTTA. *(Very coy)* Can you ever forgive me, John?

JOHN. I'm sorry, ma'am, I don't know what yer talking about.

HOLOTTA. John, I've been very dishonest with you. I wanted you to come work at the university with me and sell your farm to Chick, but you see, he wants to contract your chicken farm out and then he plans to take over the hogs, followed by the cows, then all the gardens and grain. But now I see how much the small farm is needed and I must tell you that Chick is a very, very, very...

JOHN. Very?

HOLOTTA. Very bad man. You must never sell to him. We must keep America's farm communities together.

(There is a strong chord on piano.)

JOHN. You're a good woman, Holotta.

HOLOTTA. You have no idea, John. But please just call me Ho.

JOHN. I can't wait to tell Missy about my new friend...Ho.

HOLOTTA. Well John, I'd just forget that part. Anyway, I've done something terrible. You know your uncle, Ole?

JOHN. Sure, why?

HOLOTTA. *(Ashamed and embarrassed about what she's done)* I...I...I pushed him down a one hundred foot well.

JOHN. Oh, don't worry about that Ho.

HOLOTTA. But won't he drown?

JOHN. Naw, that well's been dry for years.

HOLOTTA. Then you forgive me, John?

JOHN. Why of course, Ho.

(She grabs him in an embrace just as **MISSY** *enters.* **JOHN** *and* **HOLOTTA** *never see her.)*

MISSY. *(To audience:)* What is this I see? My husband in the arms of another woman. *(She looks at them in anger.)* It looks like K-State finally scores. What can this mean? The shame. The disgrace.

(She runs off crying.)

HOLOTTA. Now John, remember you or your uncle must never sign that contract.

JOHN. You're so right, Ho.

*(***CHICK*** enters with a dusty and dirty* **OLE** *looking very bedraggled.)*

CHICK. Too late, you Kansas Crackhead! Your uncle has already signed the contract.

JOHN. But why, Uncle?

OLE. I had to, John. He threatened to leave me in that well and make it a tourist mecca and put Greensburg out of business.

CHICK. And you Holotta, I heard everything at the door. So you've turned against me, too. Well, I've got the contract, and you've got the shaft.

*(He laughs and exits stage left. He tries to push **JOHN** out of the way, but he is too big and solid and he won't budge, so he throws **OLE** out of the way. He exits laughing.)*

*(**MISSY** enters from stage right with hobo baggage.)*

MISSY. Well, John Deere, you can have your hussy. You can have the farm. I'm leaving you.

(She hands him piece of paper and exits crying.)

JOHN. *(To the audience:)* Is this a bad day or what?

HOLOTTA. John, she doesn't understand. I'll go explain it to her. Don't fret. Just like the Governator says...I'll be bock.

(She exits.)

*(**JOHN** reads note and sits at table and puts his head in his hand.)*

JOHN. Oh no.

OLE. *(Crossing to **JOHN**)* What is it, John?

JOHN. It's a Dear John letter.

(Blackout. Sappy music during scene change.)

Scene VI

*(**MISSY** enters crying. She crosses to centerstage.)*

MISSY. That two-timer! How could John have ever done this to me? Well, there's only one way to get back at him. I'll make him jealous. I'll find a gorgeous hunk of a man for myself.

(She grabs a man from the audience and stands him up. She looks at him and says.)

Well, maybe not.

*(**HOLOTTA** enters and crosses to **MISSY**.)*

HOLOTTA. Missy, wait, I must explain everything to you.

MISSY. Please, Miss Trouble.

HOLOTTA. Call me Ho.

MISSY. You said it, not me.

*(**MARY** enters and crosses to them.)*

MARY. Missy, are you okay? I just heard about John and that hussy.

*(She notices **HOLOTTA**.)*

There you are, you homewrecker! We got a name for women like you in these parts.

HOLOTTA. What's that?

MARY. Well, we calls them...*(She is looking quite puzzled)*... homewreckers.

("America the Beautiful" is played under this next speech.)

HOLOTTA. Please, Miss Mudge, let me explain. It's not what it seems. Yes, in the beginning, I was in on this dastardly deed, but I've seen the light, the light in the window, the light at the end of the tunnel, the light in the farmhouse window. I'll do anything to help get that farm back. John was just showing me his gratitude. He loves you, not me.

MISSY. He does?

HOLOTTA. Yes.

MARY. Well, never let it be said we ain't a forgiven group. Shake on it Miss Trouble.

*(**MARY** extends her hand as **HOLOTTA** just shakes her whole body.)*

Wow, you could get a job at Sears in the paint department.

HOLOTTA. That's the way we do it in the big city. But we have to act fast, though. I just received this telegram for Chick.

*(She hands it to **MISSY** who reads it aloud.)*

MISSY. Lie-Some Foods. To Mr. Chick Lie-Some: Chick... Come back to the research lab fast. Stop. Scientists have developed the super chicken. Stop. All poultry farms could be put out of business. Stop. Stop reading this telegram. Stop. What can we do to get that contract back?

MARY. I got it. It will take a lot of cunning and guile. But here's the plan. I'll grab Chick and throw him to the floor and beat the snot out of him.

HOLOTTA. *(After some thought:)* I like it, but may I help?

MARY. Sure, honey. Now come on girls, let's break wind.

MISSY. Eh, Mary, that's run like the wind.

MARY. Whatever.

(They all exit fast. Blackout and scene change music.)

Scene VII

(**JOHN** *enters with* **OLE** *stage right.*)

JOHN. Mr. Chicken. Where's that coward? I must stop him before he ruins America's chicken farms.

OLE. Yes, John, we must tear up that contract.

(**CHICK**'s *voice through the PA system.*)

CHICK. Too late, you graduate from Silo Tech. *(He laughs.)* I've got the contract and a new secret formula for the super chicken. I've already developed the first chicken and now all I have to do is mass produce my formula. Now if you don't mind, I'd like to give you the bird.

(He laughs and enters riding a big chicken. Costume is a big chicken with a pair of man's legs on each side as if it's **CHICK***'s legs. The actor playing* **CHICK** *then puts his own legs in the chicken's legs.)*

JOHN. You coward. You tricked my Uncle Ole into signing that contract and now we're here to ask you to be a man and tear it up along with that secret formula and destroy that KFC monstrosity.

CHICK. HA! You bumbling plowboy. Nothing could make me do that.

JOHN. Very well then, I must ask you to step outside and settle this like gentlemen.

(**MISSY** *enters followed by* **HOLOTTA**.)

MISSY. John dear.

JOHN. Missy, what are you doing here, this is no place for a lady. *(He crosses to her.)*

*(***MARY*** enters with a rolling pin.)*

MARY. Yea, but it's a great place for me. *(She approaches* **CHICK**.*)* Now you either give me that contract and secret formula or you and this giant feather duster will be the main ingredients in my next chicken a la compost.

CHICK. All right, just don't hurt me. I just had my beak done.

MARY. Did you keep the receipt?

(CHICK gives contract and formula to MARY. She hands them to JOHN, and he and MISSY tear them up and throw them into the air as they hug.)

CHICK. I hope you're proud of yourself, Mary.

MARY. That's me, proud Mary.

(The song Proud Mary *plays during the Blackout and bows.*)*

The End

---

*Please see Music Use Note on Page 3.

OTHER TITLES AVAILABLE FROM SAMUEL FRENCH

THE MOSLEY STREET MELODRAMAS VOLUME I

Tom Frye

Melodrama / Various m and f roles / Simple set

With the *Mosley Street Melodramas* you'll sigh for the dainty Heroine, cheer for the righteous Hero, and boo and hiss the dastardly Villain in plays with a contemporary twist on the traditional version. These hysterical, audience-participation plays are perfect for community theatres, churches and schools to perform. Especially for fundraisers! These ain't your Gramma's melodramas!

Plays include *The Lost Samantha Treasure, The Plague on Madison Avenue, The Mystery of Baby Leah,* and *Another Kennedy in the White House.*

"*The Lost Samantha Treasure* is nothing if not memorable - and hysterical. Frye has certainly penned a good one this time around, tossing some of the more well-used melodrama jokes out the window in favor of a humor that requires timing and talent
- Sharon Faith Levin, *Wichita Old Town Gazette*

"Melodrama fans are happily cheering it again. *The Lost Samantha Treasure* is terrific fare for the whole family."
- Jacqueline Boudreau, *Wichita Old Town Gazette*

"Like most modern melodrama scripts, Frye's *Samantha* is pretty much just a vehicle for slapstick silliness, but the dialogue in this one is darned funny...Frye had a blast...the d'enouement...features *Saturday Night Fever* - style dance numbers. The audience certainly enjoyed watching the show the evening I attended.
- Terri Mott, *F5 Newspaper*

SAMUELFRENCH.COM

OTHER TITLES AVAILABLE FROM SAMUEL FRENCH

THE MOSLEY STREET MELODRAMAS, VOLUME II

William P. Johnson and Rosemary Willhide

Melodrama / Various m and f roles / Simple set

The laughs never stop with this collection of four Holiday themed Melodramas. No holds are barred as television favorites to some traditional Christmas classics get skewered in these light-hearted parodies. Each show has a diverse set of characters designed to put a modern spin on the spirit of the Melodrama. CHEER for the heroic, but frustrated Prairie Magician. BOO the villainous land baron with the hypnotic hairpiece, and OOH-AAH the four young single ladies adjusting to life in Manhattan (Kansas). These interactive Melodramas are simple to produce and appeal to all types of groups. Both cast and audience alike will have an uproariously good time!

Santa and the City - *3f, 3m (some doubling)* - The Old Mid-West will never be the same when four young single ladies in Manhattan, KS try to open a shoe store. Little did they reckon a greedy land baron, whose hair has hypnotic powers, would try to take over the town just before Christmas.

The Holiday Surprise - *3f, 3m* - It's the day before Christmas and Santa is nowhere to be found. The residents of Goosebump, Alaska (the first town South of the North Pole) try to find a substitute. Only a Canadian Mountie can save the day!

The Grouch Who Couldn't Steal Christmas - *3f, 3m* - The Annual Holiday Pageant in the town of Whooterville goes awry when Phineas P. Grouch seeks revenge from a broken heart. But who is the real villain here?

The Magical Christmas of Mistle Toe, Kansas - *3m, 3f* - The town of Mistletoe is broke and the land rights are up for grabs. Mayor Georgette Bradley pins all their hopes and dreams on a one night only benefit performance by "The Amazing Ricky and His Magic Wand." You won't believe the magic that occurs when they discover the true meaning of the season.

SAMUELFRENCH.COM

OTHER TITLES AVAILABLE FROM SAMUEL FRENCH

THE MOSLEY STREET MELODRAMS, VOLUME III

Tom Frye

Melodrama / Various male and female roles / Simple set

This new collection of campy, sassy melodramas from our beloved Mosley Street series will have audience booin', hissin' and knee-slappin'! Four all new plays in the Melodrama tradition, complete with audience participation. A riotous time for any theatre!

Booze and Kisses *Melodrama / 4m, 2f, 2 non-gender / 3 Interior* - With a hero named John Wilkes Booth, this story is bound to take off like a shot. This actor who falls into the depth of degredation with the help of the evil villian, Lawyer Cribbs, manages to ford along with the help of his darling wife Lucy. Along the way we meet his daughter Little Orpha Annie, who tried to save her father from the evils of "drink."

Crouching Santa, Hidden Reindeer *Melodrama / 8m, 2f, 1 non-gender / 2 Interior, 2 Exterior* - When a mail-order bride, Sushi Sue from Japan, arrives in Nasal Drip, Kansas, the culture shock begins. This beautiful bride controlled by her boss Sackapoopoo, desperately falls in love with her hunky groom-to-be, Rex the wonder Sherriff. Together Sackapoopoo and his equally evil wife, Shanghai Sal steal the town reindeer and try to rob all the merchants. Hold on to your kimonos, the climactic martial arts fight makes this show a kick in the pants.

My Daze in Doo-Dah *Melodrama / 3m, 2f, 7 non-gender / 3 Interior, 2 Exterior* - A strip club, a lawyer, an Englishman, a dead doctor and an old fashioned shoot-out at the funeral home. Now that's entertainment. Lizzie Botox, our vamp, and Booley Buttboil, our villian, do their best to cheat our sweet Polish family, the McTavishes out of their rightful inheritance.

There's a Villain In My School *Melodrama / 5m, 2f, 3 non-gender / 1 Interior* - If this doesn't set back education a hundred years, I don't know what will. The first day of teaching, our heroine, Goody Twoshoes, must come to grips with a looney parent, twin juvenile delinquents, an evil banker and a 22 year-old kindergardener. This makes the twenty mile walk to school, in the snow, uphill both ways, well worth the effort. Their combined IQ is just over 38, you do the math.

SAMUELFRENCH.COM

www.ingramcontent.com/pod-product-compliance
Lightning Source LLC
LaVergne TN
LVHW011716060526
838200LV00051B/2920